Tilli of

Altered Creatures
Final Days

by

A.G. Wedgeworth

A.G. Wedgeworth

Copyright © 2024 by Anthony G. Wedgeworth
Published by Anthony G. Wedgeworth
Cover Artwork by Jason Longstreet
Illustrations by Steve Ott
Edited by Deborah Murrell
Paperback ISBN: 978-1-7369704-6-1

Altered Creatures Epic Fantasy Adventures
Historical Date 2.0601.0222
Tilli of Kingsfoot Series, Revision 1.0
Final Days
www.AlteredCreatures.com

Printed in the United States of America

Without limiting the rights under the copyright reserved above, no part of this publication may be reproduced, stored in or introduced into retrieval system, or transmitted, in any form or by and means (electronic, mechanical, photocopying, recording, or otherwise), without the prior written permission of copyright owner of this book.

The scanning, uploading, and distribution of this book via the Internet or via any other means without the permission of the copyright owner is illegal and punishable by law. Please purchase only authorized electronic editions, and do not participate in or encourage electronic piracy of copyright materials.

Your support of the author's rights is appreciated.

This is a work of fiction. Names, characters, places, and incidents either are the product of the author's imagination or are used fictitiously, and any resemblance to actual persons, living or dead, business establishments, events, or locales is entirely coincidental.

No Thrashers or Chuttlebeasts were harmed in the making of this book.

Tilli of Kingsfoot – Final Days

Dedication:

This book is dedicated to all of you who have dealt with the slow painful loss of a loved one, be it family or friend, due to physical or mental illness. These are the people that were there for those struggling with disease and organ failure over months or years. You are my heroes. My heart goes out to you, as you handle all of the related challenges.

In my case, I dedicate this book to my stepsister, Angie Butler, and a young man named Nick Fohey, as well as all of their loved ones that stood by them along the way. Both Angie & Nick lost their battles this year after a long arduous fight. Both of you will be missed, but never forgotten. You have made our lives better and we thank you.

Acknowledgments:

My lovely wife, Tami, for putting up with the years of me working in my office on these stories, and for believing in me.

Our kids and grandkids who inspire me to make the world a better place, even if only through the stories I tell.

My mother, for nurturing good values and helping me establish a strong moral compass, as well as allowing me to fail at times in order to learn valuable lessons in life.

My dyslexia, for this gift has taught me compassion & empathy for others, drive to conquer my struggles, and creativity to survive outside the norm. What a wonderful set of life lessons to have.

Everyone who took the time to read my manuscript to help me work out the details and issues, as well as those who I counsel with on various aspects of the series. These include Tami Wedgeworth, JoAnn Cegon, Sarah Wedgeworth, Darci Knapp, Pat Mulhern, and Tracy (Tillman) Weiler.

I couldn't have done it without you.

A.G. Wedgeworth

www.AlteredCreatures.com

Altered Creatures Epic Adventures continues with the following books:

Nums of Shoreview Series (Pre-Teen, Ages 9 to 12)
Stolen Orb (Book 1)
Unfair Trade (Book 2)
Slave Trade (Book 3)
Baka's Curse (Book 4)
Haunted Secrets (Book 5)
Rodent Buttes (Book 6)

Thorik Dain Series (Young Adult and Adult)
Treasure of Sorat (Prequel)
Fate of Thorik (Book 1)
Sacrifice of Ericc (Book 2)
Essence of Gluic (Book 3)
Rise of Rummon (Book 4)
Prey of Ambrosius (Book 5)
Plea of Avanda (Book 6)

Tilli of Kingsfoot Series (Young Adult and Adult)
Hidden Magic (Book 1)
Final Days (Book 2)

Santorray's Privations Series (Adult)
Betrayed
Hunted
Outraged

Look for other upcoming stories of
Ambrosius
Darkmere
Myth'Unday
Dragon & Del'Unday Wars
and more…

Tilli of Kingsfoot – Final Days

A.G. Wedgeworth

Introduction
Where did we leave off?

In the book Hidden Magic, Tilli had escaped her time-traveling master, Schullis, with several of his items in tow. In her haste, she was given direction from Gluic to travel with a giant sloth named Pruva and a warrior creature named Goothr, into the Govi Glade. The last we saw them, they were making a run for the time portal sphere before an evil black dragon could follow them…

Prologue
It was a Time of Magic

Hundreds of years after the Mountain King War, civilization was no more than scattered villages of humans living between the great Luthralum Tunia Lake and the mountains to the north. Most species of Altered Creatures had migrated to the far east, with the occasional Del'Unday and Ov'Unday living on their own in the wilderness.

E'rudites had long been forgotten about, as well as their powers. But the teachings of Irluk had slowly made their way into the hands of several who were able to replicate some of her magic. In doing so, they used the techniques to devise their own brand of spells. Eventually, they learned how to embed spells within items for the use of others without such skill. The process was difficult, and few had mastered it.

Alchemists began springing up across the land, with new spells and enchantments. Some were enthralled by the possibilities, while most feared this new untamed power and shunned it from their communities. A slow rift divided the cultures between those that allowed magic and those who didn't. It even became an emotional topic of discussion and was avoided when possible.

Then a city was formed that pulled the resources of the spell casters together in order to grow their powers and to develop even greater accomplishments from this new skill. The greed for power grew and war didn't lag too far behind.

Chapter 1
Govi Glade

A giant sloth-like creature stepped out from a swirling mist of a magical sphere. Snowflakes instantly began to attach to its thick fur, as the creature's feet sunk softly into the untouched blanket of snow. The morning sunlight glistened on its wide eyes as it looked around in awe, taking in the fresh scent of pine needles and melting frost. Pruva uttered a single word of admiration: "Breathtaking."

He found himself at the foot of majestic, white-tipped, wooded mountains, standing in an expansive grassy glade. Cushioned by a dense forest, the glade seemed like one of those snow globes set upon a shelf after a friendly shaking. But this was no ordinary glade. It was a place where time could bend and twist. This place was known as Govi Glade and it was believed to have been born out of a long-ago battle between Alchemists and E'rudites. The only one who had ever mapped it just arrived - Pruva. Everyone else who dared step inside the glade had absolutely no idea what may await them or if they would even make it out alive.

Treerats were lurking just outside of the glade as the morning sun began to peek out from behind the clouds. From their hiding places, they watched nearly invisible spheres appear from the ground, soar up above the glade, and then sink back into a different part of the field. It was a peaceful place, but it was also a death trap. One mistake with an orb could lead to dismemberment or death, with body parts scattered through different periods in history. The treerats watched silently, waiting for opportunities to scavenge their next meal.

Suddenly, a thunderous wail echoed across the glade from inside the sphere Pruva had just left. A giant, red-skinned warrior tumbled out of the sphere. With one arm he clutched onto a panicking young lady, and with the other arm he held a large spiked wooden club. With an almighty crash they smashed into Pruva, sending him sprawling! Cooking pans, bags and a satchel were sent flying everywhere - their contents spilling across the snow-covered grasslands with a huge poof of enchanted-looking dust, and then all went silent.

A heavy hush remained after the fall, punctuated by moans from the trio as the mystical sphere they came from continued to settle into the earth.

The young lady's body snapped upright in fear as she searched the skies. "Did Mel'tayn follow us?" Tilli swept her long multicolored ponytail over her shoulder as she spun around, looking for another traveler. Birthmark-like sections of her skin, known as soul-markings, created patterns on her face, down her neck, and on her arms. Whirling about, she panicked at the idea of being followed.

Prior to their sphere disappearing underground, a small black dragon bolted up from it. If it had been a moment later, only half of its body would have made it through the fracture in time. After making the successful exit in the opposite direction to the prior three within the tall grass. Mel'tayn raced away from them at first, and then he took a wide turn until he raced toward the other travelers. His speed and the dark shadows of morning prevented Tilli from seeing his arrival at first.

Then she noticed snow tumbling away from the grassy surface as it parted in a path toward them. She knew it had to be Mel'tayn, and he was heading for her satchel. "Goothr! Get up!" she shouted. "He's going after the Runestones!"

Goothr sat up upon her command. A glaze of white frozen dust covered his large red dragon head and muscular human torso of the same color. He was already as tall as Tilli without even standing up on his thick wolf-like legs. "Mel'tayn?" he asked while shaking off the unexpected landing. "Where?"

The question didn't need to be answered as Mel'tayn reached Tilli's satchel, grabbed it, and then rose out of the tall grass.

"Stop him!" Tilli screamed as she slipped her way to her feet and began running. Unfortunately, she was too late. The dragon had become airborne and was already too high for her to grab him.

The black dragon's yard-long wings were just large enough to lift the weight of the satchel filled with Runestones. If left alone, he would have the strength to make it to the trees and then a bit beyond, but he was at his limits for carrying.

Success was nearly at hand for Mel'tayn until Goothr grabbed the satchel. Standing at an impressive three yards tall, the warrior's long arm and massive hand wrapped around the leather bag and snapped it out of the dragon's grasp.

The motion redirected Mel'tayn back into the tall grass. A shower of white crystals splashed outward upon his entry, along with several of the Runestones as they spilled out of the leather bag.

"NO!" Tilli screamed as she witnessed her items fling from the satchel.

Thinking quickly, the black dragon grabbed two of the stones before launching himself back into the air. Another burst of snow blew outward as he escaped from the grassy area and angled upward. Within seconds, he flew out of the glade and onto a nearby tree to rest and secure his stolen treasure. But even that was not to last. Treerats began to make their way toward him, jumping from limb to limb and tree to tree. The black dragon knew enough to continue moving, so he launched and flew off into the forest.

"I hate dragons!" Tilli cried out as she watched it disappear from her sight. Taking several steps forward to chase the dragon, she realized there was no way she could catch him. Besides, she couldn't leave the rest of the Runestones in the glade, nor her friend, Pruva. Stopping, she screamed in anger for a moment before returning to the scene of the crime.

Goothr stood proud of himself, while holding the satchel out for Tilli. "I saved most of your Runestones." Being a blothrud, he was a ferocious-looking beast who could fight and conquer just about any other creature that came along. But Goothr was a bit more simple-minded than the average super-warrior and empathy and care could be heard in his deep voice.

"I said stop Mel'tayn!" Tilli was upset and frustrated as she began picking up the other Runestones as well as the gear she had dropped upon falling out of the sphere. "Now we have a bigger problem!"

"I don't understand."

"I don't have time to explain right now. A new sphere could rise up from under our feet at any moment. We need to get out of this glade."

Goothr looked down at his wolf-like feet and pushed them as close as he could together to minimize the risk of one touching his foot and cutting it off.

"Don't just stand there. Help Pruva up and to the edge of the forest while I collect the rest of our items." Her voice was stronger than expected, but she was still upset about Mel'tayn.

Nodding that he understood, Goothr followed her orders and bent down to help their friend stand up.

The large brown sloth-like creature slowly rose from the landscape. Clumps of snow fell from him, exposing twisting and circling markings across his facial skin and hands. Pruva was a gathler, and like those of his species, they moved and talked in a slow and methodical way. He was almost as tall as Goothr, if he stood up straight, but he stayed hunched over and stood just a head taller than Tilli.

Blood ran down Pruva's head. It appeared he had cracked his head on an exposed rock when he fell.

"Pruva! Are you alright?" Goothr asked with significant concern. He hated to see anyone hurt or in pain. Again, this was uncommon for a blothrud.

Tilli lifted her head above the grass level to see what the issue was before ordering, "Get him out of the glade and I'll look at it once we're on safe terrain."

Goothr nodded again to follow her orders. Grabbing Pruva's arm, he helped him slowly escape the grassy area as several more magical orbs lifted from the depths near to where they had been standing.

Before sitting on a nearby log, Pruva removed his overfilled huge pack. It had odd items stuffed in it, tied to it, and poking out of it. None of which was for traveling. Instead, it was a collection of different types of sticks, metals, stones, and plants that he had collected along his journey.

By the time he had settled in, Tilli had already arrived with an arm full of other items that had been scattered upon their landing. "Are you okay?" she asked as she piled up her findings near him.

Pruva took a deep breath and raised a hand. "Let me rest."

"Tilli, are you mad at me?" Goothr asked.

"Yes," she snapped as she started digging around for something to clean Pruva's injury. Softening her tone, she continued, "I know you were doing what you thought I wanted, but I asked you stop Mel'tayn."

"Why? I got most of your family's Runestones back. Those are very important to you."

She sighed and tightened her lips. "Yes, they are." She began cleaning Pruva's wound, only to find it to be a scrape. "And I'm grateful that you saved most of them for me, Goothr. But we're here on a mission to obtain Irluk's Charm Runestone before it changes the future. Now the same is true with the ones Mel'tayn stole from me. In a way, we have tripled the threat."

Goothr nodded to please her and to give her a feeling he understood, but his words made it clear he didn't. "I don't know what that means or what it has to do with Mel'tayn."

"Mel'tayn worked for Irluk, and he is trying to find her Runestones to get them back to her." Grabbing a small vial from Pruva's pack, she removed the cork and poured some of its liquid on a cloth before dabbing it onto the gathler's scrape.

"Okay." Half smiling, he wanted everything to be okay. "Sooo…"

She finished his sentence for clarity. "So, now we have competition in finding the Charm Runestone, but Mel'tayn has a head start on us and he has two more stones in his grasp."

"Ah! Now it's clear." Goothr nodded with a contented look that lasted less than two seconds. "Why do we want Irluk's Charm Stone if it doesn't belong to us?"

Tilli looked at their injured gathler friend for the answer as she placed her thin fabric over the scraped area on his forehead. "Well, Pruva, Goothr has a good question. Why are we interfering with this time in history to remove this Runestone?"

"It's not right," Pruva replied.

Tilli tilted her head while inspecting her work on his wound. "It looks fine."

"No," he replied. "My history did not have the Charm Runestone. Recently it filtered into my history. Many of those from my time would say it was always there, but I know it wasn't."

"Well, if your history changed, wouldn't you only know the new history?"

"Truth be said. Truth be heard," Pruva replied, which was a common phrase among his people. "Unlike others from my place in your future, I have been traveling back and forth through time during the modification of events that led to this. Changes in history struggle with known history for dominance in my mind. These conflicts lead me to know when events were changed, which led us here, but something is wrong this time."

"What's different?"

"Normally when I arrive, I can recall both paths of history, but once you and Goothr stepped through I felt overwhelming confusion and irritation. There are now several potential outcomes, most with terrible consequences for the future."

"Are you sure it wasn't just us falling on you?" she replied, eyeing Goothr for his clumsiness.

Ignoring the question, Pruva slowly pulled out a gyroscope-looking device with hundreds of thin metal rings on it. He had built it to navigate the Govi Glade orbs. However, some of the rings had been bent from the fall into the glade. "Based on my calculations, we entered a time when the Charm Stone first appeared in my new line of history. If this is not stopped, the results will be catastrophic."

Goothr's eyes were wide with fear, despite not understanding the idea of time travel. "Will people get hurt?"

"Worse, many will never be born. The future will completely change and great events in future civilizations will never take place."

Goothr nodded. "Is that bad?"

Pruva sighed and answered, "Yes, that's bad. It may prevent my culture, my people, and even me from existing in the first place. Now, with the addition of the Runestone taken by Mel'tayn, it will most likely only get worse."

Tilli scoffed. "How can something happen that would prevent you from existing when you're right here with us?"

Pruva placed his large sloth palm on her hands. "Trust me. This change can even prevent you from being born."

His serious tone gave her goosebumps down the back of her neck and spine. Her friend was not overexaggerating and needed her help. "If we're going to find the Runestone before Mel'tayn, then we need to know what direction to go and get started."

Pruva raised an arm and pointed south. "Travel a week or so to our south to the E'rudite coliseum. The stone will be used by someone from that location soon if they haven't already begun."

"Understood," she replied as she began getting her items packed. "Let's get started."

"It's a week or so for you. It will take you over a month if I travel with you. You could easily be there and back before I made it to the coliseum. Besides, I need to repair my glade mapper if we plan to leave this place and return you two to your rightful place in history." He showed them the bent rings on the metal gyroscope he used to determine where each orb would go to and when they were above ground.

"I'm not leaving you here by yourself."

"You have to go, for you are the only one that understands how the Runestones work. Goothr has to go to protect you."

The blothrud stood up straight with pride. "I am taller than Tilli, so I must protect her."

Pruva cracked a small grin. "See, he must protect you."

"But you are—"

"My role in this is to bring you here and to get you home. And you know I'm right."

Tilli wanted to argue because she didn't want to split up. After a few quiet moments, she had an idea and began digging in her pack. Pulling out a thin, long black crystal, she asked Pruva, "Do you recall how this works?"

"Oh! I do!" Goothr said with excitement. Grabbing the crystal from her, he pushed it halfway into the ground and then turned back to Tilli with the widest grin she had ever seen. "Tilli, where's the metal stick?"

Chuckling at his enjoyment of the process, she pulled out a two-pronged metal fork. "Do you mean this tuning fork?"

"Yes!" He grabbed it and then held the end ever so gently between two of his massive fingers. Getting down on his knees, he lightly tapped the crystal with the metal tuning fork.

A high-pitched tone vibrated from the metal tool and the crystal.

Goothr smiled with delight. He had been part of the process in the past, but this was the first time he had done this by himself. He then turned his large dragon head toward Tilli. "Can I break it?"

She nodded. "You've done everything else. You might as well finish it."

He agreed. Returning his attention to the half-submerged crystal, he grabbed the exposed part and snapped it off. Taking a moment, he studied the half-crystal in the palm of his hand. "I did it."

"Yes, you did," she told him before looking back at Pruva. "Once we get the Runestone, we'll use our half of the crystal to open a portal to return here. Just make sure you're not sitting near the buried half when we do."

Pruva was busy plucking petite tools from his large pack in order to work on the fine and miniscule adjustments to the sensitive gyroscope tool. "You should be aware that this time in history is very adversarial when it comes to the topic of magic. Some see it as a tool for the masses while others forbid it and even punish those who use it."

"I don't know how to perform magic, so it shouldn't be an issue," she replied.

Pruva slowly and delicately held the small tools in his large, sloth-like claws. It seemed like such a mismatch, but it worked flawlessly for him. "True, but E'rudite powers could be seen as magic to those that live in these times."

"I'll be careful." She left some gear for him and prepared for her travels through the woods to a place she didn't know how to get to, other than the instructions of 'go south and look for a coliseum'.

She watched him tinker with his tools and miniature mechanical gears. She had seen him create unique machines from nothing more than scraps and an idea in his head. It was incredible to watch as he lost himself in his work.

"Why are you still here?" he asked after glancing up for a different tool.

"Are you sure you'll be safe here by yourself? There are many tiny eyes watching us as their mouths drool with anticipation for fresh meat."

"I'll create a barrier of traps from the treerats and there are plenty of fungi in these woods to keep my belly full until you return. I'll be fine. Get going."

After giving him a hug goodbye, she led the blothrud warrior into the forest.

Chapter 2
The Forest

Drool dripped from the rotten teeth of a treerat as it watched a new prey enter the area below. Its back lifted as it prepared to spring off the limb and down onto its latest victim. The mangled hair across the rat's body was matted down against its skin, and nearly blended into the bark of the local trees. It was ready for a fresh kill, but it wasn't alone. Dozens of other treerats all stood ready to leap down on the stray travelers for their own mouthful of flesh.

Each moment became tenser as the treerats adjusted their positions to make their attack. Scars covered their body from prior attacks as well as fighting among themselves for their portion of the remaining meat and internal organs of the victim. Meals were rare, so every part of the prey was consumed if possible.

The time had come as they watched a young lady make her way through the forest undergrowth, holding open a large sack. It was time, as the treerats attacked from above, each timed their jump perfectly to land on her from their own branch.

Tilli glanced up and saw the first treerat jump toward her from above. Holding out her empty sack, she stretched out the mouth of the fabric bag as wide as she could.

With its mouth open to bite her and its claws poised to dig into her flesh, the rat was suddenly shot with a burst of high-pressure water, knocking it unconscious and in a new direction, right into Tilli's open sack.

Goothr shot one intense spray of water after another from his powerful mouth. Each hitting his mark and each rat landing in the sack as Tilli walked along with her arms out straight until all of the local rats had jumped down or run off.

"I will never get used to you doing this," she said with a slight laugh.

"Don't tell anyone else," Goothr said with a mouthful of water, splashing her with some of it as he talked. "Blothruds are supposed to fight with their hands and teeth, not their spit." He then took the sack from her and gave it a mighty slap against the ground, instantly killing all the treerats inside.

Wiping off the light shower she received from his mouth, Tilli could tell the other rats didn't go far. "More will come, you know. They will be back."

"Good. Goothr gets hungry often," he said.

"That's for sure, my big friend." she replied as she noticed a small opening in the trees in the distance. "Let's camp there for the night. At least they can't jump down on us. They'll have to run across the ground like normal vermin." Her sarcastic tone was intentional.

They quickly cleared away a layer of snow before starting to make camp in the center of the small treeless area. Goothr snapped dead wood into firewood-sized chunks and Tilli made a circle of rocks for her smaller sticks to start a fire.

Reaching her hand into her satchel, she felt around for the correct Runestone. Each had a round crystal in the center of one side of the flat hexagonal stone. They all had from one to six small gems, each near one of the hexagon's corners. But most importantly, each had an exclusive pattern of harmonic ridges that made it unique and identified the vibration that was used to obtain each E'rudite power.

She pulled out the Runestone she was looking for and held it with both hands, extending them toward the sticks she wanted to light on fire. Closing her eyes, she focused on the harmonics drawn on the stone and envisioned pushing out mental thoughts of energy that would conjure that action. After a minute of focusing, the wood in the firepit began to turn red from the inside, and worked its way out. Soon after, a flame burst forth and the sticks carried the energy on their own to the rest of the sticks and then branches as they were added. Tilli no longer needed to use the Runestone to keep it going, so she tossed it back into the satchel.

Goothr was always amazed at her powers. "Can you teach me to do that?"

She laughed. "I'm still learning myself. I don't know how to use most of these. The ones I do, I need to learn how to use those E'rudite powers without the help of the Runestones. Maybe someday I will be skilled enough to train others, such as yourself."

He smiled only for a moment and then became quite serious. "Tilli," the blothrud asked in a soft deep voice.

She gave a deep sigh, as she knew he was about to ask her something emotional that had been on his mind. "Yes, Goothr?"

"Can I ask you something without you getting mad at me?"

"Why would you think I would get mad at you?"

"Because you don't like me asking questions that you think I should already know the answer to."

"Well, there is some truth to that. I don't like repeating myself over and over again."

"Oh," Goothr said, and then put his head down. "Never mind."

"Spit it out," she said before realizing that wasn't the best choice of words, knowing his talent of spitting at birds and treerats, as well as her. "What's on your mind?"

"Tilli?"

"Yes, Goothr?" Her patience always started to run thin when he danced around something instead of just telling her his thoughts. "Just say it."

"Okay." He nodded and the 9-foot-tall, battle-ready blothrud spent a moment to gain the strength to ask her his question. "Why are we here?"

It took her a moment to let the silliness roll off. "To be honest, I'm not entirely sure, my friend." Her words made Goothr feel better about not asking a stupid question. "It all happened so quickly. I lost everything in my life and then the next thing I knew I was told to follow you and Pruva into the Govi Glade sphere before it was too late." This was the first time she had had the chance to think about it. "I'm following Pruva's plan to help him, because he's our friend and it's what he wants."

Goothr nodded in agreement. "He is our friend. But you are my friend as well. What do you want?"

"Me?" She was a bit taken aback by the question. "All I ever wanted was to be the first Num E'rudite. But now that my master betrayed me and with the E'rudite temple gone, I'm not quite sure what I want."

Goothr looked up into the clouds that still had a bit of red glow from the sunset. "Goothr wants to make others happy," he said with a sigh. "Goothr has hurt many in battles, but wants to hear laughing and see smiling."

"That's very noble of you, but those things are fleeting moments that disappear when real life comes back into play."

"Why?"

"Well, because real life isn't always fun and filled with laughter. We have work to do in order to stay alive and feed ourselves. Just like we're busy right here, making fire and preparing to roast up some rats." Her face gave away her lack of interest in eating such things.

"Why can't we smile and be happy while we do these things?"

"True. But sometimes bad things happen. For example, Pruva got hurt. That's not something to smile about."

"We can smile that he's okay and didn't hurt himself worse."

"I guess. But my point is, life is hard and filled with things that aggravate us or make us sad. I give you that we need to enjoy life as well, but it's not realistic to think we can be happy the majority of the time."

"Goothr wants to try. Is that okay?"

Tilli smiled at the silly request. "Of course, it's okay. Just know that it's unrealistic."

"Okay. Thank you. I will be happy as I break limbs for the fire because it will give us heat and keeps the rats away." He then proceeded to wear an oversized smile on his muzzle as he pounded limbs across his leg to break them down to size.

Tilli chuckled at the goofy sight of the silly expression on the massive warrior as he was hard at work. Getting back to her own duties, she asked herself out loud, "What do I want? I want... stability... security... and people I can trust." With a sour look upon her face, she plucked the first treerat from the sack and started preparing it to be cooked over the fire. "I don't want to live not knowing where my next meal is coming from, or if there is a next meal available. I've lived on the streets with no home, and I don't ever want to go back to that, and yet here I am once again." Using her knife to prepare the rat, she glanced out into the forest to see if any more were planning on attacking during the night. "I want a safe place to live and sleep, where I don't fear for my safety all the time." She thought about her statement for a moment. "After we complete this task for Pruva, I should go back to the temple and help rebuild it in order to reclaim the lifestyle I once had."

"Anything else?" Goothr asked.

Slightly startled, she didn't realize he had been listening to her ramblings. Slightly embarrassed, she shook her head no, but then stopped as she glanced at her satchel of Runestones. "I want to be strong enough to protect myself and those that I care about. I never want to live in fear again."

"Goothr is strong enough to protect us."

She laughed. "I know. But there are times that I want to be strong enough to live without being at the mercy of others."

Finishing his duties with the firewood, the blothrud sat next to Tilli and smiled at her attempt to skin and prepare the rat for cooking. "Let Goothr do this. I've done this all my life."

She knew this wasn't a strong skill of hers and she had only done this a few times in order to survive in the wild. The opportunity to hand off the task was not one she would mind.

Grabbing the knife and sack of rats, Goothr began his work like a professional. With lightning speed and precise cuts, he had all of the treerats prepared and hanging over the fire in no time. Once done, he looked at her and increased his awkward smile. "See. I stayed happy."

They both laughed and she moved back from the fire to allow him to continue with his tasks. Reaching into her pack, she checked to see what had survived the trip so far. She had packed in a hurry and then items were tossed about or crushed while landing in the Govi Glade. It was worth taking an inventory.

For the most part, everything was still functional. The portal crystals appeared to be fine, the camping gear was functional, and the few medical supplies were still available. It was then that she pulled out a small wooden coffer and sat it on her lap and stared at it.

"What's that?" Goothr asked.

"It's a box of notes from my grandfather. He actually grew up in the future and then used the Govi Glade to come back in time, much like Pruva did." Her hands gently touched the box, in hopes of feeling his presence. She had never met him. In fact, up until moments before falling into the glade, she didn't know who he was. Using her limited E'rudite skills, she relaxed and tried to connect with the item. And, to her surprise, it worked. She had visions of her grandfather carrying the box across the lands and in various cities and caverns. She could feel his emotions tied to the wooden coffer as he protected it and filled it with his thoughts and records of his journeys. But then, she also felt another owner of the item with more devious motives. This final vision snapped her out of her trance, just as her friend spoke to her.

"What did he say in the notes?"

"Um, I don't know yet. I haven't had time to read them. All I know is that Master Schullis had these so he could foresee the future based on what events were recorded on the papers within."

"I don't read well. Do you have anything better than things to read?"

A slight pat on the wooden coffer and a deep breath allowed her to end the emotional connection and set aside her visions for the moment to see what else was in her pack. "Oh, look. Here is a ring that once belonged to Irluk."

"Is it magic?"

She took a moment to think about how to answer the question. "Well, it's kind of the opposite of magic." Seeing his confused expression, she continued. "If you have the ring, you can't be affected by magical spells."

"All spells?"

"I would assume so. That was why Master Schullis got it to protect himself." Slipping the ring on her finger, she showed him. "See? Now I can't be affected by magic."

"Would it protect me?"

"I don't think it will fit on your fingers, but perhaps if you held it in your fist or wore it as a necklace. Perhaps we could try…" She stopped her sentence upon hearing rustling in the forest by something much larger than a treerat.

Goothr heard it as well and instinctively stood up in a battle-ready pose.

Talking could be heard from the darkness as several voices were now heard on one side of the camp and then the other. They were surrounded.

They didn't have to wait long before a half dozen young men slowly walked out of the darkness and into the open area. Wearing dark leather hooded cloaks, it was difficult to see their faces. Each carried some type of weapon or enchanted items that they held ready to use.

Tilli spun around to get a count of seven intruders that had completely encircled them. "Who are you? What do you want?"

Goothr instantly became protective of his friend and growled at the young men as he prepared to do battle.

One of the taller thugs stepped forward. "I never thought I'd see a blothrud and a Num traveling together."

"What's a Num?" the youngest of the lot asked.

"They are lessor humans. Smaller. Frail. Pale skin with dark emotional markings. You should be able to take her all by yourself."

The youngest lad nodded and moved in to grab her.

Tilli knew she didn't have time to calmly summon her E'rudite harmonics, so she grabbed a log from the fire and waved the flaming end toward him.

Jumping back, the boy fell to the ground with a surprised look, while his friends laughed.

While Tilli's attention was on the boy on the ground, two others rushed in from behind her and grabbed her.

Goothr immediately leaped over to save her, only to find himself stuck in midair.

The leader of the batch had said a few magical words and snapped open his enchanted folding hand fan. Waving the fan gently in the direction of the blothrud, he was able to keep the creature in mid-jump.

Goothr reached out to Tilli in a desperate attempt to continue his movement to save her, but he no longer had control.

A shift of the leader's wrist caused the magical field holding Goothr to then push him up against a tree.

The loud crash of the blothrud's back slapping against the tree trunk echoed in the forest. It was a wonder that Goothr and the tree endured the impact.

Continuing to wave the fan back and forth with slight wrist movements, the leader walked over to the blothrud. He then pulled back his hood to expose his long black mohawk haircut, a puff of hair between his lower lip and chin, and black tribal tattoos on his cheeks under his eyes. "That's amazing. I've never had anyone survive that."

Goothr was in pain, but he was more concerned about his friend. "Leave her alone!" he growled as he tried to lean forward.

"Miv, tie the beast down so I can get on with business."

"You got it, Durren," the other lad said. Stepping next to his leader, he pulled back his cloak to expose the bracelets around his wrists. Moving his arms in circles, he started chanting in a foreign tongue to activate the enchanted bracelets.

Nearby limbs and vines reached out to capture the blothrud. Vines twisted around his limbs as branches piled across his chest. The pressure continued to increase until Durren nodded and snapped his folding fan closed. With Durren's spell ended, Miv now held Goothr with his magic over the local plants.

Tilli continued to struggle, as the two young men had a firm grasp of each of her arms. She hadn't let go of the log yet, and was still trying to wave the burning part at them. In addition, she had kicked the youth back to the ground twice since the incident had started.

The youngest was clearly embarrassed, as his friends laughed at his inability to take control of a girl who was already being manhandled by two others. With a new passion, he ran up and threw his fist at her, but the Num ducked and one of the boys was smacked across the jaw, knocking him to the ground.

Tilli used the opportunity to kick the youth in-between the legs and then shove the fiery end of her log in the face of the other. And before she knew it, she was free and standing firm with her log overhead, ready to swing.

With a youth rolling around on the ground, a second tending to a potentially broken jaw, and a third packing snow onto his burnt eyebrows, Tilli watched two others pull out enchanted items to cast their spells upon her.

The first attack was simply expanding the flame on her log so quickly that it exploded with enough force to rip open her hand and knock her to the ground. The second spell was cast at the same time, and grabbed every pine needle in the area and shot it at her. The two at the same time caused a massive explosion near her head while thousands of needles covered her from head to toe.

Goothr wailed in horror at the scene. He could move his hands, but the rest of him was pinned to the tree. As hard as he struggled, he couldn't get free to save her.

It took a few seconds for the smoke to clear and the needles to drop once the spells ended. And it was then that they were all surprised to find her unscathed. Aside from the destroyed log she was holding, and thousands of tiny holes and rips in her clothing, she had no injuries.

The young men were in shock. They didn't know how to react.

Taking advantage of the situation, Tilli made a dash for Goothr, but was stopped by Durren, who grabbed her and tossed her to the ground.

"What the hell are you?" Durren asked in disbelief. "You should be screaming in pain from those spells, if not dead!"

Tilli ignored him and rolled to her feet to try to get past him and to her friend. But she was stopped again, and this time he tossed her into the campfire.

Goothr roared as loud as he could but was still unable to break free. He was furious.

Falling into the hot ashes, Tilli screamed and rolled out as quickly as possible. She stayed crouched down and grabbed handfuls of snow to rub on her hands to cool them down.

"What do you know? She can burn!" Durren said with a laugh as he walked up to her. "Why does this fire affect you, but magical fire does not?" He then grabbed the helpless girl by the shoulders and lifted her up to her feet.

Not wasting time, Tilli threw a handful of snow in his face. This blinded him just long enough for her to run to her blothrud friend, where she latched onto him with a hug as she held his hand as a child would the hand of their parents.

Miv laughed as he continued to work his spell to force the limbs and vines to do his bidding. And while his friends gathered their bearings, he used the spell to have the vines grab her as well.

By the time Durren had brushed most of the snow from his face and approached the two travelers, most of his team were standing there waiting for his orders. The only one that wasn't was the youngest who was busy going through Tilli's packs to find things of value. His discovery of the satchel filled with Runestones was the first thing he raised over his head as a victory.

"This was supposed to be a fun little excursion for us. We thought we'd rob you and then be on our way." Durren dusted off his cloak and raked his fingers through his thick mohawk. "But you had to make this painful. So, we're going to have to give you what you deserve."

Tilli kept her clutch on the blothrud and her hand in his. "If you leave right now without our items, I'll tell Goothr not to harm you."

As his team laughed, Durren was in no mood to play this game. "That's good of you, but I'm not so kindhearted. You're going to pay dearly for what you've done here. Do you not know who I am?"

"No," Tilli answered. "And I don't care." Taking a deep sigh, she looked up at her friend and said, "Okay,

Goothr. Teach them a lesson." She transferred Irluk's ring of anti-magic from her palm to his, and the blothrud instantly felt the magical forces controlling the branches and vines fall away.

Stepping forward, the foliage fell to the sides and the enormous dragon warrior was free. With a powerful roar, he sent chills down all of the young men's bodies.

Durren and a few others ran as their friends used their various enchanted items to cast spells upon the warrior beast, but none worked. One after another, they were grabbed by Goothr and tossed around the camp until they all had enough sense to run away. Most got away with limited injuries, but had permanent scars and a few broken bones. It would not be an evening they would soon forget.

After letting loose a few overwhelming war cries that carried deep into the forest, Goothr turned back to Tilli. "Goothr is so sorry!" Lowering himself to one knee, he gave her the ring back. "Goothr let Tilli get hurt."

"No. You saved me."

He shook his head, disappointed in himself. "I couldn't save you. You had to help Goothr with that ring."

"Yes, but we're a team. No, we're more than that. We're family, and family helps each other."

"Goothr is taller than Tilli, and should protect her. That is the only value I bring to you, and I failed."

"Oh, Goothr. You have never failed me." She gazed up into his sad eyes. "Can you help me now?" Knowing his need to feel valued, she played slightly on it. "I need some fresh water to clean out some blisters on my hands from when I fell into the fire. I can't do it myself. I need your help. Can you do this for me? Can you protect me by keeping me healthy?"

The blothrud nodded. "Goothr will help keep Tilli healthy," he replied in a halfhearted way. The act of watching the young men attack her while he did nothing hurt his heart and pride. It would take more time to repair than any cuts or burns they may have received. "Tilli?"

"Yes, Goothr?"

"Can I tell you something private?"

"Of course."

"I'm afraid."

"Of what?"

"This place scares me."

"Why? Because of those few bad men?"

"Yes. But not just them. If Pruva is correct, most people here have magic."

"I know."

"Goothr is strong, but I can't fight magic. That means I can't protect you or anyone else. I am weak in this place, and that scares me. I've never been weak before."

"Oh, Goothr." Tilli hugged her giant friend and thought about the situation, until an idea popped into her head. "What if you didn't have to worry about their magic?"

The blothrud nodded. "I would like that."

Pulling away from him, she found some string in her supplies and made it into a necklace long enough to hang from his thick neck. Reaching behind him, she tied it off nice and tight, after she added an item to it. She had threaded the string through Irluk's anti-magic ring.

"See this ring?"

He gave his normal quiet nod instead of saying yes.

"Anytime someone tries to cast a spell on you, just grab onto it and it will protect you from any enchanted item or Alchemist spell."

"His head changed from nodding to shaking. "No. This is Tilli's ring. Now you will be in danger."

"Not as long as I have Goothr with me," she said with a wink. "You will protect me."

He lifted up the ring in his palm. "Goothr will no longer be afraid." He lifted his chest slightly. "Goothr will protect you."

Chapter 3
Eldor'Craft

Tilli and Goothr had been walking for several days when the sounds of nature within the forest were slowly being interrupted by distant music and laughing of villagers. As they continued south, the town's festivities were heard clearer and then seen as they approached. The locals' preparation for a celebration was in full bloom, with banners being hung and flowers being set out. A wooden stage was set at one end of the open area, and benches were being set in place for everyone to attend.

Only humans were seen within the town's common area, so Tilli could fit in with a hood covering her colorful hair and facial soul-markings. Even if discovered to be a Num, hopefully they wouldn't have any prejudice against her. However, she knew better about her friend, Goothr. Blothruds were feared by most, and for a good reason. Most blothruds demanded obedience and dealt with issues through fighting. They added stress wherever they arrived.

Crouched down and hiding within the forest, just outside of town's common area, Goothr and Tilli were in awe at the excitement in the air. Minstrels practiced various instruments with music that sprang out in exciting tunes that caused children to dance, teenagers to flirt, and elders to tap their toes to the beats. The smell of freshly baked pies and bread wafted out of the open common. Chickens were scattered about looking for food, while several cats sat up on barrels and roofs as they watched a dog play with one of the children. Hammering fell in sync with the music as benches were assembled for spectators to watch the upcoming event, while some people climbed up ladders to hang vines from the buildings and the arches. Everyone was preparing for a festive occasion.

Tilli was mesmerized at the energy within the town they had stumbled upon. It was good fortune to find such a place to gather food and information for her journey to the coliseum.

Happy at first, Goothr's feelings changed to sadness as he watched one of the townsfolk sit idle and not participate in the merrymaking. It was a young, fragile girl sitting upon the short wall that surrounded the town's well. Bony and with greyish skin, she appeared sick, with sunk-in eyes and thinned hair. A crutch leaning against the well's wall implied she struggled to walk, and her torn clothes made one question if she was homeless.

The blothrud's heart sank as he stared at her. Why wasn't anyone paying attention to her? Being larger than her, he felt he should help. Without thinking, Goothr stood up straight with desires of rushing in to aid her. He was now exposed over the top of the bushes he had been hiding behind. And then, for an instant, their eyes locked, as he nodded to the sickly child that it would be okay. But as he did so, he saw the expression on her face turn to fear as she lost her balance and fell backward into the well.

The splash at the bottom of the well was muted by the activities in the common area. No one had seen her fall in. No one except Goothr.

Leaping out of the forest, Goothr raced toward the common area with a roar to get everyone out of his way.

The locals screamed at the charging three-meter-tall red warrior with a dragon head and wolf legs as it used its massive strength and sharp spikes to knock everything out of its path. The howling cry from the blothrud sent shivers down their spines as the thundering of his steps could be felt in the ground throughout the common area. A giant beast was attacking their town.

Goothr charged across the open area to save the sickly girl in the well, not realizing his demeanor appeared aggressive. Knocking a wagon, a few barrels, and several benches out of his way, he inadvertently destroyed anything in his path.

Chickens and cats scattered while the dog held his ground and barked at the intruder. People fell from ladders, tripped over benches, and dropped whatever they were carrying in order to escape the unexpected attack. Pandemonium erupted.

Focused on his task, Goothr had no idea that chaos reigned upon the townspeople as they ran for safety. Once Goothr reached the short stone wall surrounding the well, he stuck his large dragon head as far down into the well as he could. "You okay?" he roared.

Tilli followed in his wake. However, she was very cognizant of how the blothrud's entrance appeared to the locals. "Goothr!" she called down into the well where his head still was hanging. Not receiving an answer, she took a quick glance around to see if any of the locals had been injured. What she found was the residents were slowly changing from being fearful to being angry, and it wouldn't be long before they would try to hurt or capture the two travelers after they had disrupted their festivity preparations. "We need to get out of here!" she yelled down to him.

Goothr quickly popped his head out, accidentally breaking the wooden beam over the well that held the rope for the water bucket.

Tilli was relieved he was out. "Let's go, while we still have time!"

His attention wasn't on her words as he searched his surroundings. He then grabbed the water bucket and handed it to Tilli.

Instinctively grabbing it, she was completely confused. "We don't have time for…"

Goothr picked Tilli up before she could finish her thought and turned her upside down. Holding her with one large hand, he used the other to wrap the rope around her ankles.

Screaming, she began to panic and clutched the wooden bucket as she didn't know what was going on.

He then spun the loose rope around her chest and under her arms before flipping her right-side up again. Lifting her up over the stone wall, he let go and dropped her into the well.

Screaming the entire time, Tilli fell into the darkness and then splashed into the cool water below. She was fortunate that she didn't hit anything, but the uncontrolled landing knocked the wind out of her. Returning to the surface, she shook her hair out of her eyes to look up and see the silhouette of her friend's shoulders and head at the top of the well. But before she could call up to him, she felt a movement within the water. She wasn't alone! Tilli screamed as a head rose from within the water in the very dim light. Something was down there with her!

"The beast threw someone down the well!" shouted a townsperson, who was backed up by a few other observers of the scene. "Stop the creature before it destroys the town!"

The local dog continued barking as several of the residents grabbed whatever they could use as a weapon to stop the massive beast from hurting anyone else. Those without weapons threw lumber scraps and plant pots, which smashed into pieces as they hit the strong spikes across the blothrud's back.

Once again, Goothr stuck his head as far as he could down the well. "Grab each other! I'll pull you up!"

"Stop him!" yelled the butcher as he grabbed a boning hook and a bone saw from his shop.

Others followed suit. A farmer snatched up a three-tine manure fork from his tipped-over wagon, a baker collected a rolling pin and pastry knife, another picked up an axe, and another took up a log grabber. More locals were collecting weapons and joining the circle around the beast within the common area.

"Are you hurt?" the frail girl in the water at the bottom of the well asked Tilli.

Tilli stopped screaming as she attempted to process what was happening. She wasn't expecting to meet someone living in the bottom of a well. "How did you get down here?"

"I saw a creature standing in the forest and then I lost my balance and fell."

Realizing what happened, Tilli nodded. "That very creature is about to save your life. Grab onto me."

Goothr's focus was on the darkness below him. "Did you grab each other?" He heard some splashing about and some distant mumbling. "You ready for me to pull?"

"Yes!" Tilli shouted upward.

Goothr, not realizing his own strength, pulled as hard as he could.

Tilli and the girl were jolted up half the way in a single pull. Unfortunately, it caused them to be airborne for a moment while he changed his grasp on the rope for a second pull. In that time, the girls fell back down the well a few yards. The rope snapped taut and dug under Tilli's armpits, causing her to lose her grip on the girl who slid down to Tilli's legs before she could stop her fall.

"Goothr! Hurry!" Tilli yelled up before looking down at the girl hugging the Num's legs for her life. "Get ready for another quick pull up," she instructed the frail girl. And at that moment, they both dropped back down the well and hit the water with a hard splash.

"Ouch! Stop!" Goothr roared and he knocked the weapons away from him. The locals had him surrounded and were trying to gain the courage to fight the beast, but instead it became more of a bunch of pokes with sharp items while yelling at him. That said, it was enough to cut into the blothrud's skin and painful enough to stop him from pulling up Tilli and the girl.

"Get out of here, creature!" one man yelled.

"Don't let that beast grab you and throw you down the well," said one from the back.

"Go away!" several chanted as the others kept poking him.

Each time Goothr tried to turn back to the well, he received more cuts and gashes on his sides and back, causing him to turn back around to defend himself. But upon hearing a distant "Pull!" from Tilli, he reached out and swung his massive arm out at the crowd, knocking the front line off their feet. He then twisted around and began pulling on the rope, hand over hand, as quickly as he could.

By the time Tilli and the girl reached the top, they could see the locals hitting and stabbing the blothrud, while he never lost focused on the rope. One final pull caused the two girls to pop out of the well and land on top of Goothr as he fell onto his back, nearly squishing a few of the villagers and the local dog.

"Stop!" the sickly girl yelled to her people as she rolled off the beast and onto her knees. "Don't hurt him! He saved me!"

Both Tilli and the girl were soaked and now had blood staining their clothes and skin as Goothr's open injuries spit red fluid.

A sense of caution and disbelief filled the crowd until a middle-aged woman ran over to them and placed a warm hand upon the frail girl. "Ayva, are you okay?"

"Yes, mother. I am now."

Ayva's mother, O'vette, was dressed in quality clothes and a few nice pieces of jewelry. A subtle upper middle-class citizen feeling was present in all aspects of her speech, behavior, and appearance. Her dark brown hair was properly tied up with ribbons that matched her outfit.

"What happened here?" she asked in a very commanding voice.

"I fell down the well," Ayva replied. "And this creature was the only one that saw me fall in, so he saved me."

Looking about at the destruction to the common area, the weapons in everyone's hands, and the blood dripping from the blothrud's body, O'vette asked, "How does Ayva's fall into the well explain all of this mess?"

One by one, the locals turned down their eyes and tucked their weapons away from her sight. Most were embarrassed to explain their actions.

Seeing everyone's head down, Goothr did the same; he dropped his head in shame even though he didn't understand what he had done wrong. He just had a feeling he was in trouble.

"This is our fault," the Num said after catching her breath. "I'm Tilli, and this is my friend, Goothr. We were traveling through the forest, and we heard such beautiful music and joyful spirits that we stopped to view your festivities. We meant no harm." She reached out to shake O'vette's hand, only to spray water and some of the blothrud's blood on her stunning outfit. "I am so sorry."

O'vette stepped back and closed her eyes. It was clear that she was holding back her anger over the staining of her wardrobe.

Ayva stepped away from the well, toward her mother, to keep the focus on what the outsider had done. "If they had not been passing by, I may have never been seen again. No one could hear my cries for help. They saved my life."

"You shouldn't have been out here in the first place, especially in those ratty old garments. You need your rest!" O'vette's stern motherly words were to be heard and obeyed, not to be argued with, and Ayva knew better. "Now you're soaking wet out in this cold air. You're just asking for this illness to get worse."

Once O'vette felt she had gotten her point across, she looked about the common area and shook her head at the mess. "Put those weapons away and use that energy to clean up this area," she ordered the villagers. "We have a lot more to do before the celebration takes place." Swiveling her head to find a few key people, O'vette continued with her orders.

"Give these two young ladies something warm to cover up with before they freeze to death."

Most of the locals nodded and went about the task of cleaning up the mess and putting things back in place. However, a few stood their ground. "O'vette, what about the beast? Surely, we can't allow a blothrud to roam our streets. What of our wives and children? What if it gets hungry and takes one of them as a snack?"

O'vette considered their words and eyed the tall warrior creature before her. "Why did you come here? What was your purpose?"

Goothr was on the defensive and his head lowered a bit when he pointed at the frail girl. "She fell into the well. She needed help."

O'vette nodded. "Why did you want to help her? You didn't know her."

"She is smaller than I am."

O'vette looked confused.

Goothr went on to explain. "My mother told me I should protect those smaller than I am, because I am bigger and stronger, so it's my responsibility."

At first, she thought the beast was joking, but O'vette finally realized he was serious. "You saved her because of what your mother said?"

With a few strong nods, he added, "She wouldn't lie to me."

"Of course not," O'vette said with an enjoyable chuckle at his innocence. "Seeing that everyone in the town is smaller than you, does that mean you'll protect all of us?"

He took the time to look around to make sure everyone in the common area was shorter than he was. Most were just over half of his height and none came close, so it was a bit comical to see him take the time to study each of them. Standing up straight, he gave a firm nod. "I would."

"What would you protect us from?" O'vette asked as she watched his reaction as well as the small group of men fearful of the blothrud.

"Hmmm… Goothr would have to think about that," the blothrud answered. "I would protect against bad things that are bigger than you."

"Would you fight dragons and Alchemists for us?" one of the men blurted out. But he was scolded by O'vette's eyes the moment he did.

"Goothr has fought dragons and Alchemists."

"Wait a minute," Tilli finally stepped in. By this point the adrenaline was wearing off and her wet clothes in the cool air were making her shiver a bit, in spite of now being covered with thick blankets. "Goothr is here to protect me on my mission, not to help you fight your enemies. I'm sorry for the disruption, but we are not here to get involved. We will help clean up and then be on our way."

O'vette held out her hand to stop Tilli from leaving. "It was simply a question. An inappropriate one, but just a question." Once she saw the Num relax, she continued. "You have been traveling and need winter clothing. Please take time to stay with us long enough to eat, sleep, and prepare for the rest of your journey. You're welcome to restock your supplies before you leave. Perhaps you would like to stay long enough to join us for an upcoming celebration."

"I would hate to impose," Tilli said, even though she would enjoy some fresh baked bread and cheese. But then again, she could find out more about the area and see if she was heading on the correct route to the coliseum. "Although, I could use some guidance in planning the next leg of our travels."

"Good. Then it's settled." O'vette turned to the remaining men. "All we need now is a guide to show you around town and to stay with you to make sure this…", she glanced around the common area that was being cleaned up, "…doesn't happen again."

The men looked at one another with wide eyes as none wished to take on the tasks, but they were relieved to hear someone else volunteer for the job.

"I'll be their guide," Ayva announced. Her hands shook from the chilly air against her wet clothes under the dry blanket. "I'll show them around and they can stay in the town hall. It's the only place large enough for Goothr to stand up straight in."

"You?" O'vette didn't like the sound of this. "How many times have we had this conversation? You should be resting."

"That's all I've been doing. I sit around and watch others contribute. I want to help."

"You need to help yourself by spending more time in bed. Now, go dry off and get some fresh clothes on before you make things worse for yourself."

"Mother, please. I promise not to overexert myself. I'm just going to show them where they can stay. I'll have others deal with gathering food and clothing. I spend most of my time sitting anyway. Why not let me sit with them and get to know them?"

It took her a few moments to agree. "You will be their guide. But I expect you to head home the first sign of you being exhausted from this."

"Thank you, Mother." Her lips were shivering, and she was more than ready to get indoors near a warm fire.

Turning to Tilli and Goothr, a smile finally grew upon O'vette's face. "I will plan to eat in the town hall with all of you tonight." She then glanced down at the red spots on her white robe and dress. "But right now, I need to go home and change into something with less blood on it."

Chapter 4
Ayva

The town hall was the only public building in the community. Above its entrance was a decorative 'EC' symbol which stood for their village's name and the items they created. The Eldor'Craft symbol was renowned across the lands and only the finest of items could bear it.

The hall was a large two-story stone building with one tall main room, a few small rooms in the back and then a staircase leading to a loft above. The main room was equipped with tables and benches for social gatherings, town meetings, concerts, and a host of other indoor activities. A large fireplace was placed in the middle, where the staircase separated the main room from the smaller rooms in the back. Over the mantel hung several tools normally used for the various trades performed within the village.

In general, the décor was rustic but in very good shape, and clean. Hides from various animals covered the chairs near the fireplace as well as some benches, but it didn't give off the feeling of a hunter's lodge. Instead, it was clear these people appreciated the long-honored traditions of the town's basic trades. Symbols were displayed on the walls that represented blacksmiths, glaziers, woodworkers, jewelry makers, and so on. There was a lot of pride taken in using their hands and long-established methods.

Ayva had instructed a few locals to start a fire and gather some dry clothes as she led Tilli to a back room to dry off and change.

The room in the back provided a few chairs, a table, and shelves of supplies. It would have to make do as a dressing room. Within minutes, dry outfits were dropped off.

The fresh, finely crafted items were a blend of stylish and yet naturally rugged. Tilli received nice thick hides with the fur inside and exposed along the trim. The garments were fashioned into a mid-length skirt and crop top.

Ayva had received a finely decorated full dress that was more appropriate for her age and covered her thinner body from the cool nights.

Tilli began unbuckling her belts and removing her wet items as she glanced over to see Ayva's depleted body. The color of her skin and the whites of her eyes appeared slightly jaundiced with a yellowish gray hue. In addition, there were bruises and lesions throughout her body and her hair had thinned slightly in a few areas. As tempting as it was to ask questions about her problems, it would be out of place to potentially embarrass the frail girl.

She wasn't the only one looking on with questions. After removing her dress, Ayva pulled on a garment and asked, "What's wrong with your skin?"

Tilli looked down for potential cuts or bruises, but didn't see any. "What do you mean?"

Ayva stepped over and pointed at her dark markings that ran down the length of her body. "Do they hurt?"

A coy smile lifted upon one side of Tilli's face. "No. They are my soul-markings. All Nums receive them when they come of age."

"How do they apply to your skin?"

"What? No. We don't receive them in such a way. They grow from within us as we learn and accept who we are. Each of us has a different pattern, based on our personality and they darken when we are filled with emotions."

"Does it hurt if you touch one?"

Thinking it was an odd question, Tilli replied candidly, "No, but these areas are more sensitive." Seeing that Ayva wasn't shy about asking personal questions, she thought she would as well. "What exactly are you suffering from? Is it the oma'haige?"

The girl lowered her head as her shoulders rolled in. "I will leave, if you would like."

"Leave? Why?"

"I know how many fear that they may catch it from me. I don't want you to be uncomfortable."

"I'm not. I've seen a few people with it over the years. Who is helping you recover from this?"

"It's not treatable."

Tilli was surprised by the answer. "Of course it is. I've seen cases cleansed."

Ayva's eyes grew large with excited skepticism. "Really?"

"Yes. This is not a death sentence."

"This is amazing news! We've tried everything and haven't found anything to help."

"Well, we're more than happy to help."

Ayva rushed over and gave Tilli a tight hug, nearly squeezing the air out of her. "I can't wait to tell Mother at dinner. She will be so excited to hear the news!" But her own excitement was having an adverse reaction on her frail body as she started to wheeze and struggle to stand up straight.

"Calm down," Tilli said, as she helped her into a chair. "Do you want me to call for help?"

"No." Ayva breathed heavily a few times before continuing. "I just need to rest a moment."

"Take all the time you need." Once she was sure the girl was okay on her own, she focused on cleaning herself up before trying on her new clothes.

Chapter 5
O'vette

It wasn't long before Tilli and Ayva made their way back into the main hall, where Goothr was stoking the fire inside a grand fireplace, which was nearly big enough for Tilli to walk into.

Ayva casually grabbed a handful of cinnamon sticks out of a nearby hanging pouch and tossed them onto the burning logs to give the room a spicy and sweet aroma. She then made her way to a seat to rest her frail body.

O'vette arrived just as food was being delivered. She was dressed in an elegant gown with a furry, open front bolero shrug. Walking prim and proper, she was in control of every movement she took. "I hope these accommodations meet your needs. I'll have one of the back rooms made into a bedroom for you, but your large friend will need to sleep out here. It's the only room large enough for him."

Tilli was quick to respond. "You have been very generous. I will make sure I return these garments before we continue on our way."

"No need. I picked those out specifically for you. I'm glad they fit." She lifted her hand and twirled her finger to indicate she wanted Tilli to turn around.

Tilli complied, and spun around. "I can't believe you had these available."

"They were made for Ayva for her next birthday, but unfortunately Ayva hasn't been taking good care of herself, and it's unlikely she will survive that long."

The cold words struck Tilli hard as she watched the girl sink into her dress. "About that. It's my understanding that she is suffering from oma'haige."

"It's true. But she would live longer if she would stay in bed and rest more. Unfortunately, I would have better luck herding cats."

"I'm going to die anyway, Mother. Why not let me live some before I go?"

A strong scowl from her mother ended the remarks from her daughter.

Tilli knew she was stepping into an emotional subject, so she attempted to tread lightly. "May I ask what remedies you tried to cure it?"

"No, you may not," O'vette replied. "We've tried everything, and nothing has worked. Some actually made it worse. We are no longer going to experiment with her life."

"How do you know you've tried everything?"

O'vette veered her eyes away and straightened her clothes. "My mother had the same infections in her body. I spent years searching for a cure, only to see her pass away in pain from the treatments. I won't put my daughter through that agony."

Tilli realized that O'vette was most likely more knowledgeable about the topic than she was. "Curing illnesses is not my forte, but I have seen others treat people afflicted with the oma'haige."

"Perhaps it was a different disease. What Ayva has is not treatable with any ointment, root, or natural elixir."

"That might be true. But where I come from, some of the E'rudites were able to heal tumors and diseases such as this one. Do you know where we can find an E'rudite?"

O'vette's face hardened at the question. "E'rudite? Do you mean a spellcaster?"

The staff setting out the food froze in motion at the topic, before quickly removing themselves from the room.

"No." Tilli thought about how she can quickly define the difference to help O'vette identify an E'rudite that she may have heard of. "E'rudites tap into harmonics of their surroundings and become one with the natural forces of the world in order to create, repair, or remove what is needed.

Spellcasters learn to mix a combination of physical objects, noises, and an energy source. They don't know why the combination reacts to make the spell it does, but they know how to combine them. They also like to create enchanted items to allow them to perform the spells without even understanding the basics."

Ayva and Goothr gave each other confused glances before they looked back at Tilli and O'vette.

"I've never heard of anything like an E'rudite," O'vette said with a dismissive wave of her hand. "But we have more spellcasters than you would ever want to see. They live within Stone'Ring."

"Hmm, I don't know if they can cure your illness. Have you tried asking them?"

Ayva's eyes lit up again as she watched her mother's reaction.

"We do not deal with spellcasters. It's forbidden." Her gaze slowly lifted to the tools hanging over the massive fireplace as memories of lost ones filled her thoughts. "I'm not willing to lose more of our people at the hands of unorthodox ways."

Tilli followed her gaze to the items and wondered about their significance. "Did something happen to trigger this belief?"

"Yes, something that is in my power to ensure it never happens again. Those tools represent a mistake I made long ago. They remind me and our people to never let our guard down again."

"May I ask what happened?"

"No. It is not of your concern." O'vette could tell her harsh tone was more abrasive to the outsider than she expected. "We have a history of excellence without trying to cut corners and add magic. We have no interest in it, and those who use magic must leave."

"Why?"

"Because it is our law." O'vette's voice had lowered and was sharp. Her strong voice resonated with authority. "Spells and magic are dangerous and can't be trusted."

Tilli thought the comment was a bit odd. "Is it the spells that are dangerous, or is it those using magic who can't be trusted?"

"Both. There is no room for any unnatural activity in our society. They are forbidden."

"But there could be some spells that could make life easier, such as conjuring food and water for those who are hungry."

O'vette shook her head in disagreement. "If we work together as a society, why would we allow some to starve in the first place?"

"How about healing potions? Surely, it couldn't be bad to utilize such magic on those that are injured."

"We don't know the side effects it could have on our people. It might be different if we could trust the spellcasters, but each time we've tried to build relations with them it has ended in pain and death for our people. Even when we leave them alone, they attack us."

"Attack? For what purpose?"

"Our resources. Our craftsmanship. As they rely more on their spells, they have become lazy in the basic trades, so they find towns and villages that have what they want, and they burst in to steal our goods." O'vette walked to the dining table and poured some hot tea into several ceramic cups for everyone to help them warm up. "Apparently, the quality of our goods enhances their spells. They've learned to bestow spells within our finely crafted items to be saved for later use. You should never purchase their jewelry or blades. Not only are they most likely stolen from us, but a spell is likely to have been embedded within them."

Finishing her first sip of tea, Tilli enjoyed the fragrance and warmth it provided as she contemplated O'vette's challenge. She had a natural tendency to try to solve whatever issues she came across, so she provided a suggestion. "Can you work out a trade? Can they purchase items from your people to avoid raiding them?"

"That's how it started, but it led to them demanding lower prices. Once we refused, small bands of looters started showing up at night. It quickly led to them showing up during the day with magical weapons that we could not fend off. They no longer fear us catching them as they come and take what they wish. At least they did."

"What does that mean? Has it stopped?"

Refilling Tilli's tea, she used the time to consider how to reply. "It is about to change. We have taken steps to stop them. We have started making sure we have weapons available on or near our people at all times, which is why they we so quick to respond to your blothrud crashing into the common area."

Goothr had been attempting to hold one of the tiny teacups in his massive hand and press it up against his lips as Ayva was quietly instructing him how to do so. His thick fingers kept getting in the way, so he finally decided to tip his head back and pour it straight down his throat. It was at that very moment that he heard O'vette talk about his unexpected arrival, causing him to drop the cup down into his throat along with the hot liquid. Snapping his dragon jaw shut, he stared at O'vette with wide eyes as he pretended that nothing had happened.

Ayva busted out laughing at the action and his expression of innocence, before leading him off to one side to allow him to cough the cup back up.

O'vette attempted to ignore the massive warrior creature choking on the ornate teacup. "True, we have much more practicing to do to learn how to fight, but it is an unfortunate reality that we must live within nowadays."

Tilli watched Ayva attempt to loosen the cup from the creature's throat by patting his back at first, before opening up the two large front doors and leading him out of the building. Once they had left, she asked O'vette, "You mentioned steps. What other steps have you taken?"

The town leader grinned. "Let's hope we don't have to find out."

There was clearly an air of secrecy that wasn't going to be shared with an outsider, so Tilli nodded and changed the subject. "Well, I appreciate you putting us up for the night, especially with winter weather on our heels. We will be on our way in the morning."

"So soon? Where are you heading?"

Beyond the open doors, Tilli could see Goothr in the dirt street on his back while Ayva instructed children to jump on his stomach in order to get the teacup out of his throat. It didn't take long before the cup shot up in the air and was caught by Ayva. Even though the task was completed, Goothr and the children continued to play as they jumped on him and he tossed them high into the air. It was good to see the blothrud having some fun with others with the same mental acuity.

Tilli returned her attention to O'vette. "Actually, I'm currently on a mission."

"I'm intrigued. Do tell."

"We are trying to stop a small black dragon from finding a Runestone that could change the balance of power. It is extremely important to me that he does not obtain it before we do. Once we have it, I'll hide it so no one can use it."

"Dragon, you say? We have seen more of them in the past few months than we have in the past several decades. They are now in league with the spellcasters and help protect the Stone'Ring."

"Stone'Ring?"

"Yes. It is where the spellcasters live and practice their Alchemy. It is an impenetrable fortress protected by dragons, casters, and their spells. If your treasure was taken to the Stone'Ring, then it is gone for good. You will never be able to get in, let alone find the stone you're looking for and then get out." O'vette could see the disappointment in Tilli's face. "I'm sorry, but even if everyone in our town raised up their weapons against them, we'd never make it beyond the exterior wall."

"But I have to retrieve it."

"Then I hope your little black dragon finds that luck is not in his favor."

Chapter 6
The Dragon

As the warm sun started melting the snow on roofs and the base of the homes, the sound of dripping into puddles and the splashing of footfalls could be heard in every direction within the village.

One set of tracks made a distinct noise, as the blothrud walked across the muddy streets from the melting snow. He carried Tilli in order to prevent her from getting her new clothes dirty. It was his suggestion that he do this, and Tilli felt it was very valiant of him to do so.

Arriving at one of the homes in the area, Goothr lowered her so she could knock on the door. After a little bit, she knocked a second time.

Tilli was a bit confused. "This is the one she told me."

"Maybe she isn't home," Goothr suggested.

"No, I think she is, and I'm worried about her. Let me poke my nose in to make sure she is well." Opening the door, she hopped out of Goothr's arms and into the front room. "Ayva?"

The shades were closed, and the only light was coming from the open doorway she just walked through. It allowed her to see a table with chairs, a fireplace and hearth, and shelves filled with plates and containers. The rooms beyond the various doorways were dark. She couldn't tell which one would be a bedroom for her friend. "Hello?"

The sounds of small feet ran across the room, near her. It startled her, but she remained still. It could have just been a cat or dog. Then the movement happened again in another part of the room. It was followed by a flapping sound as a large dark creature flew across the room up onto a tall cabinet.

Tilli held back a scream. Her first instinct was that it was a giant bat, but then she wondered if it could be Mel'tayn.

Up in the dark, near the ceiling, the creature perched on the cabinet and hissed at the intruder. "Go away!" it barked at her.

She stood absolutely still as she squinted her eyes to see what she was talking to. As it moved, she could make out a long neck and tail, and then a set of wings. She was now sure it was a small dragon. It had to be Mel'tayn. "You low-life thief! Return what you stole and leave this house!" She pointed at the open doorway with Goothr's backside blocking the exit.

"That's rich coming from someone that doesn't live here."

There was just enough light for Tilli to see into Ayva's bedroom. "My friend does. And I am here to protect her."

"You're a bit late for that. She's dying as we speak."

"What!?" She sprinted toward the room and ducked her head to avoid any attack from the dragon. "Ayva!" she yelled as she entered. "Are you okay?"

The dark bedroom had just enough light for her to see a bed and someone in it, so she rushed over to the bedside.

"Go away!" screeched the dragon as it flew into the room and grabbed Tilli's hair.

"Stop!" Tilli screamed and fell to the ground as she fought off the little beast. Freeing herself from its claws, she grabbed the first thing she could in order to use it as a weapon, which unfortunately, was a pillow. That said, she swung it several times as the dragon continued to try to attack her until she finally made contact. Once she did, the pillow exploded, and she heard the winged creature smack against the far wall and then down to the ground.

Taking the opportunity, she reached down to Ayva to see if she was still alive, only to find that it was a few pillows stuffed under the sheets. With no one in the bed, she pivoted around to face the dragon. "I don't know what type of game you're playing with us, but you can't stop us. We already know where it is. We'll have it and be back before you realize it. Then you'll be trapped here. Give back what you stole, and we'll take you back with us."

"Game?" the dragon hissed. "You break into our home, attack me, and destroy Ayva's room and then accuse me of playing some game?"

Tilli was tired of fighting in the dark. She opened the bedroom shutters to let the light in to improve her situation. As she stood there with her hair a mess and pillow feathers tossed across the room, Tilli watched as tiny dragon claws gripped the far side of the bed.

Pulling itself up, the yard-long dragon climbed up onto the bed and glared at Tilli.

Tilli squinted and blinked a few times. "You're green. When did you turn green?"

With a quick hiss, he tried to shake off some of the pillow feathers. "I was born green. Most green dragons are."

"You're a green dragon?"

"You're very observant," he hissed back sarcastically.

"You're not Mel'tayn."

A light growl was heard before he replied. "I never said I was."

"What are you doing here?"

"I'm here to protect Ayva."

"No. You said she was dying."

"She is. She has the oma'haige. She's been wilting away for years and doesn't have much time left." Stepping closer to her, across the bed, he leaned forward with his teeth showing. "What do you want with her and why are you in this house?"

Her experiences with Mel'tayn had given her a sour feeling about dragons, and it came across in her tone. "I'm just a friend who wants to help her."

"Well, friend, barging into her room and tearing it apart is not going to do that."

"No. I suppose not. But where is she?"

"She's out. She's always out, despite her mother's orders and my advice."

"Then I'll look for her elsewhere."

"Who should I tell her was here and made this mess?"

Unsure if she wanted to tell the creature anything of value, she finally spit out, "Tilli."

The name caused the green dragon to perk up. "Tilli of Farbank?"

"No. Tilli of Kingsfoot. How do you know of Farbank? I haven't lived there since I was a child."

He eyed her up and down to take it all in. "I have to say I expected more. It's about time you showed up," he said with a snarky attitude. "Nums from Farbank asked me to sit around here for years and wait for you. You sure took your sweet time to arrive."

"I doubt that very much. Who might these Nums be?"

"Your grandparents."

She was shocked by his answer. "What kind of game are you playing now? I never met my grandparents. They died long ago. In fact, if you lived in those times, you'd be long gone as well."

"Don't try to lecture me about timelines, when it's you who are the biggest violator of jumping from one time period to another?"

"What? If you're talking about the Govi Glade, I've only stepped through that once."

He growled at the comment. "You should have kept it at that. Instead, you go on using it as your portal to mess up events throughout history."

"Don't assume my future. I have no such plans!"

"I don't have to assume. Your grandparents lived through it, which is why they sent me here to stop you."

"Stop what?! You're talking gibberish!" Her head was spinning from the conversation. "I don't trust dragons in the first place, and you're not gaining any favors with this nonsense."

"I'm not looking for any favors from you. I didn't ask to come here. I was sent by Thorik and Avanda."

"Thorik Dain?"

"And Avanda. Your grandparents."

For a moment she believed him, but then was overcome with doubt. "Just because you discovered my grandparents' names, it doesn't mean you truly knew them or that they sent you here."

Pheosco was annoyed. "I don't have to prove anything to you. I traveled the lands with them and fought in battles to save this world. I've done my share in this life, and I don't owe you anything."

"If only there were some records of this, I might just believe you," she spit back at him.

Growling again at the young lady, he added, "There are, but Thorik's coffer of notes is long gone and hidden. If we had them here, you would see that—"

She interrupted him in mid-sentence. "I do," she said with slight surprise to the dragon.

"I find that hard to believe."

"I took them from… Never mind. I have a wooden box filled with notes from Thorik."

"You shouldn't have these. They shouldn't be exposed." His eyes squinted tight as he glared at her. "Someone, such as yourself, could use these to change events throughout time."

She squinted back. "If they truly were written by my grandfather, then no one should have them other than myself."

A long hiss could be heard from the green dragon. "If you've read them, then you know that I was there with Thorik and Avanda."

She wasn't sure how to reply at first. "I said I had them. I haven't actually had a chance to read many of them yet."

Pheosco liked the sound of that. "Then I'm not too late. I can remove them from you before you use them to mess everything up."

"I haven't messed with anything, and I certainly don't plan on handing over those notes to some little dragon with a grandeur complex."

"Nums!" he said in disgust. "You're all so difficult to work with!"

"Dragons are worse! Every single one that I have met wants to take something that doesn't belong to them!"

Their shouting stopped as they scowled at each other for a bit. The silence was needed for them both to calm down, as distrust was increasing on both sides.

"Hello?" Ayva's voice was soft as she entered the room. "Are you two fighting?"

"No," Tilli said, just as Pheosco said, "Yes."

The girl was disappointed. "Pheosco, please welcome Tilli to our home. She is a friend."

Lifting his gums on one side of his muzzle, he growled at the request before responding. "I know who she is."

"Tilli," Ayva continued with the introductions. "This is Pheosco. He has been my protector ever since he arrived in this village."

Her frown didn't change. "I've had trust issues with dragons in the past. It might take some getting used to having one around."

An uneasy, tense vibe filled the room as the three stared at each other.

"I'm Goothr!" shouted the blothrud through the open window. The sudden noise made all three of them jump and their hearts pound hard against their chests. It broke up the tension and nearly gave them a heart attack. "Come see what I found!" Pulling his head back out of the window, he walked away from the home.

After a few seconds of catching their breath, the little green dragon excused himself. "I have more important things to do." He then flew off into the other room.

Tilli looked around her. "Sorry for the mess. I'll clean it up."

"It's okay. Pheosco is just overprotective of me."

"I meant the mess to your room."

"Ah. Yes, we should clean that up before Mother gets home."

Chapter 7
The Village

After cleaning up her bedroom, Ayva led Tilli out into the village to show her what they had. The smells of fresh bread wafted through the air, while sounds of hammers bending metals into shapes could be heard from the next street over.

The baker tossed a small fist-sized loaf to Ayva as she passed by. It was still warm to the touch, and easy to break in half, and she handed one side to Tilli. The warmth of the soft textures inside filled their mouths with pleasure.

Seeing Goothr around the corner, they approached to see what he was so impressed with.

The roar of a fiery forge caught Tilli's attention as a master glazier pulled a glob of molten glass out of a furnace before she began blowing it up into the shape of a bowl. Behind her, shelves were filled with glass goblets, plates, and artistic items of various colors and shapes, as well as glass sculptures. The shop was busy with workers cleaning tools, stoking the fire, adding raw glass materials, and preparing items to be shipped.

Tilli found it ironic how much the massive warrior was intrigued by the frail glass items. Grabbing his hand, she led him away to follow Ayva.

Beyond the glass blowing and sculpting, was an area filled with wooden carvings. Several men and women were hard at work bringing in lumber, cutting out various shapes, sanding them down, and oiling them up to a bright shine. Everything from art and wooden bowls to carriage parts was being created in the row of buildings focused on the well-crafted exports.

The metal works and jewelry were just as impressive. Some items were built for endurance while some were made for decorations, but all were built by masterful hands and techniques to create the finest in the lands.

All trades had masters and apprentices as well as general workers who hauled materials or packaged items. It all worked so smoothly; unlike anything Tilli had ever seen. "It's almost like a dance."

Ayva was confused. "What?"

"The flow of everything in your village is so well choreographed that everyone's actions flow right into the next person's tasks. It's balanced and calming how everyone works together to ensure the pacing is right and no one is waiting for anyone else."

The sickly girl glanced about. "Is that different than other places?"

"Oh my, yes," Tilli contained a chuckle at the naïve comment. "Most places have more of a hurry up and then wait feeling." Watching the locals work, she enjoyed the harmony of it all. "This is very different."

"I wish I could see what you're talking about."

"Why? This is perfect."

"Because I've never been anywhere else."

Still gazing out at the various trades, Tilli replied without thinking. "Maybe you will someday."

"I won't be around someday."

"Oh, Ayva, I didn't mean to upset you."

"You didn't. It's just the reality of it. I'm dying and I'll never get a chance to live my life."

"If you had to be stuck in one place your entire life, this would be a wonderful place for it to happen. I wish I could have grown up here."

"But you didn't. You have travelled. You've seen other places, other cultures, other creatures. You've explored, while I've never been on an adventure and, as my days grow to an end, I now realize that I never will."

"Don't say that."

"Why? Because it makes you feel sad for me?"

"Because it's not true. There is still a chance to find a cure."

"It is true. There is no cure." The stress of the conversation was showing on her body, and she let out a few dry coughs.

Tilli didn't like the sound of that. "Let's get you home so you can rest."

"No. That's what everyone wants me to do," Ayva complained. "I need to experience life before I die. Resting may extend my life by a few weeks or a few months, but what good is that if I'm just lying there by myself? I'd rather have a short life with an adventure thrown in instead of a longer life in which I become a burden for others."

"Don't say that. You're not a burden."

"Every day I get weaker. It won't be long before I can't get out of bed. Others will have to tend to me as they extend my life to watch me slowly wither away." Ayva had clearly thought hard about this. "I don't want to go, but I have no choice. I want to live before I die, Tilli. Even if it's only for a day."

Tilli understood her challenge, but knew it was unlikely that a cure was available without the help of E'rudites. Perhaps the Alchemists could do something, but that didn't seem to be an option at the moment.

"What would you do?" Goothr asked Ayva. "If you had one day to do whatever you wanted."

"Goothr!" Tilli tried to hush him from causing the girl more stress about thinking of things that would never happen.

"I would live a lifetime in that day," Ayva answered. "I would go on an adventure and see new lands, races, and civilizations. I would be a hero and save the day. I would fall in love and get married." She smiled at the thoughts. "I would burn so brightly for that one day that I would be remembered forever as the girl who lived."

Goothr smiled. "I like that day."

"So do I," Ayva responded as she fell into deep thought for a moment before the sounds of music floated through the air. "Let's go watch!"

"Where?"

"The common area. They are preparing for the celebration."

Not wanting to miss anything, Goothr had more of a pep in his step than his sickly friend, so he asked if she wanted a ride. She gladly accepted the offer and was placed on his shoulder. Walking with a bounce of excitement in his step, she held onto the bony spikes on the back of his head while he held onto her legs to prevent her from falling off.

Tilli trailed behind as they arrived at the common area to see people fixing the damage from Goothr's arrival as well as adding new fixtures and decorations.

Musicians were busy practicing as children danced and frolicked about. Adults were teaching a new generation the proper steps in their folk dances.

Tinted glass globes were set on tables and awnings, each with candles in them to be lit for the festivities. Wooden carvings of the trade symbols were brought in to represent each of the disciplines that were so treasured in the village.

In addition, a tall tree was being lifted into position. The trunk and main branches had been built with metal interlacing with fine wood. Thousands of glass leaves had been attached to the hooks on the limbs with fabric, and each leaf provided an array of colors when hit by light.

"It's the biggest one yet," Ayva whispered into Goothr's ear. "Put me down, I want to see it from the ground."

Ropes and pulleys strained as the locals pulled to lift the top part of the tree to stand it up straight. They had never tried to move something that large, and the crossbeams bowed and moaned from the stress. This was the symbol of the village and the most important part of the celebration. It was almost vertical when the first rope snapped, and then a second. The weight of the top-heavy metal art started falling, and there was no way to stop it.

Those still holding onto ropes were lifted off the ground, while others ran for their lives so not to get crushed. In addition to the risk of life and limb, the metal art would surely be damaged beyond repair prior to the celebration. People screamed and ran for their lives.

As the moment of the crash approached, fear of injury and the sadness of the destroyed artistic symbol was on everyone's mind. Yet, oddly, no crash occurred. No sounds of metal snapping or clanging together filled the air. Instead, they heard a low grunt, as Goothr held the metal tree up from tipping over. Then, following a squat, he straightened his legs and arms to push the tree back upright, next to the water well.

Cheers and laughter filled the air, and those that had been upset with the blothrud the prior evening were now more accepting of his presence.

Goothr gave a cheesy smile that looked forced. He didn't understand the importance of his actions.

"Nicely done, my friend," Tilli said before leading him off to the side so the locals could get back to work. "You know, I think I'm falling in love with this place. It has everything I'm looking for. I think I could live here forever."

"You don't want to go back?"

"What's there to go back to? I don't have any friends or even a place to live there. Here, I could start fresh and learn a trade."

O'vette arrived to see what all the screaming was about, only to find everyone was busy working. "What's going on here?" she asked Ayva, who was walking back to Goothr to thank him.

"Nothing, Mother. Goothr was just helping prop up the sacred tree."

"And you felt the need to watch him instead of resting?"

"It's my fault. I asked Ayva to show us around," Tilli said to O'vette. "What exactly is the celebration all about?"

"It's our annual renewal to our trades where we pledge to maintain the finest of quality to all things we make." She then looked back at her daughter. "But the event isn't today, so there is no need for you to be out here, young lady."

"Yes, Mother."

"I don't want you to overdo it and not be well enough to attend the event."

"I know. Can Goothr carry me?"

"What? No. That's inappropriate to ask."

Goothr nodded his head with delight. "Goothr carry you."

Ayva smiled. "It would give me a head start in relaxing."

O'vette's eyes darted back and forth from her daughter and the blothrud. "Fine. Just take it slow."

Before she could say anymore, Goothr scooped Ayva up and started on his way back to her home.

O'vette stood there with Tilli, watching her daughter laugh on her ride in Goothr's arms. "I know I must sound cold to you, but she is all that I have, and I want to have her for as long as I can."

Tilli nodded. "She just wants to be happy and play like all children do."

"I know, but that drains her so much that I can feel her days being stripped away each time she is away from that bed."

"Is there no possible way to save her? Can we take her to other villages to see if they have a cure?"

"She won't make the trip. And even if she does, I don't want her to pass away in some foreign place. I want to be by her side, in our home, where my mother passed. That way their souls will be together."

Tilli struggled with the idea of giving up. "What if I found an E'rudite or Alchemist that I could bring here to help her?"

O'vette turned to face the Num head-on with a stern face. "We've talked about this. We do not allow such atrocities in this town. If you were to do such a thing, you would be banished from here and you would never see my daughter again."

"But what if it could help her?"

"This is not for discussion," O'vette demanded. "You don't know our history with their type. We will not change our beliefs for you or even my daughter."

Tilli knew there was no middle ground for her, so she dropped the conversation.

Chapter 8
Goothr

Goothr arrived at Ayva's home and set her down by the front door. "You stay calm so you can live longer," he said with a smile.

"That's not my goal, but thank you for your thoughts," she replied. But before he left, she asked, "Are you going on an adventure?"

"Yes. Tilli and I are going to find an ancient building and search for a magical stone."

"That sounds fun."

Goothr wasn't sure. "I hope so."

"Can I go with you?"

The blothrud's eyes grew with concern. "Your mother won't like that."

"Well, she just wants me to be safe. Would you keep me safe?"

He nodded his head. "I am taller than you, so I will protect you."

"See? Then my mother should be happy."

After giving it some thought, he asked, "What if she comes in and sees you're not in bed?"

"I'll stick some pillows under my sheets like I usually do."

"What if you go with us and then you get sick and don't feel good?"

She knew that was most likely what would happen. "Please, Goothr. Give me one adventure in my life and then I promise I'll stay in bed after that."

Goothr pondered the thought with great strain.

Unfortunately, Ayva couldn't tell if he was thinking hard or if he was having stomach cramps.

Perhaps it was the latter, for without warning, Goothr turned and ran from her doorway, around the corner, and out of sight.

As odd as that was, Ayva wasn't overly surprised, but she was a bit disappointed. She was hoping he would commit to taking her with him. Shrugging it off, she walked into her room and sat on her bed. With a deep sigh, she lay down and stared at the ceiling. It was so familiar. The long hours of every day looking at it allowed her to memorize every crack and the number of rings in every knot in the wooden beams. It was depressing.

Soon afterward, she was startled by Goothr popping his huge dragon head through her window. "Ayva?"

It nearly gave her a heart attack, before she jumped out of bed. "Goothr?"

"Yes, it's me."

"I know it's you. What are you doing here?"

"I came back with the answer."

"The answer to what?"

"If you feel sick during the adventure."

She waited for him to tell her the answer, but it never came. "So, what's the answer?"

Squeezing one of his arms into the window, followed by his thick neck and head, he had blocked nearly all the light coming in. Extending his arm and hand, he unfolded his fist near her face. There in his palm was a thin, long, black crystal. Once he had shown it, the blothrud smiled from ear to ear.

"It's a crystal."

He nodded his head, causing the wooden window frame to moan from his movements.

"How is this crystal the answer?"

"We plant half of the crystal here in your bedroom. When we spin the other half, it opens a magic doorway to go to bed."

She was in shock and slightly confused. She had never heard of such a thing. "Are you saying that if we travel and I need to come home, I can use this to just step back into my bedroom if I feel ill?"

He nodded again, as her wooden window trim cracked.

Fear of her mother finding out about her using a magical item such as this caused her to pause, before it was overtaken with the excitement of having one last chance to see the world outside of her village. "How does it work?

"I'll show you." With that he started to pull back out of her window, only to find himself stuck. The bony blades on the back of his neck were catching on the window frame as well as his arm had created too much pressure on his ability to move his neck free. Pulling and twisting, he grunted and made a series of odd faces in his attempts to break away. "I'm stuck."

"I noticed." She started pushing his arm and his snout, with little success. She finally gave up and said, "Just fall backwards."

Nodding, he just let his own weight carry him back, taking the window frame and part of the wall with him. He was lucky he only made a large hole in the home instead of taking the entire wall down as well. "I'm free," he said with the window frame still boxed in around him like a wooden tutu.

Ayva burst out laughing at the sight. "Yes, you're free. You'll need to show me that crystal trick after we get help fixing this."

Goothr nodded. "We'll plant it in the ground some place special, where no one will find it, except us, because we know where it will be, because we planted it."

As harsh as it was on her body to laugh so hard, she treasured the feelings Goothr was bringing into her normally bland and cautious life. "Thanks for the excitement, my big friend."

Chapter 9
The Request

Dinner was served in the great hall for a second evening. It was the only indoor location that Goothr could comfortably fit in. Tilli was there, along with O'vette, Ayva, and Pheosco.

"Thank you for your hospitality," Tilli said to O'vette. "You've given us food, shelter, and the opportunity to see your amazing village." Glaring over at Goothr, she continued talking to the village leader. "We also want to once again apologize for destroying part of your home."

"It's our pleasure. The reconstruction of my home is a small price to pay for Goothr's help in saving the day in the common area today."

Tilli's disappointment in her blothrud friend, quickly faded.

"But I do have an ulterior motive in all of this," O'vette stated. "I am hoping that you would be willing to stay here and live among us."

"We would love to!" Tilli erupted before thinking about it. "I can't think of a better place to live. We will definitely consider it once we finish our mission."

"Perhaps you'll think differently about that after a few more weeks of living with us."

"A few more weeks?" Tilli was a bit surprised at the assumption. "We should have stayed only the one night and been on our way."

"Why the rush?"

"I can't really say, but it's time sensitive."

Pheosco glared at her across the table. "You should avoid making changes in these parts when you don't know what the ramifications are."

The dragon still rubbed her the wrong way. "I didn't ask for your approval. This is something I was asked to do by a dear friend in order to save his life. Once I'm done with this task, I can't think of a better place to settle down in."

"Tell me, must you both go on this mission?" O'vette asked. "Could Goothr stay with us while you're gone?"

"Why would you ask?"

O'vette motioned toward her daughter. "Goothr and Ayva have become very close. I'd hate for him to be gone if something were to happen to her." She took a sip of wine before finishing. "None of us truly know how long she has."

It was a gruesome comment that Tilli didn't like. "How can you say that while she sits at this table with us?"

"She knows her time is limited. The lesions I found this afternoon, before coming here, are the same kind my parents received just a few weeks before they passed." She tried to stay strong in front of everyone as tears formed in her eyes while looking at her frail daughter. "Ayva and I have talked about this. We knew this day would come."

Tilli took in a cleansing breath. "I'm sorry to hear this news. But we can't stay for the next several weeks before completing our mission. In fact, I hope to be back within a week or two. We could be back in time to say our goodbyes."

"I understand." O'vette was more understanding than expected. "I just hope we're all still here when you return."

Confused, Tilli took the bait. "What does that mean?"

"This village that you are now so fond of is at a crossroads. Do you recall when I informed you about our adversarial relationship with the spellcasters?"

"Yes."

Her eyes drew back up to the tools hanging above the fireplace. "As if we haven't given enough, they want more. If they don't get more, they will take everything we have."

"Then give them more."

"If we do that, we may not have enough left for us to survive on."

"Then fight for what you have."

O'vette moved her focus over to Goothr. "That's our only option at this point, and we need a warrior strong enough to fight them off."

"Goothr's not a fighter."

"He said he's fought dragons and Alchemists before."

"He has, but he doesn't want to."

"Nor do we. But if we don't fight them, they will take everything. They will destroy our village and our lives. Isn't that worth fighting for? You've seen what we have. You know its value. Stay and help protect us."

One after another, Tilli made eye contact with everyone around the table. Her emotions swayed her decision back and forth, but without a firm commitment.

Pheosco finally spoke up. "I was asked by your grandparents to come here to stop you from changing things. Neither of you two should be here. You have no idea what damage you can do by staying here and helping O'vette or going on your mission to help a friend. Both could have devastating consequences." He could tell Tilli didn't trust him. "You should go back to where you came from and avoid both events. You're not mature enough to make these decisions."

Tilli bit her lip as she listened to the green dragon, but she took it all in. She had to be willing to listen to all points of view and all needs to understand the risks. "I love your daughter, Ayva, as well as your village. It is a place I truly would love to live in. With that said, Goothr and I will make great haste in our mission so we can return here before your enemies arrive and before we lose Ayva."

The sound of distant music could be heard within the silent hall as everyone sat quietly, waiting for their leader's response.

O'vette set her silverware down to end her meal. "I'm not happy with your decision, but I accept it."

"We'll leave tonight to expedite our plans."

"Nonsense," O'vette replied. "Come. Enjoy the festivities of our trade celebration this evening. Perhaps it will change your mind. If not, we will give you shelter, food, and gear for your travels to improve your likelihood of returning to us in a timely manner."

A thoughtful nod from Tilli was given to the village leader.

Chapter 10
Celebration

Music from the celebration wafted through the open window and into Tilli's room as she read a few notes from her grandfather's wooden coffer. She had already packed her backpack and gear for an early start in the morning. She had also taken out her Runestones from her satchel to take an inventory and was looking forward to finally having some more time to read the notes within the wooden box from her grandfather.

As she did, Pheosco flew in her window and landed on her bed. "I didn't travel all this way just to let you make bad decisions."

Tilli didn't turn to acknowledge him. "I didn't ask you to."

Eyeing the exposed notes and Runestones, he was instantly agitated. "Do you not see how dangerous this is? Where did you find Thorik's notes? In the wrong hands these could give power to favor an evil future. Even in the right hands the knowledge within them is dangerous!"

"I wouldn't know," she grumbled. "Every time I try to read them, I get interrupted."

"And where did you get those Runestones? Please tell me they aren't the ones that the Mountain King used."

She shrugged. "Okay. I won't tell you." She wasn't in the mood to fight. The stress was getting to her, and she fought off the urge to cry. Every direction could cause someone pain. "Besides, it's not all of them. A black dragon, named Mel'tayn, stole two of them upon our arrival."

Pheosco's eyes grew large as he stepped back. "This is exactly what I've been warning you about! You need to rethink this mission of yours before it's too late and you've put things in motion that you can't stop. Between Thorik's notes, the Mountain King's Runestones, the two stones that Mel'tayn has, your mission to remove the Charm Runestone, and your interest in saving this village and Ayva, you are looking to rewrite history that once allowed the Mountain King War to take place and free you from the Notarians. I don't know how this won't end badly."

She was upset. "It sounds like no matter what I decide, it's going to end badly." She wiped her eyes before closing the coffer and placing it in her backpack. "If I don't get the Charm Runestone, my friend Pruva may not survive. In fact, he and I might not even be born if I mess this up. If I do find and steal the Runestone, I might be changing the future of those that get hurt along the way. If I don't save this amazing village, it might be wiped off the face of our land. If I do save it, I could stop this civilization from expanding the way it was supposed to!" The volume of her voice continued to increase as she talked. "There is no right answer! I can't play this game with you!"

"This is no game. You're talking about wiping out all known history, which could include the Mountain King. You can't dismiss that."

"Thanks! No pressure there!" She started tossing the Runestones back in the satchel.

"It's a lot of pressure, and you better toughen up to handle it. The world's fate is in your hands. Thorik and Avanda had the same level of responsibility, and they did the right thing. Now it's your turn to figure it out and move forward."

"They also had each other, so it must have been much easier. I don't have that luxury. I don't have anyone to consult with. It's all on my shoulders."

"I wouldn't say they had it easy or luxurious. They had hard times that you can't even imagine. They went through hell, but they worked together and listened to their friends."

"I don't need friends, especially like you," Tilli spit back.

"You need to grow up and stop feeling sorry for yourself. You have more ability than your grandparents ever did."

"You don't know the first thing about me or my family!"

Pheosco growled at the statement before replying. "I traveled with your grandparents for years. I even fought in the Mountain King War with them. I was there when both you and your father were born. I protected you from storms, thrashers, and even traveled to the far reaches of our lands to find antidotes to save you from a childhood disease that nearly took your life."

Tilli struggled to accept him. "Where were you when I lived on the streets, starving and homeless? Where were you when I was fending off creatures near the Govi Glade and trying to stay alive?"

"I'm not your personal attendant. I had my own missions and tasks to perform. We all have a role to play and I'm doing my part. Now I'm here to make sure you do yours."

After placing the last Runestone in the satchel, she tied it off. "And what is it you expect me to do?" Her shoulders slumped in defeat.

"I expect you to understand the risks and ramifications of your actions." Pheosco then lifted off the bed and landed on the windowsill before giving her his advice. "The decisions you make will have huge impacts. Choose them wisely. Remove your personal wants and desires from the equation before deciding." He then flew out into the night air.

Tilli took a huge sigh, tossed the satchel near her gear, fell onto her bed, and dropped her head into her palms. The emotional pressure was immense, and she wasn't sure she could handle it.

"Tilli?" Goothr asked as he approached her room. "Can we go to the celebration now?" he asked like a child wanting a treat.

She could hear the excitement in his voice, and quickly sat up while wiping her eyes. "Yes." Even if she bore a mask of happiness for the night, she didn't want to prevent others from having a good time. Besides, she knew how much this meant to him, and the blothrud's goofy smile was contagious. "Okay, let's get going."

With that, they were off; out the town hall building, across various streets, and into the common area where they first met Ayva.

Art from the various trades were on display and joyful music filled the air. Adults and children danced in the open spaces while others carried in food for the event. Laughter and friendly chatter were warm and hearty as hugs galvanized relationships. It was going to be a night of grand celebration for the villagers that had learned to work with each other and produce the finest crafts throughout the lands.

It only took a few moments before Tilli realized how much Goothr wanted to join in. And with a nod of her head, he was released to go play.

Rushing over to Ayva, he picked her up and began to escort her around. She hadn't been able to participate in many of the games with the rest of the children her age, but with the blothrud's help, she was at least able to be out there with them playing tag, dancing, and chasing one another. Although now she was doing it while being carried by Goothr. This greatly improved her odds of winning, except, of course, when they played hide-and-seek.

Several of the parents were nervous about the massive warrior racing after their children with one of his powerful arms stretched out in front of him, but Goothr was careful never to accidentally scratch or step on any of them. Although a few local cats weren't as lucky.

Tilli watched her big friend enjoy the culture. In fact, it seemed like this big blothrud dragon warrior was fitting in better than she was. But that's not to say she didn't feel a connection. In fact, she was craving the chance to settle down with these people, but Pruva's and Pheosco's words were constantly nagging in the back of her head.

Sitting down, she took the time to absorb the experience. Everything was perfect here at that moment and time. People were happy and Goothr was accepted by most.

For that brief moment, all seemed far too good to be true. Assuming it wouldn't last, Tilli took the time to treasure the moments.

Chapter 11
Unwelcomed

Moonlight drenched the village square in a silvery glow as the festival's final notes echoed through the night. Laughter and cheerful banter filled the air as villagers, their bellies full of ale and roasted meats, began to disperse towards their homes. The once raucous atmosphere transitioned into an exhausted lull.

From the shadows of the surrounding forest, an unnatural silence fell. Suddenly, the ground trembled beneath the villagers' feet, and their laughter died on their lips. A twisted mixture of growls, hisses, and cackles filled the air as an army of creatures burst forth from the tree line.

"Run!" someone shouted, but it was too late. Chaos erupted as creatures of various shapes and sizes invaded the village from all sides.

Hearing the commotion, Tilli and Goothr ran out of the town hall to see what was happening. "Where are they coming from?" Tilli gasped, her eyes darting in search of answers.

"Greyson's beasts," O'vette stated as she approached, yet her voice was barely audible above the pandemonium.

Mutant creatures swarmed into the village. It was a nightmarish tide of scales, fur, and claws. Villagers screamed and stumbled over one another in their desperation to escape. Amidst the frenzy, Greyson appeared above them, riding atop a massive blue dragon that dwarfed the surrounding beasts. Its mighty wings cast an eerie moon shadow over the terrified villagers below.

"Please, no!" a man cried out as a mutant creature lunged for him.

"Help!" an old woman sobbed, clutching her shawl tightly around her frail body.

"O'vette!" Greyson called as his dragon landed with a thud in front of the town hall, a wicked grin plastered upon his face. "So nice of you to be up waiting for me."

"Waiting isn't the right word," O'vette spat back, her hands clenched into fists.

"Enough!" Greyson yelled at his army, raising his hand. The creatures halted their rampage, still snarling and snapping at the fearful villagers they were rounded up in the street.

"Citizens of Eldor'Craft," Greyson bellowed, his voice echoing throughout the village. "If you wish to live well under my rulership, you must learn to obey my commands!"

The creatures finished herding the villagers like cattle, their snarls and roars filling the air with dread. A menacing beast with crimson eyes sank its claws into a man's shoulder, dragging him to join the others in the main street. The smell of blood and sweat filled the night as Greyson's army continued their relentless torment.

O'vette stood upon the few steps that led up to the town hall. Tilli stood in a small group next to the village leader, while Goothr crouched down off to the side, holding and protecting Ayva. Other trade leaders flanked both sides of O'vette in a show of unity.

"Silence!" Greyson commanded, dismounting the massive blue dragon with the assurance of a skilled predator. His boots hit the ground with an ominous thud, and he strode towards O'vette, a twisted smile on his face.

He enjoyed the tense environment within the crowd while he slowly approached their leader. "O'vette, is this really necessary? You know how to stop these brutal events from happening," he said, reaching out to touch her cheek.

"Don't touch me!" O'vette snapped, swatting his hand away. Her heart raced, but she refused to let him see her fear. "State your demands."

"Very well," Greyson sighed, a hint of disappointment in his voice. He pulled a scroll from his cloak, unfurling it to reveal the list of demands. "I've come to collect what is rightfully mine."

"Nothing here belongs to you," Ayva spat, her anger boiling over.

Greyson glanced over to see the sickly girl being carried by a massive blothrud. His expression gave away his feelings as he eyed the menacing dragon warrior as it stood up straight and tall. "I see you have a pet for your village," he said to O'vette. "Just make sure you have the Fesh on a tight leash, or I'll have to release my companions upon him."

Goothr set Ayva down behind him before flexing his muscles and snarling at the outsider.

"Speaking of leashes. What demands do you have for us this time?" O'vette snatched the scroll from Greyson's hand. Her eyes scanned the list, disbelief etched upon her face. "Your lists get longer, and your visits become more frequent. Is your goal to destroy this village?"

"No, of course not. This is like home for me. I love this village, just not the old and outdated policies you cling to for no reason other than to spite me."

Ignoring him, she read through the list on the parchment. "You expect us to give you all of this?"

"Indeed," Greyson replied, his tone cold and unwavering. "And if you don't, I promise you that the suffering we bestow upon your people will be felt for generations."

O'vette clenched her jaw, her mind racing. "How could we possibly comply with your demands? You're asking for most of the goods we've made for trade. Without them, we will have nothing to sell and therefore no funds to buy new materials for future items to be crafted."

"You're resourceful people. You'll find a way."

"Even if we could handle that part, you've added a special dagger to be built that could take weeks to engineer, let alone construct."

"Yes, that's for my private collection. I'll want that ready with everything else in one week, when I send my dragon to pick up all of my items in a single crate. As usual, have it equipped with ropes for her to grab."

"I don't think you heard me. It's not possible to get this accomplished in that time!"

"Then I will be forced to break some bones and crush some skulls until you figure out how!" he yelled in anger.

Goothr stepped up right behind O'vette, towering over her as he roared at the man. "Leave her alone!"

Nearly falling backward, Greyson caught himself and straightened up, but it was too late.

Making his way past O'vette and the trade leaders, Goothr stepped forward grabbed the man with one hand, and lifted him into the air to look him in the eyes. "Go Away! Never come back!" He yelled as his spittle coated Greyson's face. "Leave my friends alone!"

Fearing for his life, Greyson clinched something hanging from his neck and focused his thoughts on controlling the blothrud. "You will do as I command!" The object within his grasp began to glow and pulse.

"No!" Goothr growled. "You leave or Goothr will get mad!"

Shock appeared upon Greyson's face, as he had honestly thought he could control the beast. Realizing he could not, he glanced to the side at one of his own mutant creatures. "Kill."

Without hesitation, the creature leaped upon an old man and raked his claws across his face and then down his chest before sinking his teeth into the man's neck, killing him instantly.

The Eldor'Craft citizens screamed at the sight of one of their beloved friends being murdered before their eyes. The horrific scene played out as the old man's body was tossed into the street by the creature who had just killed him.

"O'vette!" Greyson yelled. "Have your pet release me or I'll order my army to kill every last villager.

A range of emotions flooded within O'vette as she forced herself to stay strong in front of her people. She knew the blothrud couldn't protect them all. This fight needed to wait until they were prepared. "Goothr! Set him down and return to protecting Ayva."

The blothrud was too upset to listen to her orders. "I must protect you as well. This man is bad."

"Goothr." It was Tilli this time who spoke. "You've shown your valor. Please drop him and come back to us."

The sound of his dear friend allowed him to relax, but it wasn't until he heard another friend that he finally let go.

"Come back and protect me, Goothr," Ayva said with a soft voice that barely reached his ears.

Releasing his grip and dropping the man to the ground, the blothrud turned around and made his way back to pick up Ayva in the comfort of his arms.

Greyson brushed himself off as he gathered his thoughts and composure, while eyeing the beast, before returning his attention to Eldor'Craft's leader. Approaching her again, he stepped in close enough to her that their noses nearly touched, and they locked eye to eye. "If all the items aren't on that delivery, then I will release my army of creatures upon your backwards-thinking village, starting with that blothrud." He stayed firm for several moments until her eyes lowered. "There is always the option to stop all of this, and you know how. Just say the word."

O'vette stared at him for several thoughtful moments before replying. "We will find a way to make it happen."

Disappointed with her answer, he growled at her. "No cutting corners on that dagger. I expect it to be perfect!" he demanded before turning his back on her and walking away.

Greyson raised his hand, silencing the whispers that had erupted among the villagers. He scanned their fearful faces, drinking in their terror like a fine wine. "Now," he continued, his voice dripping with menace, "Your leader has agreed to my demands. If you don't fulfill my list in one week, my friends will be back," he said as he motioned toward the army of creatures, "and I won't be here to restrain them."

He smirked at the terror-stricken faces of the villagers, their fear feeding his insatiable hunger for power. He turned away from them and gracefully climbed onto the back of his blue dragon, its scales shimmering like water under the moonlight.

"Not one item can be missing," he warned, his voice echoing through the village as the dragon spread its leathery wings wide, casting a shadow over the trembling crowd below. Tossing his cape over his shoulders, he exposed his leather armor covered in jewels, and several necklaces of various lengths.

Tilli squinted against the darkness, and suddenly, she saw it: the Charm Runestone, hanging proudly from a silver chain around Greyson's neck. The stone glowed faintly, pulsating with an eerie, otherworldly energy.

Tilli's gaze met O'vette's, and without speaking a word, their eyes exchanged a silent determination. This tyrant's reign of terror had to end – and they would be the ones to figure out how to stop him.

"O'vette..." Tilli whispered urgently, her heart pounding in her chest. "Look at the stone on his necklace."

O'vette squinted. "Is that...?" She couldn't finish her sentence, but Tilli knew exactly what she was asking.

"Yes," she replied, her voice barely audible. "It's the Charm Runestone. He's using it to control that dragon and his herd of creatures. Without it, he has no power over you or this village."

"But as long as he has it, we must do as he asks to survive."

"At least until I retrieve it."

"Retrieve it? How?" O'vette asked, panic rising in her voice. "We can't possibly fight against his army."

"Trust me," Tilli said, her mind racing with thoughts of the responsibility that weighed heavily on her shoulders.

"Focus on fulfilling his requests while I come up with a plan to take that stone."

As Greyson's dragon beat its powerful wings, lifting him into the air, Tilli clenched her fists, her resolve solidifying like iron. She knew the risks she was about to take, the danger she was placing herself in—but this was a battle she could not afford to lose. With the Charm Runestone in Greyson's possession, the future of the villagers was at stake, as well as the future of all the people throughout the lands. This is what she came for, and now she knew where it was. It was just a matter of getting it.

Chapter 12
The Demands

By the time everyone looked back down after watching the dragons leave, all of the creatures had vanished. The townspeople were alone with one less resident as a reminder of what Greyson could do to them if they opposed him.

"Trade leaders!" O'vette announced. "Meet me in the town hall immediately. The rest of you return home and hug your families. Be thankful we are still with the living and we only had one casualty for the night." Her sad eyes stared at the remains of the old man. "Tosh, grab a few others and respectfully remove old man Binks from the street. We will plan his funeral tomorrow morning."

Taking a deep breath, she pulled her eyes away from the horrible scene before she turned to walk up the steps to the town hall along with a dozen others. Consoling a few with a hand on their back or patting them on the shoulder, O'vette did her best to focus on her people instead of her own emotions.

Tilli and Goothr came in as well, as the blothrud carried Ayva to the back of the room, near the fireplace. Ayva knew when the trade leaders were called, others were allowed to listen and sometimes speak, but they could not vote on key topics.

Tables and benches were quickly moved into an organized rectangle and the leaders of each trade sat near the symbols of their trade upon the walls. It was organized enough to show structure, but casual enough for all to feel comfortable. Most sat on benches and leaned on the tables before them, while others stood, leaned against the wall, or sat upon their table with a leg dangling. It was more about being present than looking professional.

O'vette waited until everyone was in their own trade area before starting. "You all heard his demands. What say you to them?"

"I say we chop up that dragon and have ourselves some grilled steaks!" the butcher announced.

"I ain't gon'a to let him do to my family what he done did to old man Binks," said the farmer.

The jeweler shook her head. "He's not bluffing. If we don't comply, we'll end up dead, or worse." Her eyes veered up to the tools hanging above the fireplace.

The blacksmith stood proud, confident of his ability. "The Fesh ain't inhuman. He can be hurt just as you and I. He just has magic. We could make better weapons to match his!"

The baker stepped out from his table into the center. "So, we think we can become warriors? Are we going to set aside our lifelong trades to become fighters and killers? And do we expect to do this overnight?" Removing his hat, he scratched his head as he thought before placing it back on his head. "Fighting is its own profession that is mastered over years just like our own trades. We all know what happens when we try to learn something new. We look like fools for the first few months and then nothing but apprentices for the first few years. Do you honestly believe that swinging a sword is all it takes? It's a skill that must be mastered, which none of us have."

"He has it!" the blacksmith said, pointing at the blothrud. "You saw the concern in Greyson's eyes when our beast stood head-to-head with him. We can use this to our advantage."

Tilli and Goothr were getting nervous about where this was going. They hadn't come to fight a battle for them. They had come to retrieve the Charm Runestone.

The grumbling by many of the trade masters filled the hall in several side conversations as ideas and concerns were shared. It was part of their normal process.

Once she felt enough people had expressed their thoughts, O'vette pulled the meeting back in order. "I have read through the list of items Greyson demands, and for the most part we could have these ready for him in time, if we don't already have them in our shops right now."

"If the list is easy to provide, then let's give them to him and be done with it," the farmer said.

"That's easy for you to say, he's coming after my wares, not yours!" the master jeweler replied.

O'vette stepped in before the leaders began to argue with each other. "It's not about this list."

The trade leaders gave her blank stares.

She held the list up for all to see as she slowly walked around the room. "Why would he give us a list of items that are for the most part simple to obtain for him?" She paused to let them think about it. "Because it's not about the list. He wants to see if we are, once again, willing to give in. If we continue to give, we will eventually become part of Greyson's community. If the list was hard, he knows we would say no because we would have no way to comply. Giving us an easy list allows us to learn to be compliant. So, this is a test."

"Are you saying we must say no and risk his vengeance?" one asked.

O'vette shook her head. "My goal is for us to live in peace and continue our trades. The goods that leave Eldor'Craft are shipped across the lands and known for their quality. I want to continue this reputation, but I do not wish to live in fear of being raided and our people hurt. That said, we don't know what Greyson's plans are. If lists such as this continue, we could potentially live in harmony even though we know we are not getting paid for some of our work. Putting our foot down could lead to him blocking all our trade, or worse, sending his creatures in to raid our goods and harm our people."

"What if he makes a deal we can live with and then changes it?" another said.

"We know the outcome if we say no. Saying yes could lead to something tangible. But like you said, he could change his mind. The truth is he could change the deal before tomorrow. We know he wants our merchandise so he's not going to jeopardize not getting them by killing us all off. I feel he simply wants the items without cost and once he obtains this he'll move on to other issues."

The pottery leader finally spoke up. "Other issues?"

"Yes, I have heard rumblings of battles to the south that he has been struggling with. A smart leader would try to minimize the fronts they fight so they can focus on the important ones."

"Are you saying we give in?" the carpentry trade leader asked. "We allow him to take over the village? I can't believe I'm hearing you say you're giving up on us."

"I am not. I'm trying to make a decision that allows our families and trades to continue to flourish. A successful plan of resistance has not been available yet. I suggest we continue in our efforts to develop a better path as we fulfill Greyson's demands. Remember, just like Greyson can change his mind, so can we."

The hall fell silent as they considered the path they may be headed down. It sounded safer, but at what cost?

Tilli had been quietly listening and had been waiting for a long pause, such as this, to ask a question that had been eating at her. "O'vette, you mentioned the items on the list were simple, for the most part. What items is he requesting that are not?"

O'vette opened the second page of the large scroll. "There is only one item that I see that would require us to develop a new technique to create. It is a dagger with thin twisting blades and a handle that holds two identical crystal spheres. A challenge to say the least, but it specifies that the blades, cross-guard, and hilt must be made from only one piece of metal."

"What?" The blacksmith grumbled as he and the jeweler walked over to see the diagram. "This must be ornamental, for using this dagger in battle would be foolish. The thin twisting blades would surely break after a half dozen blows. I doubt the grip would last that long."

The jeweler scoffed at the design. "What fool would use two round crystals as a grip? You'd be covering up the most beautiful element of the piece with your palm. We need to move the crystals to the cross-guard."

"Agreed," replied the blacksmith. "Then we can strengthen the hilt and wrap it in leather for a firm grip. But even still, the blade needs to be filled in. They have it hollow throughout the entire length." He nodded as he considered the options. "With enough changes, we could come up with something much better than this."

"No." O'vette was going to nip this thought process in the bud. "Someone clearly went to a lot of effort to design this dagger in a specific way. This is another test."

"I have never made anything like this. Just the calculations needed prior to starting would take a week on their own. Unless we decide to guess."

"There will be no guessing. Our town's name is on this dagger so it will be the finest possible product that it can be."

"If you can find someone to develop these extensive calculations, we can make just about anything."

O'vette searched within the eyes of the trade masters for a ray of hope, but she found none."

"I might have someone," Tilli quietly said. "I have seen him devise more complicated designs than that with much less to work with."

She had everyone's attention, including Goothr's.

"His name is Pruva. I will bring him here. But I must warn you, he's a bit different."

Chapter 13
Pruva

Morning rays of sunrise glimmered down to the forest floor in thin angled columns for light. Dew upon the underbrush glistened and slowly dripped to the forest floor where Tilli stood, several minutes walk from the village.

Goothr stood behind her, carrying Ayva. Both were excited to see Tilli perform magic.

Removing the upper half of the crystal that once attached to the lower half in Pruva's camp, Tilli held it firmly in her hand. She could feel the vibration within the black crystal that was added before the two were separated.

Adjusting the object amongst her fingers, she then gave it a quick twist and tossed it forward into the air.

Flying a yard forward, it stopped and held its position as the spinning increased in speed. Around and around the crystal spun, faster and faster until the darkness with the crystal started to bleed out into the surrounding air.

Panning out from the twirling stone, the darkness grew to a sideways funnel nearly three yards in diameter before the crystal was completely drained of color and was sucked into the funnel.

Ayva was amazed at the sight as well as fearful of what could be on the other side of this gateway. She could only see a faint view of a grassy meadow with a glass-like globe floating over it. "Goothr?" she asked as she tightened up against him.

"I know," the blothrud said without recognizing her body language. "It's pretty."

Tilli turned to give her friends instructions. "Stay here. I should be right back." Not waiting for a reply, she stepped into the sideways vortex and disappeared.

Ayva gasped at seeing her friend vanish before her very eyes. "That was amazing."

***

Stepping out of the funnel, Tilli found herself next to the Govi Glade, just as expected. A few slow-moving semi-transparent spheres floated above the grassy area on their normal trajectory as they arched up and then back down under the ground. She was in the right location and just needed to collect her friend and bring him back to Eldor'Craft.

Excited to greet Pruva, she spun about to find him.

The remains of a campfire with long-dead coals had a veil of white snow-cover over them. Several traps around the camp had done their job to stop treerats from invading the small region next to the Govi Glade. It clearly was the right location, but Pruva had not waited for them.

"Pruva!" Tilli yelled into the forest. "Where are you?"

No answer came, as she continued to search in all directions. But her time was limited before the portal would close.

Calling one more time only seemed to catch the attention of local treerats. He was nowhere to be found. It was time to return to Eldor'Craft.

Quickly pushing another thin, long, black crystal into the ground, she tapped it with her tuning fork and then broke it in half. She needed an easy way to return to search for him again.

"We must hurry before your portal terminates," Pruva said as he stepped out of a sphere within the Govi Glade, just yards from the forest's edge.

"Pruva! Where were you?"

Pruva didn't answer as he moved as quickly as his sloth-like body would allow him. "No time to talk," he said as he moved past her with the most momentum she had ever seen from him.

She then heard a noise from the same portal he had just exited, and she turned to see what was making it.

A massive beast with long tentacles was coming out of the magical orb while it descended into the earth. It roared as it chased Pruva through time. Slapping the ground near Tilli, one of the appendages knocked her down and grabbed her leg.

Tilli screamed in horror as the beast pulled her into the glade.

The creature's roar suddenly changed to a hideous scream as it was pulled into the ground, chopping off the limbs that made it through the orb's surface from the body of the creature that was stuck inside.

Muscle spasms within the freshly severed tentacles caused them to flop about as the sphere finished its journey underground. The one wrapped around Tilli's ankle was no different.

The next sound Tilli heard was even more deadly, and her heart sank. A thousand treerats raced toward her to feed upon the remains of the beast that never made it all the way through. From branch to branch and through the underbrush, the swarm of ravenous rats headed toward her as four thousand little feet clawed their way to her, while screeching with high-pitched voices. It was a wave of furry rodents that were going to crash upon her and the glade's shoreline.

Giving up on trying to kick the tentacle off her, she leaped to her feet and through the vortex just as the rats arrived for their long-overdue meal.

The crystal-formed portal shrunk and faded from existence.

***

Goothr had set Ayva down so she could get closer to the vortex in an attempt to yell through to see if Tilli was okay. Cupping her hands near her mouth, she yelled to her friend.

But instead of Tilli stepping back through, a giant sloth-like beast stepped through, nearly stepping on Ayva.

The girl screamed in terror as the wide, hairy creature arrived when she was expecting Tilli.

Ignoring her, Pruva stepped past before stopping to take a breath. He was not built for running and even a short sprint was more than he could handle.

Just as Ayva calmed herself down, Tilli rushed through the portal with a long, slimy tentacle grasping onto her ankle, causing Ayva's level of fear to explode again.

Fumbling her way toward Pruva, Tilli tripped and fell, flinging the tentacle off her leg and onto Ayva.

Slapping against her, the muscle's reflexes compressed and wrapped around her chest and neck. Falling backward, Ayva didn't have the strength to pull it off, and she started gasping for air. Her frail lungs struggled on a good day, so this was quickly causing her to lose consciousness.

"No!" Tilli yelled as she ran over to help, only to be pushed aside by Goothr.

Scooping her up with one arm, the blothrud grabbed the tentacle with the other hand and squeezed. The appendage popped and sprayed fluids in every direction before the remaining parts flopped onto the ground.

Resting on the forest floor after being pushed by her friend, she was a bit surprised that he shoved her away. "Goothr?"

Picking pieces of tentacle off Ayva, he glanced over at the Num. "I'm sorry, Tilli, but I am taller than Ayva and I have to protect her."

Sitting there, she realized that things had changed. He had found someone else to protect. Someone that needed it more, and perhaps even deserved it more. Ayva had been giving Goothr more of her time, which he craved. But even with the rationalizing of it, she still felt left behind and slightly jealous of Ayva's relationship with the blothrud becoming stronger than hers.

Ayva coughed a bit before she regained her composure. "Thank you, Goothr. I love having you around."

"Goothr love being around," he replied.

Tilli had enough of the love-fest. "As you can see, Ayva, leaving your village and going on a journey isn't as exciting as you had hoped."

Ayva's head tilted in confusion. "It was the most thrilling event I've seen in my short life. Sure, it was scary, but I haven't felt scared in years. I haven't felt anything in years. I'm so isolated from any strong excitement that I want to feel it all. I can't even imagine this level of exhilaration while lying in bed all day, just waiting for the end. I want to live before I die."

The blothrud nodded to support her. "Goothr protect you."

"I think this was enough excitement for today. We should head back into the village." Uncharacteristically, no one reached down to help Tilli up. Goothr was busy with Ayva and Pruva was still catching his breath. "Pruva, where were you?"

"Needed to test my Govi Glade map device…" he took a few breaths before continuing, "…to ensure it was working properly."

"Was that creature chasing you?"

"Yes." He took in a cleansing breath as he started to regain his normal breathing. "I needed to obtain this chest for our mission." Within his grasp was a decorative wooden box with metal trim.

"You stole that wooden chest from that creature?"

"No. I took it from the owner of that creature."

Tilli was confused. "Why did you need to risk your life to do that right now? You could have jeopardized our mission if you didn't make it back."

"Truth be said, truth be heard."

"Then why did you?"

"Because you asked me to collect it for you."

Completely confused, she searched her memory for any such conversation. "I don't recall asking you for anything."

"You haven't yet. But you will. So, I went to get it ahead of time."

"Even if I pretend to understand you, doesn't that violate your own rules of not changing the timeline?"

A second deep cleansing breath was taken in through the nose and out through his mouth before Pruva finally responded. "No."

"No? That's it? I'm lectured about not changing anything that could affect the future, but you can just change whatever you want?"

"That is false," the gathler said. "I took something at the end of its existence. It was about to be destroyed and would have no more interaction with historical events. Therefore, nothing was changed."

A bit frustrated at how easily Pruva could change events without consequences while every option she had felt like it would end the world, Tilli asked, "How about that creature's future? You just cut that life short. How do you know the ramification of that?"

Pruva gave her a knowing grin and a wink. "You'll have to trust me."

"I hope you're as skillful with designing as you are with navigating through time."

His interest was piqued as he raised one eyebrow. "Truth be said."

Chapter 14
The Dagger

    The sound of hard work from every tradesman was at full steam within the village as Tilli and her friends entered the main street. Hammering of metals, cutting of wood, turning of machinery, and the loud roars of the fires could be heard as they heated and melted various materials. Workers in each craft shouted out instructions over the noise, while the clopping of faralopes' hooves filled the area as they pulled wagons with fresh supplies.

    The oddly shaped two-legged faralopes had large hairy hooves at the base of the two thick legs which held up its heavy center while the long tail acted as a counterweight to its wide and stubby neck and bird-like head. Covered in thin, coarse, white hair over black skin, they appeared to be the primary force used to pull heavy loads.

    As the outsiders approached, the noise level seemed to drop slightly as workers stopped to stare at the new creature entering their controlled village.

    The creature wasn't threatening in looks, like the blothrud, but the size was intimidating, as it could be as tall as Goothr, should it stand up straight, and it was several times wider. The new creature had long claws for its fingers and spiral markings across its face. It was something they had never seen before, and it was hard for the locals not to gaze at the gathler for a few moments as it passed by.

    Near the center of the village was a small crowd of trade masters arguing about how they could possibly build the ornamental dagger for Greyson. The initial drawings were sprawled out along with several new drafts of how they could build the individual elements before combining them. It appeared to be an impossible puzzle.

O'vette watched as her brightest minds became frustrated with the project. She could only hope that one of them would have a breakthrough.

It was then that they spotted the arrival of the slow-moving, giant sloth-like creature and parted ways as it approached the table.

Tilli quickly introduced him. "O'vette, this is my friend, Pruva. He can design and build anything."

Several of the trade masters took offense to the comment as a slap in the face while others scoffed. Eldor'Craft was known as containing the most advanced trade smiths in the world. If they couldn't figure it out, then it simply couldn't be built.

"Welcome, Pruva." O'vette opened her arms to signify to all the craft masters that the creature was now part of their research team. "We look forward to any insight you may have on building this item."

Pruva lumbered over, squinting down at the detailed drawing. His slow, deliberate movements contrasted sharply with the intense energy of the villagers. He traced one of his large fingers along the intricate lines, humming thoughtfully.

The gathler then took one of his curved bony nails and dropped it on one of the new drawings, puncturing it before dragging it off the table and dropping it onto the ground.

The metalsmith master, Bishhall, gasped at the sight of his work being tossed away like rubbish, but before he could vocalize his feelings, he saw O'vette give him the eye to keep it to himself.

Next, Pruva dipped the end of his nail into some ink and started marking up a second new drawing, made by the glazier master, Pamalia.

She also was not pleased with the crude markings he made on her detailed drawings.

Pruva continued changing or removing various papers until he was satisfied. "Now we know."

"Know what?" O'vette asked.

"We now know where Varacon was designed and built," he replied before taking a step back and closing his eyes. Placing his hands on his knees to keep his balance, he took a slow deep breath before releasing it at the same speed.

"Are you ill?"

"I must still be recovering from an injury I received in the Govi Glade."

O'vette was unsure how to proceed. "Perhaps you should rest from your travels before reviewing any more drawings."

Tilli was in agreement, and she placed a comforting hand upon his arm. "We'll find you a place in the town hall to relax until you feel better."

Pruva raised a hand to stop them. "I just needed to take a moment. It is already starting to pass." Then, after a few more cleansing breaths, he stepped back up to the table. "Interesting design," Pruva mused, tapping the paper gently. "I see the challenge."

"Can you help them?" asked Tilli hopefully, her heart racing in anticipation.

"Indeed," said Pruva confidently, his eyes glinting with understanding. "Follow my instructions closely."

As Pruva began to explain the complex process of constructing the unique dagger to the craft masters, Tilli couldn't help but feel a surge of gratitude towards him. This mysterious creature, with his vast knowledge and gentle demeanor, had become an invaluable ally to her once again.

"Remember," he reminded them, "precision and timing are key."

"If I understand you correctly, you're saying several of our trades must overlap throughout the sequence," Pamalia stated.

Pruva nodded. "Truth be said."

Bishhall shook his head. "Ya can't have detailed glass sculpturing being performed at the same time I'm poundin' metal around it. And then you're suggesting one of our fine jewelers be placing those two gems at the same moment. The heat alone will burn their hands if me hammer doesn't crush a finger or two."

"Truth be heard," the gathler added. "If you use your current practices, you will not succeed."

"We have the finest practices in the land. If we can't use them, there is no hope," Bishhall fired back.

Pruva thought for a moment as he studied the drawings. "I was asked to explain what was needed to create this dagger, not the process you would use."

"What does that do for us?" Bishhall shouted in frustration. "We're right back to where we were before he showed up!"

Pamalia disagreed. "No. Pruva has given us the design and timing. We need to improve our craft to support it."

The blacksmith had washed his hands of the idea. "Improve on perfection?"

Pruva smiled. "What are the best known methods today will be old trade practices of tomorrow."

Most of the craft masters stood silent at the comment. Some were confused, while others were agitated that the outsider would assume their ways were not perfected as far as they could be taken.

"Why?" the gathler asked. After receiving confused looks, he asked his question more directly at Pamalia. "Why can't you perform your task while other perform theirs at the same time?"

Thinking it was obvious, she entertained the question. "First of all, the glass has to be at a temperature that will bend and pull. At that temperature, it will easily stick to the metal or anything else it touches, preventing me from keeping it independent from them. Next, the metal and gems will be in my way, as well as the crafters that will be placing them. And even if I could get in there, the metal hammering is likely to hit me or the glass."

Pruva nodded. "Why? Why would it stick to the other objects?"

"Because the glass will touch them."

"Why?"

"Because when I place it inside there isn't a lot of room to work and the tolerances are so tight that it would take but a bump of the dagger and the materials will touch."

"Why?"

Bishhall crossed his arms. "This isn't getting us anywhere."

Pamalia continued as her creative thoughts started answering her own problems. "But I could make a graphite lining between my glass and the metal, then I could prevent that issue." Visions in her head raced at how to make it. "We'd have to have the entire dagger clamped down to minimize the movements and new tools would have to be designed to allow us to reach in without putting our own fingers near it…" as she continued to brainstorm the idea, others started joining in with suggestions.

Various new clamps, paddles, hammers, and other tools were crudely being drawn up on the fly as they started working out the details of how they could build it.

O'vette nodded determinedly, her mind racing with the new information. She glanced around at the craft masters, watching as they absorbed Pruva's wisdom and applied it to their work. Despite the weight of their task, hope flickered like a flame within each of them, refusing to be extinguished.

Chapter 15
Hard at Work

As Tilli observed the villagers working diligently under Pruva's guidance, her attention was drawn to a sudden burst of laughter nearby. She turned her gaze towards Goothr, who had immersed himself among the village children, Ayva included.

"Look, Goothr strong!" he announced with pride, lifting a wooden beam effortlessly above his head as the children gasped in awe. He then proceeded to balance it on his forehead, eliciting more delighted squeals from his young audience.

"Can you teach us that?" Ayva asked with a laugh, her eyes sparkling with excitement despite her frailty.

"Maybe when you're bigger," Goothr replied cheerfully, setting the beam back down and ruffling Ayva's hair.

Tilli couldn't help but smile at the scene unfolding before her, even as she felt a twinge of annoyance at Goothr's childlike nature. She glanced over at O'vette, who stood nearby, arms crossed, and raised an eyebrow.

"We have work to do." O'vette grumbled, though her eyes betrayed a hint of amusement.

"Perhaps," Tilli responded, "but he has a way of lightening the mood, doesn't he?"

"True," O'vette conceded. "But time is of the essence."

"Let the children have their moment," Tilli said softly, watching as Goothr hoisted Ayva onto his broad shoulders, causing her to giggle uncontrollably. "They deserve some joy in their lives."

"Alright, but only for a little while longer. Ayva needs her rest." O'vette replied, relenting with a small smile.

As Tilli continued to observe Goothr's playful interactions, she couldn't help but feel a pang of envy. His simple-mindedness allowed him to find happiness in the smallest of things, and in turn, bring joy to those around him. She wished she could let go of her worries, if only for a moment, and join in their laughter.

"Back to work," she murmured to herself, pushing aside her longing and focusing once more on the task at hand. There would be time for laughter and joy later, once their mission was complete. For now, they had a dagger to forge and a world to save.

The rush to get more done was adding stress to everyone. Few were taking needed breaks, as everyone understood the consequences of failing. However, by the end of the day some tensions were getting high, especially while listening to Goothr playing with the children.

Tilli gave him a frustrated look several times when the noise of laughter was louder than the banging of the hammers and the roar of the fires. But each time she stomped over to give him a stern lecture, she would find him hauling large amounts of materials along with a load of children on top or carrying lumber with several youths hanging from each side as he bounced the boards slightly to knock them off. He was getting work done, while playing at the same time. However, the laughter still seemed annoying to those dripping with sweat as they worked double-time on their projects.

There, on his shoulders, was Ayva. Laughing as she hadn't done in years. With O'vette being so busy, she had left the confines of her bed to play once again. The sight of her being happy was one of the few reasons Tilli didn't have an altercation with Goothr, who could get more done if he wasn't playing along the way.

Tilli's heart sank at the thought of Ayva not growing up, let alone not having another year to play with others. The

Num had grown up on the streets and knew what it felt like not to have a real childhood. She wished that upon no one. "There has to be a way to cure her," she said to herself.

"What's that?" O'vette asked while walking up to her with an arm full of leather hides.

"Oh, nothing." She knew not to discuss any attempt to cure Ayva.

"I appreciate you and Goothr staying and helping us instead of leaving."

"My primary mission is to remove the Runestone that Greyson is using. In doing so, it will hopefully save this village."

"At what cost to you? Didn't you mention losing some of your personal items already?"

Tilli knew how O'vette felt about magic and enchanted items, so she needed to choose her words carefully. "True, Mel'tayn stole a few of my grandfather's artifacts. They are the only things left from my family heritage."

"I understand. This village is what my ancestors left for me to watch over and to protect. It is a great burden to know that I could be the one that allows all of their hard work to fail during my watch."

"It doesn't have to. We're fulfilling his demands."

"That only provides us some time. He'll be back, and if we eventually will need a plan to stand up to him and his army of creatures. If not, Eldor'Craft will be no more, and I will have failed my family and their legacy."

"Not if I can get that Runestone away from him."

O'vette gave her a curious look. "You are brave, but not even your giant friend can fight off enough of his beasts to pull that stone from his neck. Even if you could, how would you get through his creature-filled forest and past the walls to his city?"

Tilli responded with a cunning expression on her face. "I have an idea about that. It's twofold. What if we built that crate just a little bigger than needed? Just enough room for Goothr and I to fit inside it?"

"You're not serious."

"Absolutely! The dragon would take us past the forest and the walls of his city. With any luck, we'll be set down inside his private walls to ensure none of his people grab his new ornamental dagger before he arrives."

"You'll be trapped inside the walls. Even if you did find the stone, you'd never make it back out."

Tilli knew better than to tell her about the use of her portal crystals, which would look like magic to the village leader. "I have a plan for that as well. What I need from you is to instruct the crate builders to add extra room inside. Can you do that?"

"Tilli, I appreciate you trying to help us, but you're now asking me to nail you into a box and ship you to the people who want to destroy us. It's a suicide mission." She shook her head as she thought about the idea. "We'll find another way so that you and Goothr can live among us in peace."

"I would love to live here. This is paradise compared to growing up on the streets, and Goothr has already become part of your family. But we can't send these items to Greyson and just hope he never comes back for more. Buying time hasn't worked for you in the past, so we can't bank on it happening in the future. It's time we try something completely different."

"It's too dangerous."

"It's very dangerous. But so is doing nothing." Tilli could see the worry in her eyes. "You've taken me in, and you've tolerated Goothr. I need to do this to save Pruva's future, and I want to do this to save Eldor'Craft."

The leader eyed her for a moment before giving Tilli an answer. "You said it was two-fold. What's the other part of this?"

"I think I know how we can prevent any further attacks from Greyson's creatures. He has to use the Charm

Stone on them to do his bidding. Goothr and I have a ring that prevents such magic from being affective. The crystal in the ring cancels out all Alchemist and E'rudite powers." Her thoughts raced with ideas how they could use the ring to help the entire village. "With your permission, I'll work with Pruva to extend the ring's ability to cover a large enough area to protect all the villagers."

Uncharacteristically, O'vette showed her emotions by stepping forward and hugging the Num. "Permission granted. And we will make sure there is enough room in the crate, so you're not cramped." The tight hug didn't last long before she stepped back and regained her composure in case someone was watching. And with that, she politely nodded and went about her business.

Chapter 16
The Coffer

The sound of a metal clasp was heard before the nearly audible squeezing of hinges as Tilli opened her wooden coffer. Inside was an assortment of papers filled with her grandfather's notes and maps of his journeys.

Sitting on her bed, in the back room of the town hall, Tilli finally had time to relax and uncover the mysteries of her family's past. She hoped it would answer some questions about her father, who she never really had the time to get to know very well before his death. But on first glance, the records within the box were more about Thorik and Avanda.

Adjusting her pillow, she leaned up against the wall and started putting the papers in order. Most had dates written on them, but there were a few that were simply sketches of animals and locations they had encountered.

Taking in a deep breath, she was excited to finally dive into her grandparents' adventures and forget about her own problems.

As she started to read, she envisioned a grand heroic journey with a team that pulled together to fight evil. But the more she got into it, she found that most of their struggles were within their own party. Trust issues, individuals having their own agenda, and deceptions to achieve goals other than that of their mission.

The romantic idea of them all working together to defeat an evil enemy quickly fell away as the reality of daily challenges came into play. Decisions weren't as obvious as she had assumed, and even when all was lost, they kept moving forward with those they could trust.

Rubbing her neck, she looked up from the papers now scattered across her bed after only reading a dozen pages. "They had each other and a team to help them." She sighed and watched a light snowfall collect on her window. "The difference is I'm alone."

"Alone?" Ayva asked as she stood in the doorway. She had been sitting in the large room of the building near the fireplace, as her mother didn't want her outside on the cold snowy day.

"Hi, Ayva, I thought you were resting."

"I was," the ill girl replied before correcting herself. "Heck, I always am. That's all I'm allowed to do most of the time. But I got bored and I thought I'd see what you're up to."

Tilli patted her hand on her bed, inviting the girl to hop up next to her. "These are notes from my grandparents about their life. They explored these lands and uncovered many mysteries."

Ayva's eyes lit up. "That's exciting! I wish my family were adventurers."

"I know it sounds glamourous, but it's a hard life. It was a daily challenge to travel, find food and drink, and a warm place to sleep. You don't know how nice you have it here."

"But to see the things they have must have made it worth it."

"Perhaps, but from what I read so far, they didn't travel for the adventure, they did so to help others. They were called upon for a mission to save lives and they stepped up to the challenge without even fully understanding what the risks were or how they would complete it."

Ayva picked out a few papers with drawings on them. "That sounds a lot like what you and Goothr are doing."

Tilli cocked her head a bit and smiled at the intrigued girl. "I guess, in some way, you're right. I have a mission to save lives and yet I don't fully know how I will accomplish it."

"How exciting, to go off into the unknown and live on the edge instead of sitting around here doing the same thing."

"True, but it's also a bit intimidating. There are the risks of not succeeding, or even perishing during the travels or in combat."

The girl had picked up a drawing of several Nums, a cloaked human, a dragon, and a giant. "Can you image being on a journey with this group? Climbing across mountains, fighting off beasts, and winning the day? The idea of living on the road with no idea of what the day will bring is intoxicating."

Tilli recalled her own past. "I've lived homeless on the streets begging for food and finding corners in animal stalls to sleep. There is nothing attractive about it. I fought every day to survive and then I had the chance to escape that and live inside the E'rudite temple. I had my own room with fine sheets, meals available when needed, and the security from wild animals."

"If you liked it so much, why did you give it up?"

"It was destroyed. And the next thing I knew I was asked by an old lady to help on a mission to save the future."

Still holding the drawing, Ayva said, "It looks like your grandparents had an old lady in their story as well."

Glancing over at the image, Tilli pulled the drawing closer. "Is that Gluic?" she asked herself. The art wasn't detailed enough to validate her question, but there were striking similarities. "That does look a lot like her."

Ayva coughed and then leaned back against the wall. "That would be funny if the same person sent you and your grandparents on adventures."

"Yes," Tilli replied under her breath as she continued to stare at the inked image on the paper. "That would be unlikely."

Chapter 17
Crystals

Goothr set Ayva down upon a fallen tree trunk as he prepared to help Tilli. They were just outside the village, and in a small grassy opening within the forest that was nice and flat.

"Can you move those fallen limbs?" she asked her big friend as she pulled a tuning fork out of her pack. "I don't want us to trip on them if we come through the vortex in a hurry."

Goothr easily cleared the area of debris while he watched Tilli dig in her pack for something else. A sense of nervousness was clear on his face as Ayva shook her head to make sure the blothrud didn't say anything.

"Hmm, I could have sworn I had more of those," Tilli mumbled as she pulled out a thin, long, black crystal. "Goothr."

The blothrud shot straight up with wide eyes. He was sure he was caught and was in trouble for taking one of her crystals for Ayva's bedroom. "I didn't do it!"

Ayva sunk her head into her hands with embarrassment.

"I know, but would you like to?" Tilli asked, holding the crystal out for him to take.

Confused for a moment, he smiled and quickly got excited about the chore before him. Taking the crystal, he lowered himself to his knee and cleaned a spot on the forest floor. The ground was a bit hard from the frost, so he used a stick to start a hole. Once it was to his liking, he placed the crystal inside and pressed it in until only half of it was exposed.

Tilli was impressed. "You're getting really good at that."

He nodded with excitement. "Been practicing."

Ayva coughed several times as she tried to hold back her laughs, knowing he almost blew their secret.

"Are you alright?" the Num asked the girl, who had inadvertently distracted Tilli from what Goothr had said.

"Goothr need tuning fork," he said with an open palm.

Tilli smiled and handed it to him. "You're getting good at this. One day you'll do this on your own."

"Someday," Goothr replied as he slightly hammered the fork against the planted crystal before snapping the crystal in half. "All done," he added while handing her the fork and crystal.

"Thanks." She then placed both back into specific locations in her pack so she could quickly find them when needed. She then turned to them both with a serious look. "Can you two keep a secret?"

Goothr and Ayva turned at each other and smiled before they both nodded to Tilli.

"Good. I need you both to keep this private. I don't want anyone to find out about what we just did. It's just between us, okay?"

"We promise," Ayva and Goothr said in unison.

***

Returning to the village, Tilli led her friends to Pruva, who was overseeing the work on Greyson's dagger.

"Pruva, I have an idea that I'd like you to help me with."

He slowly turned to her and waited for her to continue.

Tilli looked up at Ayva, who was being held in Goothr's arms. "Can you give me that necklace Goothr is wearing?"

The frail girl reached around his thick neck and removed the necklace which held the anti-magic ring, as a sad expression crossed Goothr's face.

"I'll give it back," Tilli assured him as the necklace was lowered to her.

Once she had it in hand, she removed the ring from the thin leather strip and handed it to Pruva. "This once belonged to Irluk as well as my E'rudite master, Schullis. No spells or E'rudite powers can affect the bearer of it."

The giant sloth inspected the item with interest. "What is it that you wish to accomplish with it?"

"Can we extend its power beyond the one with it? Is it possible we can use it to cover a large area?"

Pruva's focus never waivered from the crystal within the ring. "Harmonic reversal…" he mumbled to himself. "It could be stimulated and amplified."

"Can you help?" she asked.

Pruva turned and began walking down the street, leading his friends behind him.

Goothr's eyes grew with concern about the ring being taken away, while Ayva patted the side of his neck to calm him.

By the end of the block, the gathler stopped at the pottery area and grabbed a small chunk of wet clay. Slapping it down on a table, he then pressed the ring into the clay several times, cleaning it between each impression.

Once satisfied, he handed the clay-covered ring back to Tilli. "I will design a way to push light through the crystal extend its powers."

Tilli handed the ring back to Ayva. "Thank you, Pruva. Let me know what you come up with."

Ayva glared at the dirty ring and then at Goothr's disappointed face. "I'll clean this off so you can wear it again."

Chapter 18
Task Completed

Day after day, the villagers worked with little sleep to fulfill the order they were given. Those not crafting were hauling raw materials or packaging finished goods. The carpenters that fixed Ayva's wall and window were busy building a crate large enough to store a massive amount of supplies and nearly large enough to park a wagon within it.

The sun lowered in the sky on the final day, casting an orange glow that bathed the village in warmth. Shadows stretched long and thin as darkness crept ever closer.

"Listen up!" O'vette called out, clapping her hands together. "We haven't much daylight left. Let's make sure everything is near the center of the street so we can plan the packing of the crate!"

Tilli wiped a bead of sweat from her brow, after spending the day moving crafted items to prep for loading. She watched as villagers bustled around her, their determination evident in every swift movement. The giant crate stood at the center of it all, its gaping maw eager to swallow their hard work.

"Almost done with this one," a blacksmith grunted, putting the finishing touches on a finely crafted broad-bladed battle-axe. Tilli marveled at the intricate designs etched into the metal, a testament to the skill and dedication of the smith. He was sometimes hard to work with, but he lacked nothing in his craft.

All the items were clearly marked with the 'EC' symbol, which gave them pride. Throughout the lands, everyone knew the symbol only marked the finest of crafted goods.

"Excellent job!" O'vette encouraged, trying to keep her voice steady despite her own exhaustion. Inside, she worried about the approaching night and the uncertainty it brought. But she couldn't let her fears show. Not now, when they were so close to completing their task.

Goothr arrived with an armful of heavy items, and he also pulled a cart filled with children who cheered him on. Even though one of the youths attempted to make it harder by pressing his boot on the wheel, the blothrud grinned and jerked the wagon just hard enough to cause the hooligan to fall out and tumble to the dirt road.

The final item to arrive was the special dagger. It was carried by Pamalia, displayed on a beautiful thick cloth. Everyone stopped to gaze upon it as she walked past them toward the crate.

Pruva had been standing nearby, waiting for its arrival as he held out a well-crafted chest with unreadable markings. "This unique container was designed and built by my people in Ovla'Mathyus. It is my gift to you, for such a dagger should have nothing shy of this to be stored within." He opened it, and they could see it was lined with a fine cloth over a layer of padding to ensure the contents would not be harmed.

Pamalia and the master crafters gave one last gaze at the ornamental dagger that they all had worked so hard on. It truly was a masterpiece and one of a kind. She then wrapped the item in a fine fabric before lowering it into the small chest that Pruva held.

Once the dagger was inside, Pruva closed and latched the lid. The chest itself was of superior construction and design and was worthy of holding such an object. He then handed it to O'vette.

Eldor'Craft's leader gave a deep sigh of relief that they had fulfilled Greyson's demands and would have more time to determine how to resist future encounters. Placing the small chest into the open pocket within the crate, she stepped back out and gazed upon the villagers' faces. She had bought them time, but she had to stop this from happening again. She feared losing the village and its reputation that her ancestors had worked so hard to build. Another such demand from Greyson could cripple them and leave them with nothing.

Once the chest was put away, the final loads of goods were brought into the area and stacked near the huge crate, which was already half filled. The next step would be for them to organize the rest of the boxes, sacks, and barrels into the crate like a puzzle.

"Alright, everyone," O'vette announced, surveying their handiwork. "Let's take a break and have a well-deserved meal to celebrate your efforts over the past week. We'll load the rest and close the crate up afterwards. We have a few hours before the dragon comes to collect our offering."

As the villagers dispersed, Tilli couldn't help but feel a surge of anticipation. Their plan was coming together, and soon they would be one step closer to finding the Charm Runestone. But first, they had to face the night and all the unknowns it held.

O'vette escorted everyone down the street to the common area. Once there, Goothr helped Ayva fill a plate before setting her down near Pheosco. He then went back to make a plate for himself. Tilli was too nervous about starting her new journey to think about food, as she watched the locals relax after accomplishing their mission.

Once Pruva arrived, he stood near his friends and opened a parchment with a design of a lantern. "This is what I have to amplify your ring's power." The drawing showed where the ring would be placed within the top of the lantern, above the flame. The light would refract through the crystal and then out, giving an array of light that would spread its powers. "I will need resources to build this device."

O'vette and Tilli were intrigued as they knew that if it worked, it could prevent future attacks by magic and the Charm Stone.

"This is excellent!" Tilli said with excitement.

Feeling there might be a better future for Eldor'Craft, O'vette nodded. "You two may have just saved this village." Taking in a cleansing breath, she looked up and watched her people for a few moments, before glancing over to Tilli and Goothr. "This is your last chance. Once you're inside the crate and Greyson's dragon lifts you up, there is no going back."

Goothr was the first to reply. "Tilli told Goothr the plan and I promise to protect her, because I am taller than her."

"Truth be said," Pruva slowly nodded. "This is why we came here. Tilli must remove the Charm Runestone, or our future will be devastated."

"What's that?" Pheosco perked up from the table Ayva was eating at. "We dragons can hear better than you think." He flew up onto the blothrud's muscular shoulder and glared at Tilli. "What are you about to do?"

Tilli glared right back at him. "Keep your voice down." She glanced down toward Ayva and then back to the dragon. "This isn't for everyone to know."

"Well, I'm not everyone, so spill it!"

Tilli led Goothr off to the side while O'vette sat with her daughter to keep her company.

The tension was building as Tilli took another look around.

"Oh, this should be good." Goothr could hardly wait to hear what Tilli was going to divulge.

"You've already been briefed on this mission," she told him.

"I was?"

"Yes. And I hope you remembered, because it's a huge risk."

"What is?" the giant warrior asked.

Tilli sighed before looking up to the dragon still perched on Goothr's shoulder. "Goothr and I are going to stowaway inside that crate so we can get inside Greyson's fortress and steal the Charm Runestone."

"Oh! I remember now!" Goothr smiled, feeling proud of himself. "You're right. That was the secret that I wasn't supposed to tell anyone."

"No, you're not going in that crate. I won't allow it!" Pheosco spit back.

"I knew you'd be mad, which is why I didn't tell you!"

Goothr's smile faded to a frown. "Are you two going to fight?"

"Yes!" they both shot back in unison.

Goothr lowered his head before glancing over to Ayva. "Goothr needs to carry Ayva home. It's late and she shouldn't hear you fight." Turning, he walked off.

Pheosco launched off and landed near her feet. "Are you insane? That dragon could drop that crate and kill you, or even worse, you land safe and then Greyson catches you!"

"I can't just sit around here and wait for him to bring the Charm Stone to me."

"I'm not suggesting that you do. But if you get caught and he gets his hands on the rest of your Runestones, there is no end to the terror he can unfold upon these lands. You can almost bet that your friend Pruva won't survive that level of a change to his past."

"Then you keep them here, safe, where no one will find them. They're in my room right now, you can protect them until I return."

"And if you don't return?"

She didn't like that question. She had tried to avoid thinking of all the potential issues she could encounter and the true risk to her own life. "I don't want to discuss that possibility."

"Why? You have to face the fact that it might happen. You can't just rush in there thinking it's just going to go your way!"

"Yes, I can. In fact, I have to. Otherwise, I'll be too afraid to take the first step!" she said as tears formed and rolled over one cheek. "I'm scared, Pheosco. I don't know what to do, but I have to do something. So many people are relying on me, and if I start thinking of all the ways it can go wrong, it will paralyze me from even trying."

Growling at the girl, the green dragon began to pace. "Then I'm coming with. I've been to the Stone'Ring and know how to get around. That should increase your odds." He then walked off while grumbling to himself.

O'vette had noticed the two arguing after Goothr had picked up Ayva and headed home. Slowly approaching, she reached out with a gentle touch to Tilli. "What's the issue, my dear? Have you changed your mind?"

Tilli wiped the tears from her face. "I'm sorry. This is so difficult."

The village leader wiped a missed tear from her cheek. "You don't have to do this. Our safety is not your responsibility."

"I know, but I want to save this village, and Ayva, and the future."

"That's a heavy load for anyone to carry."

"I have no choice."

"We all have choices. You can do nothing, if you want to bad enough. We all have that choice every day of our lives."

Tilli looked up into O'vette's eyes, and for a moment it felt like she was talking to her mother. "But if we all did nothing, where would we be?"

"True. But I find that the key is to not just do something, but do it with intent and passion. Fill your heart with desire to accomplish it." O'vette glanced over at her villagers. "See these folks, they create the finest goods anywhere in the world. This is not accomplished just because they have to do this to survive. They are driven with pride to do their best and to know anything that they were a part of can be trusted to be the best quality and finest workmanship.

We have created a reputation and the name Eldor'Craft is synonymous with quality."

"I don't create amazing art and goods. It's just not the same."

"It is. You must make decisions in your life and live with the outcomes. If you agree to do something, then be committed to doing everything in your power to make it successful and the best you're capable of doing. Don't cut corners or take the easy way out. See it through and then be proud of yourself, regardless of how it turns out, because you know you did your best."

Tilli closed her eyes in thought before looking back up into hers. "Do you think I should take this risky journey?"

"If I make this decision for you, then it means you're not committed to it. If this is true, then don't go."

"I understand," Tilli confessed as she glanced up to see the silhouette of the small dragon fly out of the common area. "It's time I talk to Pheosco with a level head."

"It's about time," the green dragon hissed from near her feet.

"Pheosco?" Her body froze in sheer terror as though she saw a ghost.

"Yes?"

"How can you be there, by my feet, if I just saw you fly overhead?"

"Clearly I didn't."

A wave of panic ran through her body. "If you're here, that means the other dragon is Mel'tayn! And he's headed toward the town hall where my Runestones are!"

Chapter 19
Runestones

The sound of shattering glass over the evening gathering instantly caught Pheosco's attention as he flew toward the town hall. His vibrant green scales seemed to bristle as he pumped his wings to increase his speed.

Tilli snapped her head toward O'vette. "Find Goothr!" she yelled while starting her run down the street, back to her room. "We may need his help!"

As Pheosco approached the building, he spotted the broken window where shards of glass glinted ominously in the moonlight. He never hesitated. Instead, he steeled himself as he swooped through the jagged opening.

Within the room, a small black dragon had just pulled the satchel of Runestones from Tilli's pack.

"Stop!" Pheosco roared upon entering, baring his teeth as he confronted the intruder.

Mel'tayn sneered and clutched the satchel, undeterred by the other dragon's anger.

Flapping his wings, he blocked the window for any escape. "You must be Mel'tayn."

Gripping tighter on the leather bag, the black dragon glared up at the intruder. "You have me at a disadvantage."

"I am Pheosco, protector of Rummon and the Mountain King. You do not want to challenge my skills or honor," he hissed. "Drop the Runestones and the two you stole earlier, and I will let you live."

"The Mountain King is dead and Rummon is in exile, while my master, Irluk, is alive and waiting for me to return these to her."

"Her body was washed away to the distant future. You have no master any longer."

"Her legacy lives within the Alchemists and these stones will bring her back to power. You'll have to pull these from my dead claws to get them."

"As you wish!" Pheosco quickly dove down upon his opponent.

With a flurry of wings and a clash of talons, the two dragons lunged at each other. Their scales shimmered in the dim light as they twisted and turned, seeking any advantage over their opponent. The confined space of the bedroom proved to be both an ally and an enemy.

"Is that all the protector of Rummon has to offer?" Mel'tayn sneered, dodging a swipe from Pheosco.

"Far from it!" Pheosco retorted, his heart pounding with adrenaline. He needed to keep the pressure on Mel'tayn, forcing him to make a mistake.

"Pathetic!" Mel'tayn roared as he struck back, his claws narrowly missing Pheosco's head. His tail whipped around, smashing into a small table and sending it crashing to the floor.

"Careful now," Pheosco taunted. "You might hurt someone."

"Enough games!" Mel'tayn bellowed, anger flaring in his eyes. He charged at Pheosco, determined to end the battle once and for all.

"Got you," Pheosco thought, seizing the opportunity. With a flick of his tail, he sent a vase hurtling towards Mel'tayn, momentarily distracting the black dragon.

"Ha!" Pheosco yelled, using the distraction to land a solid blow to Mel'tayn's snout.

Mel'tayn snarled, shaking off the pain.

"Come on," Pheosco prodded his opponent.

"Enough!" Mel'tayn roared, launching himself at Pheosco with renewed fury. The two dragons clashed once more, their wings beating the air like thunder.

"Can't let him win," Pheosco thought, desperation creeping in. But Mel'tayn was relentless, and it was all Pheosco could do to stay on the defensive.

"Give up!" Mel'tayn growled, slashing at Pheosco with renewed ferocity.

"Never!" Pheosco spat back, his vision blurring as exhaustion threatened to overtake him. "I'll die before I let you have this satchel!"

"Then so be it!" Mel'tayn snarled, lunging forward for the final blow.

The harsh sounds of shattered glass and splintered wood echoed through the narrow hallway, reaching Tilli's ears like a siren's wail. Her heart raced as she sprinted towards her bedroom door, fear threatening to choke her. The fate of her family's legacy and her friend's life weighed heavily on her shoulders, and she couldn't fail them now.

"Please," she whispered, praying that her precious Runestones were safe.

Tilli flung open the door, her eyes widening in disbelief at the sight before her: Mel'tayn and Pheosco, locked in a fierce battle amidst the wreckage of her makeshift bedroom. The ferocity of their strikes sent shivers down her spine, but she knew that she had to intervene.

Running through the streets and around buildings had cost her valuable time needed to prevent the black dragon from stealing her items. However, Pheosco's direct flight had stopped him long enough for her to arrive before he could escape.

"Stop!" Tilli cried out, adrenaline coursing through her veins. But her voice was lost in the chaos, drowned out by the dragons' snarls and the flapping of their wings.

She glanced at her satchel, lying dangerously close to the battling beasts upon her bed, its contents the key to everything she held dear. A spark of determination ignited within her, driving her to act.

"Enough!" Tilli bellowed. With a swift and agile leap, she dove into the fray, narrowly dodging a swipe from Mel'tayn's razor-sharp claws.

"Are you insane?" Pheosco hissed, his eyes wide with shock.

"If that's what it takes!" Tilli shouted, her conviction unwavering. She ducked under another vicious strike from the black dragon, using the distraction to snatch her satchel from the floor.

"Got it!" she cried triumphantly, clutching the satchel to her chest. But her victory was short-lived as Mel'tayn's fierce gaze locked onto her prize.

"Give me that!" he roared, lunging at Tilli with terrifying speed. Her heart leaped to her throat as she narrowly dodged his attack, rolling out of the way and catching her breath.

"Never!" she spat back, her eyes blazing with determination. "Over my dead body!"

"With pleasure," Mel'tayn snarled, preparing for another strike.

Tilli's mind raced, searching for a strategy to protect her precious Runestones. The weight of responsibility bore down on her, but she refused to let fear cripple her resolve.

"Come on, Tilli. You've faced worse," she told herself, gritting her teeth. "You can do this."

With Pheosco's help, Tilli fought against the onslaught of Mel'tayn's fury, their movements swift and calculated. Each strategic strike, each desperate dodge, brought them closer to victory – or defeat. Slashes across her arms, legs, and neck made it clear that the black dragon was a dangerous adversary that could potentially kill her. And if it were not for the green dragon, that could have already been the case.

As the battle raged on, Tilli's thoughts drifted to her father, her mother, and all those who had fallen before her. She couldn't let them down. Not now, not ever.

"Fight, Tilli. Fight for your family," she whispered, her voice barely audible above the noise of the battle. And with renewed vigor, she charged headlong into the fray, determined to protect the Runestones at any cost.

Tilli's heart raced as she parried Mel'tayn's razor-sharp claws, barely dodging each swipe. Pheosco, hissing and baring his teeth, lunged at the black dragon. The battle raged, a storm of scales and teeth, each movement precise and deadly. Tilli's muscles screamed in protest, but she refused to give in.

As they fought, Tilli yanked the satchel free and fell backward, her back against the wall. She clutched the satchel close to her chest, her knuckles white with fear and determination, while the two dragons fought near her. She was at her breaking point, and it was time for her to take on an offensive posture to end this once and for all.

The first moment the two dragons unlocked their talons, Tilli swung the satchel like a club. The makeshift weapon slapped Mel'tayn, sending him across the room and slamming into the far wall before he fell to the floor, behind her bed.

She then leaped up on the cot to glare down at him. "Tell me where my other two Runestones are, and I'll spare your life!"

Still stunned from the blow, Mel'tayn rolled off his back and to his feet. "They don't belong to you!"

"You don't belong in this time in history, and I won't let you change the future or obstruct my mission. I have no desire to kill you, but you leave me no choice."

The black dragon leaped at her with claws out and teeth bared.

Using the satchel as a shield, Tilli blocked the attacks from his claws while using her free hand to grab the dragon's neck, as he attempted to bite her. "Not this time!"

Pheosco then leaped on Mel'tayn's back, covering the black dragon and holding him firm against the leather fabric, preventing him from hurting her or escaping.

Aside from snapping his jaws at the Num, Mel'tayn was finally captured.

Mel'tayn tried to strike one last time just as the door burst open, revealing Goothr's massive form.

"Black dragon, bad!" His declaration made, Goothr charged forward, the floorboards groaning under his massive form. The room seemed to shrink around them, as the air thickened with tension.

"Wait!" Tilli cried out, her heart missing a beat as the sight of her giant friend racing at them. She clutched the satchel tightly, feeling the energy of the precious Runestones within.

Reaching out for the black dragon, between Tilli and Pheosco, Goothr's powerful charge unintentionally collided with all three of them, knocking everyone through the bedroom wall and into the next room. The force of the collision sent them sprawling across the second room, including the now loose satchel.

For a brief moment, everything came to a halt from the shock of the impact, while everyone shook off the unexpected events.

"Tilli hurt?" Goothr asked, genuine concern etched across his monstrous face as he momentarily forgot about Mel'tayn.

"Get... the satchel..." Tilli gasped, the wind knocked out of her as she lay on the floor, her fingers reaching for the lost treasure.

"Stupid beast!" Pheosco spat, struggling to regain his footing. "You'll cost us everything!"

The sound of shattered debris crunched beneath Mel'tayn's claws as he seized the satchel before Goothr could grab it. The small black dragon darted back to the bedroom, his wings unfurling with a sharp snap.

"Mel'tayn!" Pheosco snarled, launching himself after the thief, pain from the collision momentarily forgotten. "I won't let you get away with this!"

"Too late!" Mel'tayn taunted, as he clutched the satchels tightly in his ebony talons. He soared out of the broken window, leaving a trail of cold air that cut through the room like a knife.

Pheosco's fury boiled within him. He couldn't let that vile excuse-for-a-dragon steal the Runestones – the future depended on it. With a determined growl, he shot out of the window in pursuit, his lean green body cutting through the night sky like an arrow.

Tilli's heart pounded hard against her chest and her breath was labored as she rushed to the window. The cool air chilled her hot cheeks, but she barely felt it. Desperation gripped her as she watched Mel'tayn and Pheosco shrink into the distance among the dense trees, their forms barely distinguishable. She knew there was no way to chase them through the forests, nor could she just allow them to fall into the wrong hands.

"Sorry," Goothr murmured, his eyes downcast. The weight of their situation bore down on him. "Goothr just trying to help."

"We have to stop him!" Tilli shouted, feeling helpless.

"He is too fast through the forest." Goothr rumbled beside her, his massive form looming over her like a protective shadow. "Pheosco will catch him."

Tilli clenched her fists, frustration growing inside her. "He has to."

"Runestones... are important." Goothr's quiet voice was filled with concern.

"I know!" Tilli snapped, then instantly regretted it. "Sorry, Goothr. I'm just angry... and scared."

"I know," he admitted, his dragon-like eyes glistening. "Goothr will protect Tilli and help get stones back."

"Thank you," she whispered, touched by his loyalty. Emotions swirled within her – fear, anger, guilt. Why had she been so careless as to leave them in her room? Was this the reason her grandparents sent Pheosco? Did they know the Runestones would be stolen and start changing history?

"I can't lose them," Tilli muttered, as if saying the words aloud would somehow make a difference. "They're all I have left."

"You still have Goothr," the giant blothrud said softly, placing a large, gentle hand on her shoulder.

"Always, Goothr," she replied, forcing a smile. "But we need to get those Runestones back. For my family. For the future." Glancing at the mess in her bedroom, she started to pack gear.

"Tilli can't leave at night. Too dangerous in the forest."

"We can't just let him fly away. We have to head out after them!"

"We will help," Goothr vowed, his deep voice filled with determination. "But if we go tonight, we can't get in crate. If we don't get in crate, we can't get Charm Stone to save village, Pruva... and Ayva."

Tilli took a deep breath. She knew he was right. Between the dangers, the slow travel, and the risk of getting lost, leaving as night rolled in was pointless. Besides, this was their only opportunity to get inside Greyson's fortress. "Damn. You're right. Let's make short work of this at the Stone'Ring so we can get back here to help Pheosco find my satchel."

"Maybe he'll have it here waiting for us when we get back."

Tilli grabbed a hooded cloak for the cold night to be spent in the crate. "That's a little optimistic, but we can always hope." Heading out of her destroyed bedroom, she waved for him to follow. "We don't have much time to get in that crate before people start finishing their meals and return to start loading."

Chapter 20
Time to Leave

"What happened?" O'vette rushed in through the open doorway leading into the town hall.

"Mel'tayn stole my items and Pheosco is now chasing him through the forest." Tilli was in a rush as she marched past her toward the street while putting on the hooded cloak for the cold night ahead of her. "Tell Pheosco to stay here, once he returns. We'll have to do this without him."

Nearly being run over by the blothrud, O'vette grabbed a few supplies before following them into the street.

A smile grew upon the Num's face as she saw Pruva standing at the enormous wooden box just before them.

He had been hunched over, struggling with a headache and vertigo, but fought through it to stand up straight before Tilli arrived. "Something isn't right," he mumbled to himself.

"Came to see us off?" Tilli asked while approaching.

"Truth be said."

Once Tilli arrived and gave her friend a quick goodbye hug, reality started setting in. This could very well be the last time she saw Pruva, O'vette, Ayva, Pheosco, or even the village. She took a deep breath, her heart pounding in anticipation. This was it – the night they would infiltrate Greyson's fortress.

"Ready?" Tilli whispered to Goothr, who nodded solemnly in return.

"Follow Goothr," he said, his voice hushed yet reassuring. He led the way into the mouth of the giant crate, now shrouded in darkness under a moonless sky.

"Help me in," Tilli instructed, offering her hand to Goothr. His grip enveloped her small hand, and with ease, he lifted her over a few large boxes into the depths of the crate. The scent of wood, metal, and leather filled her nostrils as she landed softly on the items below.

"Okay, Goothr, your turn," Tilli called, feeling a mix of anxiety and excitement course through her veins. She heard the creaking of wood as the large creature climbed in after her, his movements surprisingly graceful for his size.

O'vette arrived and stepped inside the crate before handing them a few items. "Here are a few bladders of water and another blanket for your journey. It will be a cold night."

As the village leader stepped out, Tilli and Goothr hid the best they could as they heard a few large boxes pushed into place by Pruva to ensure the villagers wouldn't see the stowaways when they came back to finish packing. After that, Pruva and O'vette walked back to the common area.

It got eerily calm and every little movement they made seemed more intense than ever. The sound of their breathing alone was nearly enough to give their location away. Tilli was starting to panic.

"Goothr will protect Tilli." He placed a calming hand upon her to ease her nerves. "You're safe. Goothr is safe. Pruva is safe. O'vette is safe. We are all safe."

"Is Ayva safe?" Tilli asked, concern lacing her words. "I could never forgive myself if she passed while we were gone. I hope you didn't have her out playing too much and she over did it."

Goothr hesitated, then nodded, his face etched with worry. "Ayva is tired, but Goothr protects her. She is lying down and resting," he replied, though his voice wavered slightly.

Tilli sensed something was off but pushed the thought aside, focusing instead on their mission. "Remember," she whispered, "we stay hidden until we're inside the castle. Then we find the Charm Runestone."

Goothr nodded, his fierce loyalty evident even in the darkness.

The sound of the villagers returned as they worked hand-and-hand to fill the rest of the crate. They had more than enough room as they finished stuffing in the last few sacks between the boxes and barrels. Their task was now completed, and a sigh of relief could be felt by everyone.

O'vette was lifted up upon the crate to give her words of thanks to everyone, specifically honoring several of the masters of trades and those that went above and beyond to ensure they were successful in not only delivering everything on the list, but also ensuring the items were at a level they were all proud to be associated with.

After the brief speech, they helped her down and the final thick ropes were tied to the metal hooks on top of the crate. Once everything was ready for Greyson's dragon to arrive, they all went home except for O'vette and a few of her closest friends, who sat on the steps leading to the town hall. They would wait and watch to ensure nothing went wrong.

The minutes stretched out inside the crate, punctuated only by the sound of Tilli and Goothr's breathing. They waited in silence, listening for the approach of the dragon. And after an hour, the ground beneath them trembled as the winged beast landed nearby.

Tilli's heart raced as the dragon's claws closed around the ropes that held the crate. Then, with a jolt, the parcel was lifted into the air. The sensation of being airborne was both exhilarating and terrifying. She clutched Goothr's arm, seeking comfort in his presence.

Just as they began to ascend, Tilli heard a light cough from within the crate.

"Was that—" she started, her breath catching in her throat.

"Sorry," came Ayva's small voice, trembling with fear and excitement. "Goothr said I could come on one adventure."

"AYVA?!" Tilli hissed, her shock quickly turning to panic. "But how? When did you?"

"Too late now," The giant warrior interrupted, his voice heavy with guilt. "Goothr protect Ayva."

As the crate continued its ascent, Tilli realized there was no turning back. They would have to carry on with their mission – the life of a dying child now hanging in the balance.

"You helped her sneak in here instead of taking her home from the common, didn't you?"

Ayva couldn't let the blame fall on her friend. "It's not his fault. I talked him into it."

"I doubt that took much prodding," Tilli whispered, steeling herself for what lay ahead. "Your mother is going to kill me."

The night grew darker, and the cold wind howled through the slats, as the dragon carried the crate and its occupants toward an uncertain fate.

Chapter 21
The Flight

The cold air whipped through the open slots between the boards and against Tilli's face as they soared higher and higher, while the dragon carried them effortlessly through the night sky. She questioned her decision to make this trip and her heart pounded hard against her ribs. Ayva's presence weighed heavily on her, adding a layer of responsibility she hadn't anticipated.

"Are you scared?" Ayva whispered, her voice trembling between coughs. Going the night without any sleep had taken its toll on her.

Tilli handed her one of the blankets. "Terrified," she admitted, allowing herself a moment of honesty. "But we can't let fear control us."

"That's how good adventures start, right?" Ayva's eyes wide with hope of one of her dreams being fulfilled. It had already been more excitement that she had experienced in the past year. Her wishes were coming true, and she had her giant friend to thank for it.

Goothr sensed Tilli's unease. "Goothr will watch Ayva. And I'll keep her happy and healthy."

"Easy for you to say," Tilli muttered under her breath, though she appreciated his attempt to calm them. She then turned her attention back to the stowaway. "Why did you do this? You know you're not healthy enough for this."

After trying to hide a few coughs, she pulled the blanket tightly around her. "I'll never be better than I am right now. Each day I get worse. Waiting until I'm up for this is just a way to lie to myself."

"But to do something this dangerous? Why not focus on your other dreams?"

"None of my other dreams were any closer. It's too late for me to find the love of my life and get married. I won't be here long enough to have any children I can tuck in bed and tell bedtime stories to." Several more coughs forced their way out before she could continue. "My time is up. I asked Goothr to take me along so I could at least see life outside of Eldor'Craft. It was my dying wish."

"Stop saying that. There is still a chance I can save you."

"I used to think so as well. I've moved on from the false hope. So has my mother. If you're truly my friend, you will as well."

Her words stung. Tilli knew someone out there could heal her. She just needed to find the right person. "In a way, I'm glad you're here with us."

"Really?" Ayva and Goothr said in chorus.

"Yes. We will be around Alchemists, and one of them is bound to have a cure or know how we can treat you to extend your life."

"Stop!" Ayva yelled, before starting a coughing fit. "Stop trying to save me and start being my friend." Strained breathing tensed every muscle in her torso as she tried to continue. "Give me this last wish for excitement before I go."

Goothr pulled her in and cradled her while rocking back and forth. His concern for her was obvious.

Tilli grimaced. "I understand, Goothr. You simply wanted to make her happy. But you may have just shortened all of our lives by bringing her. She is now a liability that will slow us down and could blow our cover." Clearing her own throat, she added, "But she is now part of our journey so let's make sure we all survive it."

And with that, the tone of the trip changed, at least for a few hours, until their destination could be viewed through the slits of the crate.

The fortress loomed in the distance, its silhouette stark against the moonlit sky. As they approached, the enormity of their task became all too real. Tilli closed her eyes and took a deep breath. The circular shape now made sense as to why O'vette had called it Stone'Ring. But Tilli could see what its true nature was. It was a coliseum, which is where Pruva said they needed to travel to find the Charm Stone. They were in the right place.

"Okay, everyone," she said, her voice steady despite her nerves. "When we land, Goothr will get us out of the crate. Then we need to stick together, because once we get what we need, I'll open a portal for all of us to immediately return to Eldor'Craft."

"Goothr protect friends who are smaller than me," the blothrud vowed solemnly.

Tilli nodded. "It may come to that. If we can't quietly get what's needed, then we may need your brute force to help us get it before we make a quick escape."

The deafening flap of wings punctured the stillness as the blue dragon swooped into the center of the coliseum. Moonlight glinted off its iridescent scales, casting eerie shadows on the ancient stone statues. With a thunderous thud, the dragon lowered the wooden crate onto a sandy pit within the walls. The impact jolted the occupants of the crate, sending a shiver down Tilli's spine. She clenched her fists, drawing upon an inner strength she wasn't sure she possessed.

They all sat in silence as they waited for the winged beast to get far enough away, while Ayva held her hands over her mouth to stifle another cough. After a few moments of silence, it seemed as good a time as any.

"Here goes nothing," Tilli murmured, her resolve hardening with every passing second.

"Is it gone?" Ayva's frail voice trembled with both excitement and fear.

"Seems like it," Tilli responded, her eyes wide and alert as she peered through the crate's thin slits. Her long blond and red hair, pulled back in a ponytail, swayed with every movement. "Goothr, can you open the crate without making too much noise?"

"Of course, Goothr is quiet like a mouse!" the giant red-skinned warrior beamed proudly and began to pry the crate open. The wood groaned softly under his massive, clawed hands, but he managed to keep the noise to a minimum.

"Alright," Tilli said as the last splinter fell away. She scanned their dim surroundings, heart pounding in her chest. "We need to move quickly and quietly. Remember, stay close and follow my lead."

"Lead," repeated Goothr, nodding vigorously. He tried to keep his deep voice low, but it still rumbled like distant thunder. Holding Ayva's hand, he placed his other hand on the Num's shoulder for comfort.

"Exactly. And let's hope the people that live in this city aren't all like Greyson's creatures." Tilli took a deep breath, gripping the blothrud's hand to follow her. "We also need some luck that they are still sleeping or too distracted to notice us."

Chapter 22
Investigation

With the grace of a cat, Tilli slipped out of the crate and into the looming darkness of the castle. Ayva followed, her pale face etched with determination, though her thin frame trembled with every step. Goothr brought up the rear, even with his hulking form, surprisingly light on his feet when he took his time.

"Stay close," Tilli whispered as they crept through the shadows to the edge of the outdoor arena. "And be ready for anything."

"Goothr is ready for anything!" Goothr echoed, trying to stifle a snort that threatened to give them away.

"Quiet, Goothr," Tilli scolded gently, the corner of her mouth twitching in amusement despite their dire situation.

"Sorry, Tilli," the blothrud mumbled sheepishly. They pressed on, the danger and urgency propelling them forward.

Goothr noticed Ayva's legs trembling, her breath shallow. "Goothr carry Ayva," he whispered, gently lifting her frail body into his massive arms. She nestled against his warm, muscular chest, her eyes filled with gratitude.

"Thank you, Goothr," she whispered back, a weak smile on her lips. With Ayva secure in his arms, Goothr followed Tilli toward an entrance into the coliseum's corridors.

The open area was filled with shops and small huts for the vendors to live in. Closed for the night, the ancient coliseum arena had been transformed into a place for commerce. Scattered about they could see small groups of mutants, like the ones that appeared when Greyson had visited the village.

"I would assume Greyson's room would be in the highest level, so he could look over everyone under his rule," Tilli said, her voice barely audible as they moved through the dark, winding corridors. Her heart raced, but she forced herself to remain focused. They couldn't afford any mistakes.

They couldn't avoid walking down hallways lit with lanterns, but the first few were empty and allowed them to relax a little before they encountered locals walking the opposite way.

Two humans chatted softly to one another as they approached. Dressed in fine robes, one stopped and gave the blothrud a startled reaction. "What do we have here?"

"He is a blothrud," Tilli replied before Goothr had the chance to open his mouth.

"I know what a blothrud looks like," he spat back. "I mean the girl? Was she injured in battle, like the rest?"

Thinking fast, Tilli felt this could work for them. "Yes."

"Then take her to the infirmary to drop her off to get healed. And then get your blothrud back on the battle front where we need him."

She nodded. "Which way? I get turned around so easily."

"Back through the main hall," he replied. "We're heading that way. Follow us."

Tilli and Goothr locked eyes at each other for a moment before she gave a soft, "Thank you." She didn't have time to think of a way out of refusing the offer that wouldn't cause suspicion. So, they turned around and followed the two men down the corridor.

All three of the outsiders kept giving each other glances as they headed away from where they believed the Charm Runestone would be kept, and closer to where a large gathering of locals would be. It was the opposite of their agreed upon plan.

The noise grew louder as they closed in on the main hall, which was filled with various species preparing for the day. Some were planning on upcoming attacks, others had just returned to report the status of the battles, while others were healed and ready to reenter the battlefield.

Amongst the humans and other species, small bands of mutants scattered about the corners of rooms and shadows in the hallways. They seemed to be everywhere, like an infestation of rats, and yet no one paid attention to them.

Beyond the main hall were several large rooms filled with injured lying on the cots and on the floor. Many were missing limbs or an eye, or suffering from broken bones. The odd assortment of humans and other creatures allowed Goothr to not stand out as unusual.

Shelves were filled with elixirs, powders, liquids, and jars of body parts that could be used for those who had lost some. Several Alchemists mixed formulas together while dozens of servants rushed around to save the lives of those they could while waving some away due to them being a lost cause.

"What's her problem?" One of the servants asked.

"Oma'haige," Goothr said before thinking it could cause any issues.

The servant seemed surprised. "Definitely didn't get that in any of the battles. Lay her over on that cot and we'll have one of our masters take a look at her."

"Can you help her?" Tilli's voice was soft but excited.

"No, I can't. But maybe one of the masters can. They are all busy at the moment, so you'll have to take your turn." He then moved his attention to the next person being brought in.

Tilli led Goothr to the bed and motioned for him to set Ayva down. Scanning the room, she saw that there was enough going on that they actually blended in within the organized chaos. "This may be exactly what we needed."

Goothr gently set Ayva down on the cot. "They will heal her?"

"I don't know, but this is the best chance we have." She looked around the busy room for some water. "Make sure Ayva has plenty to sip on. I'm going to make my way around to get an idea of how to navigate these halls while searching for Greyson's private quarters. I'll return and check on your progress."

She then placed a hand on Ayva's head. "You're burning up. Drink lots of water and stay lying down until I get back."

"I'll be fine. Go get what you came for." Her weak smile didn't give the reassurance she wanted to, but it was all she had as she watched Tilli nod and walk away and then out of the room. Turning back, Ayva watched her giant friend try to pour water into a small glass with his large clumsy hands. She smiled as he spilled half of it before getting back to her.

Goothr handed Ayva the glass. "Drink."

She sat up and then did as she was told. While still up, she gazed at her surroundings. "Thank you."

"You're welcome."

"No. Not for the water. This experience. I never knew there were so many types of creatures. I never knew there were buildings this massive or rooms this big. I'm already experiencing things I never did."

Goothr looked around the room perplexed. "This is bad stuff to experience. Goothr been in battles. Not a good adventure. People get hurt."

Seeing him slightly upset, she patted his hand. "We're not at war. We'll be okay."

"Blothrud!" a man in a full military uniform yelled over to him. "Get over here!"

Goothr sheepishly glanced around, hoping to find another blothrud in the room, but failed. "Goothr be right back." He patted her on the arm before leaving her cot.

By the time he approached the man, he was already trying to explain. "Goothr is busy taking care of Ayva—"

"I don't care!" the man barked. "Come with me." He then turned and walked out of the room.

Uneasy about the situation, he gave a quick uncomfortable wave to Ayva before following the man out of the infirmary and back into the main hall where three other blothruds were standing. They were older than him and dressed for battle.

"We're sending you to the front line to take out a new beast that has been literally eating our army of creatures. The only description we've received from the few that have escaped is that it's the size of a building and is impossible to harm." Slapping a map down on a table, he pointed at the area where the beast was last seen. "We need this new threat eliminated so we can stop their supply route."

Goothr let the other three blothruds study the map while he attempted to slowly step back away, but he wasn't going to get off that easy.

"Is that all you've been equipped with?" The man gave Goothr a disappointed glare. "Just a club?"

"My club is strong," Goothr said in response.

"Fine by me. Just get the job done." He then eyed the small group of giant warriors and gave designations, starting with the tallest blothrud. "You're in charge, Worvik, as usual. Pick your second-in-command before you reach the target." He then gave a questionable look at Goothr. "And then if three of you fall in battle, it's the responsibility of the remaining warrior to finish the job and return here to give me an update. In other words, I don't want to see any of your ugly faces back here unless the job has been completed."

The other three blothruds grunted in unison and slapped weapons high in the air to start their mission. They then fell in line to follow the man toward their transportation to the front line of the war.

With hopes of not being seen, Goothr stood idle as the blothruds began leaving before he turned to make his way back to the infirmary. Stepping inside he was pleased to see one of the cloaked masters checking on Ayva. He was an elderly man with a long gray beard who hunched over to speak with the ill girl.

Looking up from her examiner, Ayva smiled at her friend in the doorway, but she could see something was wrong. His expression was that of sadness as an even larger blothrud came up from behind and grabbed him.

Goothr's and Ayva's eyes locked in that split second that seemed like an eternity as the horror of the moment began to settle in that he was not going to be there for her. Tears welled up in her eyes as he lowered his head and was escorted from the room to be taken into battle.

Chapter 23
Separate Paths

Tilli worked her way through the labyrinth of corridors, trying to get the lie of the land. The once decorative coliseum was filled with new walls to support an environment of city living. Getting lost a few times, she managed to gain her bearings by the time the sun slowly crept up.

The market area within the sandy arena was opening and goods were starting to be hung. The wide corridors were filling up with locals as the buzz of tasks needed to be fulfilled.

It was the opposite of the harmonious flow she felt in Eldor'Craft. Instead, it was a stressful vibration of reacting to demands and everyone attempting to do their part to stay out of trouble. Piles of gear and supplies for war were stacked in random locations awaiting others to have the time to ship them.

It seemed like the vile mutants were in every dark corner within the city and everyone just accepted the parasites, even when they stole food. They were protected by Greyson himself and were to be called upon him at any time to do his bidding. It was best to just leave them alone.

After an hour, she felt it was time to check back in with her friends. She didn't know if she was blending in because of their openness to the range of races and species, or simply because everyone was too busy to notice her. Either way, she felt comfortable walking among the city of Stone'Ring as she started to head back to the infirmary.

The sound of synchronized slapping of boots against the stone floors caught her attention. She leaned forward and arched her head around a corner to watch the marching of several guards escorting Greyson.

Lumbering behind them was a hairless giant that was easily a head taller than Goothr, and twice as wide. His brown skin looked like thick animal hide and was covered by a long winter robe that nearly touched the floor. His arms and most of his chest were exposed, while his lower legs extended beyond a studded leather military kilt. His weapon was an oversized hammer attached to a wide leather strap that hung from his shoulder on the opposite side. The massive giant followed Greyson's guards while pulling a wagon, which carried the crate Tilli had traveled in from the village.

This was her chance to see where he was going. It could lead her to where he stored his most precious items.

Tossing the hood of her cloak back over her head, she followed the wagon and the procession leading it. The giant stood twice the height of most humans and wore a heavy robe-like uniform that had the city's symbol on it. In fact, all of the guards and all of the warriors had the same symbol, which was a stylized 'MC' with letters that overlapped.

A slight smirk escaped when she realized how similar the Magic'Craft marking was to the Eldor'Craft symbol. "Not very original," she muttered under her breath.

The busy locals within the wide hall parted ways as Greyson and his followers trudged down the center. Turning and walking through two enormous double doors, the city's leader led them into a huge warehouse of goods.

"I'm still furious about someone opening this crate before I arrived!" Greyson had been lecturing one of his men on the expected protocol for such deliveries. "If any of our items are missing, you will be the one to pay the price." Stepping closer to the man, he lowered his voice while adding a menacing tone to his next statement. "And it will be your head if my dagger isn't in here."

"Sir, how would we know if they were even able to create such a dagger in the first place?"

"We wouldn't!" he yelled, inches from his face. "But if the crate hadn't been opened prior to me arriving then I could blame them. But now you'll have to take the fall!"

Standing stiff, the guard knew his place. "Yes, sir."

"Dwall!" Greyson yelled to the giant while still nose to nose with the guard. "Unload and finish opening my crate so I can see what's inside."

Tilli noticed that he wasn't using his Charm Stone, so the giant was not controlled by the E'rudite powers. That said, a yellow crystal had been mounted in the back of Dwall's skull with two metal straps bolted into his head. A faint glow came from the crystal upon Greyson's orders.

The giant pulled the massive crate off the wagon with a loud crash of snapping lumber against the stone floor. He then easily grabbed the heavy panels and ripped them apart, snapping the nails like they were toothpicks.

Once Dwall stepped back, Greyson released the stone and stepped forward to inspect his gifts from the villagers. They hadn't just fulfilled the list he had given them, but they ensured the quality was nothing less than perfection. Each item was branded with their trademark EC. Allowing even one item to be average would be an insult to the entire village and their ancestors.

"Where's my dagger?" he said as he scanned the boxes. "Where is it?" His voice was louder this time as he was growing concerned. "I don't see my special gift!"

The lead guard was starting to shake as he knew the consequences of the dagger not being found, and Greyson was not known for making idle threats.

"I was promised…" And then Greyson went quiet once he noticed an ornate little chest which he hadn't expected. "…my dagger." Like a wild cat sneaking up on his prey, Greyson slowly approached the chest with anxious finger movements before he finally snatched up the chest to make sure it was real.

It was as though it was the first gift he had ever received in his life as he clutched onto it with anticipation, and yet if it was truly the dagger, then it was a gift to him from him. And yet, he was beyond excited.

Opening the clasps, he slowly opened the lid to extend the moment as long as possible. Because there, within the finely lined wooden chest, was a dagger wrapped with the finest of silks. It was the most beautiful thing he had ever seen. It meant more to him than anyone could realize.

Closing the chest with a quick snap, he pulled the box to his chest and held onto it tight. "I'll take this to my room. Sort out the rest and prepare the items for battle. Have a few dozen enchanted before they leave. These are worthy of our spells."

Tilli was stunned by what she had seen. So much so that she had forgotten she was standing completely exposed in the doorway watching, at least until she saw him turn toward her to exit the warehouse and their eyes met.

"Sir?" The lead guard said, to get Greyson's attention. "Why would they send this?"

Greyson didn't immediately place where he had seen Tilli before he turned to see what the guard was calling his attention towards.

The guard picked up some half-eaten food and a blanket from behind a few boxes. "Someone was traveling inside the crate."

In that fraction of a second, Greyson recognized the girl from the village. "Stowaway!" He spun back around to confront her, only to find she had vanished. He then ran to the large main hallway where hundreds of locals roamed in both directions, but she was lost within the crowd.

With the benefit of being shorter than most humans, Tilli scampered down the hall as quickly as she could, dodging around others while snapping her head back to see if she was being followed. And it was during one of these times she was looking backwards that she ran into someone. But not just anyone. This young man had a long black mohawk haircut, a puff of hair between his lower lip and chin, and black tribal tattoos on his cheeks under his eyes.

She had run into Durren, the leader of the thugs who had attacked her and Goothr in the forest after they had exited from the Govi Glade.

"Watch it!" Durren said, just moments before he recognized her face. "You!" he yelled, pointing at her so his friends would see her and follow in pursuit. "Stop!"

Greyson also heard the young man's yelling and charged down the busy hall. He was followed by his bodyguard, the incredibly large brown giant that towered over everyone.

Tilli kept her head down, ducking and weaving between people until she ran into a small group of large blothruds marching toward her.

The leader of the group casually brushed her off to the side as though she was nothing more than an annoying insect. However, his light sweep of his arm sent her little Num body flying off to the side and against a small pile of goods for the war.

Shaking it off as they passed, she couldn't believe her eyes. "Goothr?"

Turning his head, his eyes pleaded with her to save him. But it was clear that the others of his species weren't going to let him just walk away. Surrounding him, they were acting as escorts while one actually had his hand upon the back of Goothr's neck to keep him moving.

Tilli stood up to confront them. "Wait right there! Where are you taking my friend?"

The group stopped their march and the lead blothrud turned to growl at the little Num.

"Grab her!" Durren yelled as he approached them with his friends.

In addition, Greyson could be seen running toward her, just a few yards behind the gang of youths. "Seize her!"

Before Tilli could skirt away, the lead blothrud warrior grabbed her by the arm.

"No!" She yanked and twisted to free herself without any luck, just as Durren and his friends arrived.

"I'll take the Num!" The young thug grabbed Tilli's free arm and began pulling. "Let go of her!"

Stretched out like a rag doll, Tilli's arms were fully extended, and her feet were barely touching the ground.

The blothrud growled at the punk kid who had the audacity to tell a blothrud warrior what to do.

"What's your problem, ya rud? Get hit a few too many times in battle?" Durren laughed at his own comment.

Letting go of Tilli, the warrior grabbed Durren by the front of his clothes and lifted him up to eye level as the young man's feet dangled. Blowing out hot air through his nasals, he wanted the boy to understand who was in power.

Durren's friend jumped in to help, causing the other blothruds to corral the young men. Weapons were drawn against the blothruds, and a fight immediately broke out.

By the time Greyson arrived, the hall was blocked by the turmoil.

Tilli took advantage of the fighting to get back on her feet to make a run for it.

"Get that Num!" Greyson ordered the warriors as he approached.

Tossing the youth to the side with ease, the three blothruds turned around to charge at Tilli while everyone else in the area raced off to the side. Not even a fool would risk getting trampled by a small herd of blothruds.

She froze for a moment, as a gang of thugs, three blothrud warriors, Greyson, and Greyson's giant, Dwall, all wanted to capture her. She knew she couldn't stop them, nor could she outrun them without a good head start, along with some luck to hide in a crowd down another pathway. Her options were limited.

"RUN!" Goothr yelled as he leaped from the side, knocking all three of the other blothruds over, tumbling on the stone floor, blocking Greyson's path.

It was her only chance, and she took it. She would have to return to save her friend. Tilli was off like a bolt of lightning as she tore down the large hall and into a side passage that she had been in earlier. It was darker and filled with supplies as well as people stacking more in the confined quarters.

Dwall arrived and pushed two of the blothruds aside to make a path for his master to get to the Num. He then picked up the traitor, Goothr.

"Make sure he's on the next transport to the front line," Greyson ordered his bodyguard as he personally headed after the stowaway.

Using her small stature and quick Num reflexes, Tilli bolted out the other end of the passage and made a tight turn just as her pursuers could see which way she exited. She could hear Greyson's footsteps falling farther behind, as she headed toward the arena. With any luck, he would follow her lead and search the market area while she doubled back and headed for the infirmary to warn Ayva.

Her run slowed to a fast walk to prevent any unneeded attention from the locals as she weaved her way back to her friend. Her mind raced on how she was going to save Goothr, who was surely captured for his help in her escape. Everything suddenly seemed to be going sideways and she didn't have an obvious way to resolve this, let alone find the Charm Stone.

Chapter 24
Limited Options

Arriving at the main hall with her hood up, she worked her way around the perimeter to the entrance to the infirmary, avoiding the random mutant creatures. Taking a breath, she peered in with hopes of seeing her friend resting.

Tilli gave a deep exhale. Nothing seemed to be amiss. Her friend lay in her cot, much like most of the patients in the room, as nurses helped those in need while the masters determined what potions and spells were required to get the fighters back into battle as quickly as possible.

Walking with slight haste in her step, she worked her way to Ayva's side before kneeling so she could whisper without others hearing. "Ayva, wake up."

A gray complexion, mixed with dark circles under the girl's eyes, showed that she wasn't doing well. Her chest rose and lowered in a rough pattern and was interrupted periodically with a cough.

Tilli nudged her. "We can't stay. We have to go find Goothr and return to Eldor'Craft before it's too late." Not receiving any response, she held the girl's hand and cupped her other hand alongside of Ayva's neck. "Don't give up on me. I'll get you home."

A mixture of sadness and anger filled her body. It was devastating to see her friend lie unconscious before her and possibly on her deathbed. And on seeing this, she knew it was her fault. She should have used the portal stone to bring her home immediately.

Standing up, she waved one of the nurses over. "I need her to come with me. Can you give her something to wake her?"

The nurse glanced down at the girl. "I'm sorry, but your friend isn't going to make it."

"Yes, she is." Her voice was stern and commanding. "Just give her something to wake up long enough for her to walk out of here with me. I'll take care of the rest."

"Ma'am, she's not going anywhere. Let her die in peace."

"Don't say that!" The Num's voice was louder than she realized. "She's not going to die. At least not here!"

"Please calm down," the nurse said while others approached to help her out. "I know it's hard to lose someone, but it's best to let them go in their sleep."

"NO!" Tears ran down her face as she lunged at her friend to wake her up. "She can't die here!" she shouted as the workers began pulling her off Ayva. "I have to take her home!"

"And where might that be?" a calm voice said from behind her. "Eldor'Craft?"

Tilli shook the nurses' hands off her and spun around to look eye to eye with Greyson.

"You," he said while studying her face. "You're that little Num I saw at Eldor'Craft…" he paused as he pieced the new faces together. "…and that blothrud that helped you escape is your friend that stood up to me just outside of the village's town hall."

Then his eyes went to the sickly girl on the cot. "Is that…"

"It's Ayva, O'vette's daughter," Tilli interrupted. "She's ill with Oma'haige."

Stroking his chin, he stared at the girl with intermittent glances back to the Num. "So, you stowed away in the crate to bring her here to be cured?"

Tilli wrapped her head around his assumption before replying. "Yes."

"I doubt that. Her mother would never approve of such a thing."

"Her mother doesn't know."

His eyes grew wide as a grin pulled his lips tight. "O'vette knows everything that is going on in that village. She's in complete control and ensures nothing happens that would cause chaos, just like her parents used to."

"Well, she didn't know about this… at least until after it was too late."

"Surely she would be against what you're trying to accomplish by using magic to cure her daughter."

"She would. But at least her daughter would be alive." Tilli was shifting gears from being on the run to working with Greyson to save her friend. It didn't seem possible, and yet it was happening. She just needed to figure out how. "Can your people save her?"

Sizing the Num up, he felt there was more to uncover. "Why were you running from us, if you truly needed our support?"

The question rolled around in her head before she came up with an answer. "Once I saw you and your giant bodyguard, I panicked. The last time I had seen you, one of your creatures killed a villager. The scene flashed in my head, and I lost the courage to approach you, so I ran."

"For the record, I did make sure it was one of your least valuable residents who wasn't adding benefit to the village."

Appalled by his justification, she needed to keep her emotions under control. A slight nod is all she could muster in response as she bit her lip.

Glancing back at the Ayva, he shrugged his shoulders. "It doesn't look like she is much help to your community either."

"Can you help her?"

He sighed. "Why should I?"

"Because she is a life worth saving."

"Says who?"

"Me… and O'vette."

"O'vette has shunned me and my ways for a long time, and now I am being asked to help her. To what end?

Will healing this child bring her to listen to my ways and be a part of my future, or will she continue to argue with me over the implications of magic? I would bet on the latter, so I see no reason to use our valuable resources on curing this child."

"It's her daughter! Of course, she would be thankful, and it might be the very catalyst needed to bring her to the table to talk about these issues."

"No, I know her far too well to think she will. The negotiations would have to happen prior to curing the girl. Besides, I'm not convinced that she is even O'vette's daughter. This could be just a ploy."

"You can't just leave her here to die!" Tilli's emotions couldn't be held back any longer.

"Yes, I can. I see no value I get out of this transaction."

"Doesn't helping someone give you enough value?"

He glared at her as his face went rigid. "It used to, but O'vette taught me a lesson long ago not to make that mistake again."

"Then at least allow me to take her home so she can die with those that love her."

"Resources are limited and I'm not using any to help you or her."

"Then just let us leave. Goothr can carry her, and we will walk back to the village."

"Goothr?"

"My blothrud friend."

He chucked at the thought. "He has already left. We placed him on a wagon that is headed to the front line of our battle."

"You sent him into your war?"

"And if he survives, which is very unlikely, he will be a valuable resource that I plan to keep."

What she thought couldn't get worse, just did. Tilli had lost everything. Both of her friends were most likely to die and there was nothing she could do about it. Fighting back the tears, she glared at Greyson, who was waving over one of the masters. In doing so, she could see the Runestone hanging from his neck. "I'll teach you."

"What's that?"

"If you save my friends, I'll teach you how to use the Runestone properly."

Greyson glanced down at the flat hexagon stone as he lifted it up in his palm. "You, a Num, think you can teach me how to use this?"

"Yes."

An unexpected laugh burst out at the idea. "I already know how to use this, my little Num. In fact, I'm the only one that knows how to use it."

"I am Tilli, servant of head master Schullis within the E'rudite Temple. I was trained by him in their ways and know how to utilize these stones." She could see that he was curious, but not convinced. "This Runestone was lost many years ago during the Alchemist and E'rudite War within the Govi Glade."

His expression went cold as he stood in bewilderment as to how she knew where he had found the stone. "Are there other Runestones that were lost as well?"

Tilli didn't want him to know the truth, for fear of him obtaining more power. "No. But I must say, you are very talented to have learned how to use it without the appropriate training. But with the proper training, your abilities will grow dramatically."

Intrigued, he wasn't sure if he should believe her. "If this is true, why would you do this?"

"Save my friends, and I will teach you what I know."

"Which could be nothing," he speculated. "But I'm willing to find out. So, I'll save your friends once you train me."

"They won't last that long. Training you will take weeks or even months. You need to save them first."

"With only your promise to train me afterwards, when you have nothing to lose? I think not." He stood tall, knowing he was in control of the situation. "We will do this in unison. You start training me, and I will have my Alchemist start working on this girl. This will not happen overnight, and she could take a few months to fully recover."

"It's Ayva," Tilli replied.

"What?"

"Her name is Ayva. She's not just another person in your war machine. She's an individual that means a lot to me."

"Fine. I'll have my people start working on Ayva, while you're training me."

"And what about Goothr?"

"Who? The blothrud?"

"Yes. You need to bring him back from the front line and keep him safe while I'm training you."

He thought for a moment before replying. "Agreed." He then stepped closer to intimidate her as he looked down into her eyes. "But just know this, Num, if I find out you aren't able to train me to use this Runestone better than I currently do, not only will I allow your friends to die, but I'll make sure you join them."

She stood strong and glared back at him. "And if either of my friends die, not only will I stop teaching you, but I'll make sure you will never be able to use that Runestone again." It was a bluff that she hoped she would never have to play out.

They stared at each other until Greyson finally broke off and turned to the approaching Alchemist master. "Moordok, please evaluate this girl and report back to me what all can be done for her." He then held a hand up before the long-bearded, frail old spellcaster could start providing his earlier assessment of the girl. "When you come with your report on her, I also want you to bring the others so we can enchant the dagger I spoke of. It has arrived."

Chapter 25
Dwall

The three blothrud warriors marched out of the structure where dozens of wagons were being filled with supplies for the war after unloading the injured fighters to be taken to the infirmary. The vehicles were arriving just as fast as they were being repurposed to head back to the front lines.

The sight of those returning was horrifying. Missing legs or arms were common. Fighters with internal injuries vomiting all over themselves or spitting up blood were just as frequent. Little to no initial triage and treatment had been performed on most of them. If they couldn't fight, but weren't dead yet, they were simply tossed on the parade of wagons cycling between the city and the war.

Goothr had seen war before but had hoped to keep it in his past. Unfortunately, the view before him stirred up ugly memories of fighting to prevent the eradication of all blothruds. He had lost many of his friends and family in those wars, including his parents.

"Keep up, warrior!" Worvik ordered. He was the clear leader of the blothruds even though he wasn't the largest. Despite that, his commanding voice made it clear he was in charge.

Goothr had been lagging a bit while seeing the returning fighters, and eventually he came to a stop. In doing so, he was quickly reminded that Greyson's giant, Dwall, was following him.

An oversized hand pushed Goothr forward. "Move!"

After taking a few more steps, Goothr turned back to the giant. "Goothr shouldn't be here. I am not one of your fighters."

"Goothr!" Worvik shouted. "Get back in line and get on that damn wagon! That's an order!"

Goothr shook his head. "I must take care of Ayva. She is sick. She needs me." Nodding to himself in agreement with his own words, he began to head back.

Dwall reached out with his hammer to block Goothr's way. The hammer was enormous, and the metal head was nearly half the width of Goothr's torso as it pressed up against his chest to stop him. Within the metal, the word 'Quake' was engraved.

Goothr glared up at Dwall. "Goothr not want to fight, but I will if I have to, I'm not leaving Ayva."

Worvik found the challenge amusing and waved his other two warriors back to not interfere. It was a good chance for him to see what the new recruit could do against a giant mognin warrior with the magical hammer. "This should be fun," he mumbled.

Goothr pushed the massive hammer back and started walking again. He felt he had expressed the importance of his duty, and they would understand.

A powerful swing of Dwall's hammer hit the back of Goothr, sending him flying across the courtyard before slapping into the city's exterior wall.

By the time the blothrud knew what was happening, he was on the ground with the giant standing near him. He could see his spiked club behind Dwall, but it was out of reach.

Dwall leaned down and grabbed his leg, before heading back toward the wagons. He was ordered by his master to ensure the blothrud was on the wagon to the front line, and that was what he was going to do.

Sinking his fingers into the ground didn't stop Goothr from being dragged back, nor did the kicking and scratching of his wolf-like legs against the mognin's oversized hand. But seeing his club nearby, he came up with a plan. Rolling over on his back, he reached out and grabbed the handle of his weapon. At the same time, he arched his body so that the spikes upon his back dug in and anchored him into the ground.

Somewhat surprised, Dwall found himself unable to pull the blothrud any further. Turning around, he could see what Goothr had done, so he dropped his leg and stepped over to pick him up by the neck.

It was then that Goothr swung his club, slapping Dwall hard on the face. So hard in fact, that the club's spikes embedded into the side of the giant's face.

Dwall screamed in pain, dropped his hammer, and jolted back a few steps while trying to pull the weapon off. It wasn't easy, and it took three tries with both hands before he dislodged it. And once he did, blood poured out of the holes that had been made in his cheek and the side of his bald head.

By this time, Goothr was back up, and he grabbed the handle of the enormous hammer. It was ridiculously heavy to the point that even with his own powerful strength, he struggled to lift it over his head. Stepping forward, he swung it forward at the giant, missing him as the hammer slapped hard upon the road.

The ground shook hard, knocking nearly everyone off their feet. Barrels and stacks of goods fell and the faralopes on all the wagons screeched in panic. This was not a normal hammer. This was a weapon enchanted with superior powers.

Goothr stood stunned for a moment, his hands still wrapped around the handle of the magical hammer as he wondered just how powerful it could be.

Before the blothrud could pick it back up, Dwall stepped on the handle, pushing it back to the ground. His weight prevented Goothr from lifting it.

Still trying to pull the war hammer's handle out from under the mognin's weight, Goothr glanced up to see what his other options were. The last thing he recalled was seeing the oversized fist coming down on his face, knocking him out.

Dwall picked up his hammer and hung it back onto the leather shoulder strap, before dragging Goothr by the leg to the wagon. Once there, he tossed the blothrud onto the vehicle and gave Worvik an order. "Front line."

Worvik grinned at the giant who still had blood spilling out from the puncture wounds on his face. He always enjoyed watching a good fight. "That's where we're headed," he replied to the mognin before giving his own warriors an order to get moving. "Dirk, grab that spiked club and then load up. We have a battle to win."

Chapter 26
Training

Chanting from a small choir of Alchemists filled Greyson's quarters and echoed within his room before flowing under the doorway where Tilli sat as she waited for her turn to enter.

She could see bright lights and shadows under the two heavy wooden doors and, at one point, a shallow mist rolled out from underneath. Several hours went by as the ceremony continued behind closed doors, while Tilli feared for her friends' lives and tormented herself over the decision to train Greyson. But it was the only leverage she had to play.

Though she was tempted to depart and check on Ayva, the guards would have prevented her from leaving anyway. The stone bench was cold and hard to sit comfortably for a lengthy time. The air was dry, and her back was hurting from a night in the crate with no sleep. In general, everything seemed wrong, and she couldn't relax in mind or body.

With one final baritone blast and the cracking of stones, the sounds from the other room went quiet. Soon after, it was followed by a half dozen Alchemists, including Moordok, leaving the room and walking past Tilli and down the hall.

Tilli was tempted to ask the Alchemist how Ayva was doing, but he was in a heated conversation with two of his colleagues.

After they left, she noticed that the doors were left open, and curiosity was getting the better of her. Standing up, she casually walked to the doorway to see how the guards reacted. With no response from them, she continued her way into the leader's quarters.

Filled with finely carved wooden furniture, plush rugs, and silk drapes, the room was large enough for several people to live in. It boasted a large main room for meetings with a few side rooms for sleeping quarters. Shelves filled with unique souvenirs and several full-length mirrors were placed along a few walls. Smells of incense lingered in the air after the Alchemist's ceremony and an array of magical items had been left behind to be removed and stored by servants. In addition, the aftermath of the spell they performed had cracked several floor stones and burnt the edges of the main table and a few chairs.

Greyson stood at the window, looking out over the distant forest. "The enchantment is completed. One more step closer," he said to himself.

"Closer to what?" Tilli asked, now standing in the center of his room.

Slightly surprised she had overheard him, he gracefully turned around, exposing the dagger he was gripping with both hands. The two red orbs mounted within the handle were still glowing from the enchantment ceremony, but were fading off.

"That's the special dagger we built in Eldor'Craft. What's so important about it? Don't you have enough weapons and creatures to kill your enemies?"

He smiled as a sense of security overwhelmed him. "It's not for taking lives. It's about saving them."

"I don't understand."

"Nor should you have to. Your job is to teach me how to improve my use of the Runestone."

She nodded while eyeing the dagger as he placed it back in the wooden chest he had received it in.

Pulling the Runestone out to expose it to her, he waited to see what she knew.

She took in a deep breath as she thought how to start his training and give him just enough to keep him interested while her friends were being saved. Walking across the room to take the stone, she had planned to hold it long enough to learn how to use it herself. Eventually, if she could convince him to trust her with it, she could take it and collect her friends for a quick jump home through her black crystal portal.

Greyson instinctively pulled back as she reached for the stone. "I don't think so. No one touches this except me."

"Then that will make this more difficult to teach."

"Then it will be more difficult. I'm not handing this off to you, especially after you've told me you know how to use it."

Frustrated, she had to work on a plan for him to trust her with the stone. "Then you hold it and I'll start teaching you the basics."

"I know the basics," he spat back.

"If you knew the basics, you wouldn't need my help."

Grumbling, he finally gave in. "Start with the basics, but don't delay. I have no need for you to drag this out."

"Understood."

Holding the flat stone out in his palm, while still on his necklace, he waited for her to start.

"Every Runestone has ridges."

"There are more than just this one?"

Tilli realized her mistake and tried to cover up the potential mess. "There are several Charm Runestones, but they all do the same thing. You can only use one at a time, so it's pointless to have more than one."

Skeptical, he nodded for her to continue.

"These ridges represent the harmonics needed for the actions to take place."

"Harmonics?"

"Yes. I thought you knew the basics."

"Yes, I do. Keep going."

"I can start at a more basic level, if needed."

"No need. Keep training."

Tilli knew he was a bit lost, and she had a chance to milk the process. "As I said, the ridges are the harmonic waves. The center crystal is the primary point of these waves and should be viewed as you. Then we have several gems in the hexagonal corners. These are also harmonic starting points which interact with the waves you're pushing out from you. So, you'll need to imagine the locations of these points around you in order to have the interaction points perform correctly. Are you comfortable with that?"

Greyson had slightly glossy eyes as he tried to understand what she had just said. "I'm the crystal in the middle and other objects are the gems."

"Not exactly, you need to visualize yourself in the center of this wave pattern," she said while pointing to the ridges on the surface of the Runestone. "Then you need to create the harmonic waves from the other locations at the same time."

She could see he was starting to get flustered. "When you use this stone, what do you visualize?"

"When I hold it tight, I feel the ridges in my palm. Then I just relax as I concentrate on them. I get a strange feeling running up my arm and into my neck. For a moment, I can visualize the surface of a small body of water."

"Perfect. Let's use that image. If you toss a large rock into calm water, what do you see?"

"I see waves reaching out in every direction."

"Then if you drop in a pebble off to the side at the same time?"

"Then it creates smaller waves that interact with the larger waves from the rock."

"Correct. So, if you release the right size rock and multiple pebbles at the exact right time, you should see something similar to the pattern you have on the face of your Runestones.

Greyson glanced down at the Runestone. "Yes, that's what I visualize when I use the stone. I must feel the pattern in my palm and instinctively think about it."

Tilli nodded. "The first part of your training will be to create and control that image. Once you have more control over the various size, speeds, and starting points of the waves, then we'll be able to start applying that to improving your focus and the strength of your Runestone use.

"Fascinating," Greyson said as he tried in vain to make it happen without holding the stone's ridges facing his palm. Flipping it over, he let his mind relax and accept the pattern. But once he attempted to manipulate the waves, the feeling of energy from the Runestone faded. "Teach me how to control this power."

"That will take some time. It is not conquered in one session. It takes constant training and practice." She felt she had given him enough to believe she had the ability to train him. "Are you prepared for me to provide training every day?"

He nodded, as he once again tried and failed to master the technique to control all aspects of the harmonics.

"I'm pleased to hear. With that said, what's the status of my friends?"

He ignored her as he tried and failed again, slightly discouraged that he didn't have immediate success.

"Greyson, we had a deal."

"Yes," he replied with a dismissive wave. "I've already given orders to help your friends."

Chapter 27
The Ride

Goothr's vision was blurred at first as he woke from being knocked out by Dwall. His first thought was to leap to his feet to keep fighting. He simply couldn't allow them to take him away from Ayva. But, in spite of what he wanted, his body didn't follow through.

Everything seemed to be spinning as he squinted his eyes to see his surroundings. And once he did, he realized he was lying on the floor of a wagon that was traveling across the lands on a cool, wintery, sunny, day.

Sitting up, he searched the horizon for the sight of the city, only to find distant forests in every direction as the wagon moved down the bumpy dirt path. "What happened?"

"You got stomped by a mognin, but not before you took out some of his flesh as a reminder of you." Worvik was sharpening his blades while chatting. "That crude weapon of yours can do some damage when used right."

"Crude weapon?" The fog of being unconscious was starting to lift.

"Your spiked club. Looks like the kind of weapons they used a few generations ago."

Goothr glanced at his club that had been tossed into the wagon next to him. "Santorray made that for me."

A moment of silence broke out before Worvik started laughing. "Fine. Keep your secrets. Just have our back while in battle or I'll make sure you don't survive it."

"No secrets. Santorray had this made for me when we fought for the survival of all blothruds."

Squinting one eye, he studied the new recruit with the other. "That was a long time ago. Generations have passed.

Do you expect me to believe you're an old man in a young body?"

Shaking his head, Goothr didn't fully understand what he meant. "We fought together at the Govi Glade—"

"Govi Glade? That's no place for sane folks. Are you saying you went through one of those magical spheres and landed here to help us with Greyson's war?"

"We came here through a sphere, but not to fight a war."

"We? Is Santorray here as well?"

"No. I came here with Tilli and Pruva. We came to find a stone, but then I saved Ayva and she is now sick in the city and I need to get back to her." He started getting up to leave.

"Hold tight, lackey. We're not heading back to the city until our job is done."

Goothr wasn't happy about that. "When will it be done? Goothr needs to hurry back."

"The faster we get rid of this new beast at the border, the sooner we'll get back."

Goothr stared at the dirt path behind them. "I can just walk back the way we came."

"Not likely. Not only will you find several path intersections, you'll likely be ambushed by our enemies along the way."

"Enemies? Goothr doesn't have any enemies."

Worvik laughed at the naïve comment. "We all have enemies, son. Heck, you just made one with Dwall before we departed. But you'll be spotted as a war enemy simply because you're a blothrud. Greyson is the only one that has accepted Del'Unday, such as us."

"There are only three blothruds left? I was sure we won our battle to keep the blothrud species alive."

Worvik chuckled. "Most of our kind traveled southeast to a new Del'Unday city called Corrock."

"Why didn't you go to Corrock?"

Sitting back on the side bench of the wagon, he was beginning to fully believe this new recruit had no idea what was going on in the lands and truly could be from another time. "Lord Ergrauth and I don't see eye-to-eye on a few topics."

"You've met the lord of all blothruds?"

"Let's just say it's best if Ergrauth and I don't work together."

"Okay. Goothr will say that."

Worvik chuckled again. "You're a strange one, lackey, but you've proven you know how to slice some flesh and I can always use another set of blothrud hands under my command."

Chapter 28
Infirmary

Escorted back to the infirmary, Tilli stopped the old Alchemist treating Ayva to see how her friend was doing. "Moordok, have you seen any improvements?"

Moordok looked up from the papers he was reading. He then glanced over at Ayva and then back to the Num. "You do understand that she has oma'haige, correct?"

"Yes, I understand that. But you're treating her for it, right?"

"We are," he answered without elaborating. "Don't get your hopes up."

"Oh, but I will. She didn't have any chance in her home village. At least now she has the finest Alchemists in the land treating her."

The old man smiled and gave a soft scoff. "Finest Alchemists. It's been a long time since I was called that. Perhaps about the time I first met Greyson. He was always optimistic, much like you. After I showed him what magic could do, he came up with this grand plan to make a sanctuary for us so we could work together to make the world a better place. Instead, I spend my time healing the wounded from his many battle fronts."

The talk of battle triggered her thoughts of her other friend. "I wish I knew how Goothr was doing. Greyson said he sent word to bring him back, but I haven't heard any updates."

"I hear plenty from those that I treat. I can keep an ear open about a returning blothrud."

She peered into his sunken brown eyes. Between them and his thinned white hair and beard, it gave him a since of kind elderly wisdom. "Thank you."

Taking her hand, he patted it with his free hand. "I'll do what I can."

She nodded with a smile before she excused herself and headed to a familiar face. Tilli was pleased to see her friend awake and sipping some blue liquid. The Num raced to Ayva's side with excitement. "You're already feeling better?"

"No, but I'm awake. That's a good sign."

"I thought they were going to start a treatment to heal you."

Pulling in a shallow breath, Ayva coughed before replying. "They have me drinking this terrible elixir. I don't believe that it's possible for this to help me."

"It is. Greyson promised me."

"Greyson?"

"Yes, he said he would cure you and save Goothr."

"Goothr? They took him away. Where is he?"

"He's heading to the front line, but Greyson has sent orders to have him returned."

Ayva was confused. "Why would Greyson help us?"

"That's not your concern. I've got everything under control. As soon as you're better and Goothr has returned, I should be ready for us to go home."

"I don't know if I'm going to last that long."

"Don't say that. Greyson has his top people on it and you should start feeling better soon."

Ayva closed her eyes and lay back down on her cot. Sitting up, having a drink, and holding the short conversation was too much for her. "I want to see my mom again before I pass."

The words hit hard against Tilli's chest and her eyes swelled with tears. "I'll make sure you do. In fact, I'm making sure you'll be in better health by the time we return. Trust me."

Ayva reached up and the Num's arm. "My life is now in your hands."

"I know. And I'm going to make it better. I promise."

"Promise?" Greyson's distinct voice carried over the room as he approached Ayva's cot, while his bodyguard, Dwall, stood in the large doorway. "You're doing a lot of promising lately. What are you pledging to now?"

Tilli composed herself and wiped the tears from her eyes before turning around to address him. "You told me your people would heal her."

Greyson grinned and used her own words against her. "That will take some time. It is not conquered in one session." He then looked at the sickly girl. "It takes many elixirs and potions to stimulate her own body to stop it from killing itself."

"Killing itself?" Tilli didn't believe this to be true.

"Oma'haige is caused by the body attacking itself from within. There is war raging inside your friend that has been playing out for a long time. We are stepping in near the end of the final battle to aid the side that wants her to survive. We will not be able to win this overnight, but we can start turning the tide."

Tilli was dumbfounded at the concept of someone's body attacking itself, but it was clear that Greyson knew more about this than she did. "This is clearly not my strength."

"I'll keep it at a basic level for you," he said with a wink.

Ayva gave off a few more coughs before calming down to a labored breathing.

Greyson waved over a few nurses to watch over the child. "Tilli, rest is the best thing she can do right now. Come with me."

She wasn't planning on leaving quite yet, but once the nurses arrived, Tilli was pushed back out of the way. It seemed like her friend was in good hands who knew more about the disease than she did, so she gave in and followed Greyson out of the room.

Her mind flashed back on her friend's request to see her mom and the promise the she herself had made. She hoped she was doing the right thing. If she could gain access to the Runestone by the time Goothr returned, she could have him grab Ayva and a jug of the blue elixir.

Chapter 29
The Market

Before she knew it, Greyson had led her to the open arena, where she had originally arrived when the crate had been deposited. What was a quiet venue at the time, was now a loud location filled with merchandise and those trying to sell their wares.

"It's a little different from Eldor'Craft," Greyson mused.

"Just the opposite," she replied with a smirk. "That village is so organized and…"

"Under control?" he finished her sentence as they started to walk by the first few vendors.

"Yes. There's no confusion, like this."

"Confusion? Is that what you see?" He glanced back-and-forth. "I see freedom and innovation. I see sellers from various races and species all being able to create new things, use new techniques, and sell what they want, when they want, and as much as they want."

Tilli glanced back and forth as people yelled out to potential customers about their goods. "It's noisy. There is unused stock that has been piled up. There are many shops selling the same thing. Seems wasteful."

"You've been talking to O'vette. She said the same thing." He smiled when he said her name. "She inherited a village with a legacy of traditions and controls. It truly is a well-oiled machine."

"Is that so bad?"

"No, but it does prevent growth."

"In what way?"

"They have used the same old processes for generations. They produce wonderful goods, but they don't expand on what they have. Their skills could make this world a better place if they just opened their minds to it."

Tilli glared at the shop filled with hanging meats as the owner swatted away the flies that covered the thick cuts. "How is this madness helping the world?"

"Competition forces people to try new techniques to be better than their competitors in order to increase their sales. Sometimes these new techniques rollover to other industries which increase their quality or productivity. It may not be obvious now, but by shedding traditions and embracing new concepts, we will be changing the world."

Tilli shook her head. "I'm not convinced it's worth it. I felt so comfortable and relaxed in Eldor'Craft, while I don't feel safe here."

"Safe? What would make you feel safe? Locking yourself in a room with food and water delivered to your door?"

"No." She eyed a shop with curious blades and weapons for hunting.

"Ah! I see." He walked over to the booth with her. "A blade at your side would shed those feelings?"

She ran her fingers over a long metal blade and eyed a hunting bow.

"Do you know archery?"

Her eyes fell in embarrassment. "No. Not well enough."

Seeing the broadsword she still touched, he made a different recommendation and picked up a long and thin blade with a bright red handle. "This is more your style. It's for cleaning the skins off large prey, such as a chuttlebeast." He handed it to her handle first.

Taking the item, she inspected it. The weight was comfortable, and it fit in her palm well. "It wouldn't be a weapon I would go into battle with, but I would feel less vulnerable while walking these streets."

After tossing the merchant a few coins, he handed her the leather belt sheath that was made for it. "You'll want to cover that blade, so you don't cut yourself by accident."

She grinned at his assumption that buying her the blade would sway her. "Thank you for the gift, but the difference between the two places is more than just safety."

"Ah, I get the feeling that what you're in search of is security. The feeling of knowing that you have a soft bed, warm meal, and strong walls to protect you."

She smiled at the thought. "Is it that obvious?"

"I would assume most people want such luxuries. And they are now yours, assuming you plan to stay here and help me."

She bit her lip slightly at the thought. "It's more than just security. The stress within the environment is so much more here than O'vette's village."

Greyson nodded as he watched locals negotiate the cost of goods and services. "I can see that. But let me ask you, can the people of Eldor'Craft adapt?"

"Adapt?"

"Yes, my little Num. The villagers have been told a lie that I'm trying to destroy their peaceful paradise. The truth is that I've been attempting to save it from itself. Although my tactics may seem extreme, I'm not an evil villain here. I'm their liberator to a new generation of thinking that will keep them alive."

Tilli gave him a skeptical glance. "How do you come to such a conclusion?"

"The world continues to change whether we like it or not. What would happen if the merchants that purchased their products decided to buy them cheaper from somewhere else?"

"Then they would be buying goods of inferior quality."

"I'll give you that. But what if the customer was okay with good quality instead of Eldor'Craft level quality?"

Tilli never thought about it. "I don't know."

Reaching his arms out to his sides, he offered her a moment to look at the variety of goods. "These merchants can adapt to such changes. They continue to improve their ways, and if their goods are no longer needed, they quickly change to produce new products that are wanted."

"I think the villagers can adapt."

"Have you seen evidence of this?"

Tilli took a moment to search for an example. "Your dagger."

"What about it?"

"They couldn't figure out how to make it. They didn't have the tools or technique to build such an object."

"Yes. It was a risky test that I had for the villagers. Just how did they accomplish it?"

"They had to develop new methods."

Greyson stroked his chin. "Impressive. And they did this on their own?"

"Yes," she replied before changing her answer. "Well, no. My friend, Pruva, explained to them what needed to be done in order to build it, but then the craft masters developed the tools to support his instructions."

He let out a small chuckle at the comment. "I'm sure it was a stressful event for them to do so."

"There was some tension with the idea."

"I bet Bishhall was opposed to even trying to build it." He chuckled louder as he visualized the old blacksmith.

Tilli stopped dead in her tracks. "How do you know so much about them?"

"Didn't O'vette tell you about me?"

"Only that you arrive and steal their goods periodically."

"Steal? Ouch. Harsh words." He started walking again through the open market. "I was born and raised in that village."

"No."

"Yes," he said with a nod. "O'vette's parents managed the production of the merchandise, while my parents ran the distribution. We traveled the countryside with a team of wagons providing the highest quality of goods in the land. Then we returned with raw supplies so the villagers could make even more."

Tilli found herself intrigued by the story. "Then why did you leave?"

"Leave? I didn't want to. No. I was exiled from the village for one of the most horrific crimes one can commit in Eldor'Craft. I suggested change."

"Change of leadership?"

"No. Why would I want that? I was in line to rule over the village, once O'vette and I got married."

"Now I know you're lying."

Lifting his hand to stop her, he went on to explain. "O'vette and I grew up together. We played and courted like most youth. Seeing that our families were the most powerful in the village, it seemed like the perfect relationship to bring everything together. Eventually we got married in the largest celebration Eldor'Craft had ever held. It was amazing."

"Wait! Are you telling me you and O'vette are married?"

He smiled. "I'm pretty sure that's what I just said. And the last I checked, we still are."

Shaking her head, Tilli was confused. "You two hate each other! Why would you get married?"

"We were in love at the time."

"What happened?"

"I spent a lot of my time traveling and I became aware of many things I never saw within our village. New techniques, new materials to work with, and new goods that our customers wanted."

"And the villagers exiled you for that?"

"No, but it was enough to start driving a wedge between me and O'vette's family. Then I found a small group of people that were using magic. I was amazed by this foreign concept and wanted to learn more. The potential for improving our goods and how we made them was staggering."

"You brought magic to the village?"

"I did." His expression turned very solemn as he thought back. "I collected all the magical components and scrolls of spells that I could find. I knew they would be resistant to the idea, so I only had one chance to show them how powerful using magic could be."

Tilli stopped in her tracks. "What did you do?"

"I was young and excited about the future of our village moving forward in a new direction. It was the first time I ever attempted to embed life into an item. Just think of it, if our tools could work without us having to handle them, and if the chores could be done for us, we would have more free time to be creative instead of doing the repetitive mundane tasks over and over again."

"And?"

"And it worked, to a degree, but at a great expense." He stared out into space for a moment before continuing. "I was able to embed life into a few of the masters' crafting tools, but in doing so it stole the life of those masters within our village, including my parents and O'vette's father."

"Stole their life?"

"Their soul and very being was transferred into the items I was enhancing specifically for them. I had no idea it would happen and not a clue how to reverse it."

A sudden moment of clarity hit Tilli. "The tools hanging so proudly over the fireplace hearth in the town hall. Those are the tools you embedded. They held the souls of several craft masters?"

"And still do. Their consciousness will live within them as long as the items exists."

"And that is why you were exiled."

"Correct. It was a foolish mistake that costs me my parents, my home, and my love."

Tilli watched his expression. "You're still in love with her, aren't you?"

"Without question. She is my soulmate, and we will eventually be together in life and for all eternity."

"All eternity? How can you plan on such a..." Tilli's face went pale as she answered he own question. "The dagger. You plan to capture her soul."

"And my own, when the time is right. My Alchemists have finished their embedding ceremony on the dagger, and it is now prepared to hold two souls. Once used, the dagger will then be hidden away so we can exist forever, together."

"You're planning on murdering O'vette?"

"No. I plan to break her of the village's old ways so we can finally be together. I hope I don't have to use the dagger for many decades, until we get old and are nearing natural death. But I will use it one way or another, for we are destined to be together."

Chapter 30
Pain of Change

Pruva slowly picked up a piece of thin metal from the blacksmith's barrel of waste. There were all sorts of unused pieces tossed aside from the various projects being worked on.

Despite his huge sloth-like body and his long nails at the ends of his fingers, Pruva showed great precision in obtaining the tiny pieces that he was searching for.

He then proceeded to cut and bend the metal to his liking before adding it to the lantern he was building. The frame was completed and he was finishing up the side panels that would help focus the light from a tight beam to a wide arc.

Finding another metal that he liked, even though it had nothing to do with his project. "May I have this?" he asked a worker.

No one had asked for scrap metal before, so the apprentice shrugged. "Be my guest."

The gathler bowed his head slightly before placing the small metal piece away with the hundreds of other fragments and scrap he had picked up during his many journeys.

He then slowly walked down the street to the glass blowing workshop, where he was entertained for nearly an hour as they made countless shapes and colors. However, to the glazier's surprise, it wasn't any of the finished works that interested the outsider. Instead, he requested access to the scraps and failed attempts. Once granted, Pruva took his time to find the shapes and sizes that he felt could come in handy.

Thanking the worker, Pruva stepped into the road for the next trade. But upon getting back out into the sun, he found himself feeling sick. Another bout of vertigo spun his equilibrium around to the point where he began to lose his balance.

A few locals noticed and approached, asking if he needed help.

With blurred vision, his head swayed about as he tried to understand what they were saying. Everything was confusing, and his senses went mad, delivering incoherent information to his brain. Before he knew it, he slumped over and collapsed onto the dirt street.

***

Within the large main room of Eldor'Craft's town hall, Pruva rubbed his temples with peppermint oil in a vain attempt to control his headache, which had progressed into a migraine-like throbbing and dizziness.

O'vette had been called by the villagers who had moved the gathler from the cold street to in front of the warm fireplace. She shed her thick winter coat and hung it up before approaching, discovering him hunched over while holding onto the lantern he had built.

She struggled with expressing her feelings, so talking business was her natural tendency. "I see you've finished the lantern."

He nodded and handed it to her. "Just light the wick and place the ring into the impression on top. Although you may want Bishhall to buff out the edges so to not cut anyone."

"I'll have him do that. Everyone in Eldor'Craft thanks you for this." She held the lantern as she watched him drop his face into his palms. "You're still not feeling well?"

"Truth be said," he replied, slower than normal.

"These are getting worse as time goes on. What do you think could be causing them?"

"Change."

She crossed her arms and considered the options available to treat him. "I don't understand."

"My memories of my past are changing and overlapping."

"Your memories?"

"Truth be heard." He stretched his neck to relieve some tension. "What I know of my past is no longer the only memory of it. Several lines of history now overlap in my head, confusing me as to which one is real. They contradict each other and fill my mind with vivid events that keep growing and subsiding as though all possibilities are in flux of becoming true. I am struggling to know what is real."

"What could cause this?"

"Critical events are on the edge of changing. Someone is making a decision in the here-and-now that is changing my past."

O'vette gazed back down at what she was holding. "Could it be this lantern that is causing it?"

"No," he responded with little concern. "I know how this village will end, and this lantern plays no part in it."

Chapter 31
New Home

Within a well-lit corridor of the Stone'Ring city, Greyson and his giant bodyguard, Dwall, escorted Tilli to her room. It was on the upper level, same as Greyson's quarters, and was much quieter than on the main floor where she had attempted to escape from him. With only a few rugs and chairs along the way, the echo of their footsteps reminded her just how far she was away from her friends.

Tilli had noticed fresh deep cuts in the side of Dwall's face and head, and she wondered what type of a creature was strong enough to take on the giant.

Greyson patiently waited for her to step forward and lead them both in, while motioning for her to open the wooden door.

The room was clean and filled with quality furnishings, rugs, bed cloths, and oil lanterns. It reminded her of the bedroom she once had in the E'rudite temple. It was a safe place for her to get away and gaze out the window.

Tilli made her way over to the window and pushed apart the curtains to see her new view. "Wow," she said without thinking. It was an impressive sight over the forest with the snowcapped mountains in the distance.

"Make yourself at home." He then tossed some coins on the bed. "Go buy yourself some fresh clothes and food. I'll expect you at my quarters after dinner to continue my lessons."

Tilli glanced at the coins, as she had no idea what such things would cost. "What about my friends?"

"What about them?"

"I don't feel right about living with such comforts while they aren't."

"That's an odd perspective," he replied. "I've sent out an order to have your blothrud friend return here, at which time we'll make accommodations for his needs as well."

"When will that be?"

"As long as it takes for the carrier to travel, find him, and return with him. We are at war here and it's not as easy as you may assume to do such a thing."

Tilli bit her lip as she worried about Goothr's safety. "And Ayva?"

"She'll stay in the infirmary until she's healthy enough to leave. She needs constant care and shouldn't be moved upstairs with you until her treatments are down to a few times a day."

Tilli shook her head slightly, as she was appalled by his lack of emotions. "Don't you care about your own daughter?"

"Daughter?"

"Yes, if Ayva is O'vette's daughter, then you must be her father."

Greyson smirked. "No. I confronted O'vette with the same notion, and she made it perfectly clear that the child was not mine. That was fortunate for O'vette."

"Why?"

"Because if the child was mine, I would have taken her away from that narrow-minded village and raised her here, with the finest instructors in the lands to learn everything from running this city to the art of magic."

"Could O'vette have lied to prevent you from taking Ayva?"

"Perhaps. But I've never known her to look me in the eyes and lie. Besides, the odds were low. I was exiled before we had any children. I don't know who the father is. To me, she is the bastard child of a woman who wanted to get back at me for her father's death."

Tilli was flushed with embarrassment for making the assumption. "I didn't know."

"There is a lot you don't know, little Num. But you had better know enough to teach me to become more powerful with my Runestone."

"It seems that you are already very powerful. You have recovered from being banished from Eldor'Craft and now run this entire city."

"True, but it wasn't easy." He walked over to the window and peered out upon the distant hills and valleys. "Weeks after I left the Eldor'Craft, I found myself at the Govi Glade at night, contemplating the idea of leaping into one of those orbs. I didn't care where it led me, as long as I could start over. But upon entering the area, I stumbled upon something glowing in the thick grass. The energy of the glade was causing the crystal to glow, just enough for me to see it."

Tilli stepped near him and gazed out the window. Her hope of creating trust was essential to her obtaining the stone. Standing next to him was an opportunity to build such confidence.

"I plucked it from the ground only to find it was embedded into a flat stone with gems in the hexagonal corners. I gazed at it, wondering what it could be. Could it be what I needed to change my life? I was exhausted and heartbroken, and not in a strong frame of mind. So, when a bunch of treerats attacked me as I exited the glade, I screamed for them to stop while tightening my grip around the Runestone." He took in a deep breath as he relived the moment. "I remember receiving a rush of energy and then all the treerats stopped, just as I asked. It was incredible. Over time, I learned how to recreate that same feeling so I could use it whenever I needed it, but its strength limits me to species of limited thoughts and those of shallow willpower."

"How did you go from there to having all of this?"

"The building of this empire started by convincing those that were learning spells to come together to improve this art, to make it more powerful and useful, and to eventually make it more accessible to the average person without such training."

"How would you accomplish this?"

"We learned how to embed spells within objects so that anyone could use it."

"That's sounds a bit dangerous to me."

"You're missing the opportunity here. What if everyone had the ability to heal minor injuries, or could lift large loads into wagons without straining their backs. The ability to use magic for everyday purposes has an endless array of opportunities."

She thought about it for a few seconds then turned to look up at him. "Then why doesn't everyone have these items? I've walked these halls, and I don't see the average person using such magic."

"True," he responded in an indifferent tone. "There is a cost to these items and the time it takes to embed spells within them, so there aren't enough for everyone. In addition, the war has forced us to send many of these embedded items out to the battlefields."

"For healing the wounded?"

He paused before answering. "Some. But right now, most of the magical components are for war. It's unfortunate, and hopefully short term. My goal is to end these battles and have these items used to improve the daily lives of our people."

"So, you grew this empire by creating a training area for new Alchemists, while building the local population by promising them the chance to obtain enchanted items?"

"Yes, for the most part."

"What does the Runestone have to do with any of that?"

"Oh, that was the key to keeping us safe. The Runestone has given me the ability to create an army of misfit creatures that have been wandering these lands. They follow me to protect our assets."

"From whom?"

"From the nomads and clans that wanted to stop us or pillage our stores. From those within our walls that break our rules or steal our secrets…" His brow lowered in thought. "…and those that think they can manage this city better than me."

Tilli stood dead silent with this information of potential threats from his own people.

"Yes, this is the price I pay for creating such a successful city. Other leaders now want to take what I have built. They want to rule differently. They want us to stop these battles."

"Is that so bad to wish to stop fighting the people from other communities? Shouldn't they be free to run their lives without living under your ways?"

Greyson looked down at her. "What do you think these battles are about?"

Tilli turned away and considered her words before saying them. "Your goal is to have everyone live under your controls, to enslave them to do your bidding."

Greyson shook his head to disagree. "I don't want to fight the people. I want to fight for them. They should have the right to use magic if they so choose. I've launched these campaigns to free people from their oppressed leadership that are dictating who can have what. I'm not enslaving them, I'm liberating them."

Frustrated, he turned and walked back into the hallway, where Dwall was still standing. But before leaving, he slowly turned back toward the Num. "Take a few moments to settle in and then meet me in the main hall, outside the infirmary. I want to show you something."

And before Tilli could respond, he and his bodyguard turned and headed down the hall, as Dwall's heavy steps pounded against the stone floors and echoed back into Tilli's new bedroom.

Chapter 32
Worvik and the Beast

The driver pulled back the reins of the faralopes until the wagon came to a complete stop in a small foggy clearing. This was as far as he was willing to take the blothruds. Beyond this point would put himself in mortal danger. "Get out!" he yelled to his passengers. "I don't travel into that forest."

Worvik was the first to exit the back of the wagon as his thick wolf-like feet hit the muddy path with a squelch that splatted the dark muck in every direction. It had been snowing and raining for the past few hours and everything was saturated, including him.

Raising the muzzle on his dragon head, he sniffed for signs of the creature he was sent to kill. Within a few moments he had a general idea of the direction they needed to walk, and he stepped to the side and took command. Rest time is over. Get your ass down here. We have a job to do."

Dirk stood up from the wagon bench, leaped off and then fell in line. He was quickly followed by the other blothrud named Chaos.

Goothr sat on the bench, taking a final deep breath before leaving. "Once we finish the job, Goothr can go back to Ayva?"

Worvik tilted his head at the unexpected question. "Son, you can go see Ergrauth himself, for all I care. But you aren't going anywhere until we have eliminated this threat."

Goothr nodded. "Okay. Goothr finish job quickly so I can go back to city." He then hopped off the wagon and stood in line.

"That's the plan, warriors. We get in, terminate this beast, and then head home." Worvik gave each of them a quick review to make sure they were ready. "Dirk! Are you ready to kill some hideous creature that no one else has been able to?"

"Yes, sir!" Dirk stood at attention. He was a good soldier and followed every command without questioning it.

"Chaos! Are you ready to unleash the fires of Della Estovia on this bastard?"

The lips across Chaos' face retracted and shook as he exposed his teeth while growling, waiting to attack at any moment.

It was the first time Goothr had seen any emotion or sound out of the blothrud, which he assumed was mute. He had been sitting absolutely silent, staring into the horizon the entire time on the wagon and showed no signs of knowing what was going on. The blothrud's name, Chaos, made no sense to Goothr.

Worvik grabbed his battle-axe and pack of supplies for the hike to the front line. "We are warriors!"

Dirk and Chaos grunted and slapped their blades high in the air as their response.

Goothr didn't understand the expectations, and by the time he had lifted his club, it was too late.

"If one warrior falls, another steps in!" Worvik yelled.

Dirk and Chaos grunted and slapped again; this time Goothr caught the tail-end of the gesture with his club.

"If a warrior drops his gear, another picks it back up!"

Again, they grunted and slapped weapons, this time with Goothr in sync.

"And if a warrior dies in battle, the others take vengeance on his enemy!"

Goothr nearly moved too soon as he was now getting in rhythm with the other two.

"We are warriors!" Worvik shouted.

"We are warriors!" Worvik and Dirk yelled.

"We are warriors!" they all yelled, except for Chaos, who had yet to ever speak a word.

"We are warriors!" Goothr shouted by himself. The other three had stopped and pulled away before eyeing him for making such an odd shout after the warrior cheer had already ended. Embarrassed, Goothr slowly pulled his club down from his extended arm. It was a reminder that he was not familiar with the ways of these blothruds.

"Time to kill our enemy," Worvik said as he started heading away from the wagon, into the dark forest.

Dirk and Chaos fell in line behind them, with weapons in hand, ready for battle.

"Do we know what this creature looks like?" Goothr asked as he strolled along side of the three.

Worvik shook his head.

"Then how will we know when we see it?"

"Because it will most likely want to bite your face off!" the leader spat back.

Dirk nodded. "If it bites your face off, I'll kill it. We are warriors."

Goothr glanced back to see if it was too late to wait in the wagon.

Worvik gave his troops their orders as he led them down the dirt path, as the trees seemed to close in on them and the fog thickened. "This neck of the forbidden forest is where all of Greyson's army has been lost. We shouldn't have to travel far before we encounter the monster. With any luck at least one of use will survive to report the outcome."

Goothr's eyes grew a bit as he looked at the other two blothruds, who didn't flinch.

There were no covert operations with Worvik. He hid from no one. He faced his enemy head-on, weapon out and ready to fight. Sneak attacks were for cowards.

Goothr hugged his spiked club as his head swung back and forth with every little noise he heard. The intense nature of the situation made even the movement of a squirrel sound imposing and dangerous.

Disappointed that nothing was emerging, the leader felt he needed to take action. "Maybe it's sleeping," he mocked his enemy. "Chaos! Wake that beast up!"

Dirk quickly took a few steps back and stood behind Goothr, which confused the newest member of the party.

Chaos stepped forward and took in a long deep breath before letting out the loudest roar Goothr had ever heard. The tree branches shook and the vibration against the ground could be felt by their feet. It was as though a small explosion had gone off.

Standing stoically a few yards in front, Worvik smiled, knowing the call would draw out his opponent. "It has to know we're here," he chuckled.

Goothr was still mesmerized by the amount of sound that came out of the mute blothrud, and he was confused that no one else saw that as odd.

It was then that a mighty roar returned from the forest before them. Nearly as loud as the one from Chaos, but it was accompanied by the thunderous sounds of footfalls.

The beast was coming.

The four blothrud warriors stood ready with weapons held tight as the head of the beast came crashing through the trees toward them.

"Attack!" Worvik charged forward.

Racing toward it, Dirk followed every order by Worvik, never hesitating or wavering from his exact command. He was loyal to a fault.

The beast exposed its body as it reached the dirt path. It was a massive creature with hundreds of legs and the head of an insect. Its enormous centipede-like body was taller than the blothruds' and its length was that of a dozen wagons.

One of the four giant mandible pincers on the insect's head slapped Dirk away with little effort as it moved forward to grab Worvik.

The leader charged. It simply wasn't within him to run from any threat. Swinging his axe, he cut the end of the large pincer clean off.

Chaos stared at the monstrous insect without any emotion or movement. His normal daze was not affected in the least.

"Watch out!" Goothr yelled to Worvik as another pair of the creature's four mandibles closed in on the warrior leader. But it was too late.

Worvik's axe was pinned between his body and the thick pincer, preventing him from using it. Instead, he resorted to swinging the spikes on the back of his arms into the creature, but the thick pincer wasn't flesh and couldn't be penetrated.

Dirk and Goothr ran in to save their leader as they swiped their weapons over their heads at the mandibles holding the blothrud up in the air.

The insect used its other two pincers to knock them away, while picking Worvik up high in the air, until it was over its mouth, surrounded by hundreds of thorny finger-looking muscles to stab and drag food inside.

"Chaos! Create Chaos!" Worvik ordered.

As though a switch had been flipped, the dazed stare of the warrior snapped into a hellish fury. With more energy and speed than Goothr had ever seen in a blothrud, Chaos went berserk as he began swinging his two blades at anything in his path. Spinning, leaping, twisting. The whirlwind of rage that he had been bottling up was released.

Goothr and Dirk leaped out of the way to prevent themselves from becoming the first victims of the little tornado of death.

Chaos reached the monstrous insect. Legs and chunks of flesh began flying in every direction. Mowing through its legs like a scythe cuts down wheat, the warrior never gave the creature time to move away.

Worvik screamed as he was dropped into the creature's mouth. The large finger-like muscles grabbed at him and pulled him into the acid-rich insides.

"Dirk! Save Worvik!" Goothr commanded while he used his mighty club to start breaking one of the insect's mandibles.

Dirk did as he was told and rushed in to save a fellow warrior without thinking of his own safety. A pincer slapped him hard, knocking him down again, but this time he rolled back up to his feet.

After a third grand smack of his spiked club, the mandible Goothr had been working on finally cracked. Another few hits and it would fully snap off.

Chaos continued his insanity, inflicting damage to any part of the insect he touched until it finally fell from the lack of legs near the front of its body. Then the blothrud began burrowing, like a massive drill, into the side of creature.

Worvik swung his axe again and again as his lower half continued to be dissolved and eaten by the gigantic insect. But no matter how deep the warrior cut into its face or how many finger-like appendages he cut off, he kept sinking deeper into the mouth.

The mandible that was keeping Dirk from helping his commander eventually cracked and fell off from a final swing of Goothr's club.

This allowed Dirk to rush in and grab Worvik's arms to pull him out. In doing so, they could see that the warrior's lower body had been completely dissolved.

The colossal insect collapsed onto the ground. The internal damage from Chaos was too much for it to survive, but the sound of Chaos continuing his attack continued.

Dirk dragged Worvik's body away from the monster along the path until they were free of the large pincers.

"Chaos! Stop!" Worvik yelled to end the blothrud's out-of-control frenzy. He then coughed up blood as he realized his legs were gone and his internal organs were trailing behind them.

"Now what?" Dirk asked, waiting for the next order.

Feeling his life draining from him, Worvik had to put someone in command. He knew it couldn't be Chaos, and as great a warrior as Dirk was, he only took orders and could never give any. "Goothr is now in command."

Goothr didn't know how to react, as he had never led warriors before. But before he could reply, Worvik was no more.

Chaos sliced open the side of the insect and walked through the opening before standing near the other two. Covered with slimy chunks of flesh, he stared out in space as though nothing had happened.

"Chaos, Worvik is gone," Goothr said, but received no reaction.

Dirk confirmed it with a nod. "Goothr is now our leader."

Again, no expression could be seen, and all three stood there, wondering what to do next.

The cool wind blowing down the path caught Goothr's attention as dark clouds were starting to approach. "A storm is coming. We need to be on our way back to the city. Ayva must be worried about me."

Chapter 33
Risen

Tilli held onto Ayva's hand as the girl slept in her cot. She didn't appear any better, but she also didn't appear any worse. Her recent fever had broken, but her pillow and hair were still wet from the damp cloths used by the nurses to help her through the ordeal.

Several low footfall thuds caught Tilli's attention and she noticed Dwall standing at the doorway, waiting for her. There was nothing she could do for Ayva while she slept, so it was time to see what Greyson had to show her.

Following Dwall through the main hall and into the arena, the leathery skinned giant led her to Greyson's large blue dragon with a thick saddle strapped to it. It was the creature that she had seen Greyson ride into the village.

"Are you ready for a quick trip to see what we're trying to accomplish here?"

Tilli snapped her head around to see Greyson standing behind her. He had a way of sneaking up on her. "To where?"

"To the cities and villages you think I'm destroying," he noted as he climbed up the side of the dragon. He then reached down to help her up. "Are you open to learning the truth?"

Tilli hadn't had a history of good relationships with dragons, and climbing upon one was never something she had aspired to do, but she knew this was needed to earn Greyson's trust. She reached up, they grabbed each other's forearms, and she mounted the winged beast in front of him.

Holding the Charm Runestone, he commanded the creature to lift off and take them to one of the villages.

Extending its wings, it gave a mighty flap while pushing off with its muscular legs, and they were airborne. A series of subsequent flaps allowed them to rise from the arena area, as sand blew in every direction, until they were high enough to see over the coliseum's outer walls.

Tilli clung onto the saddle as tight as she could with both hands, as anxieties grew about falling to her death. The experience was now less about fearing the dragon and more about holding onto the dragon to stay alive.

"Hang on," Greyson ordered.

Once the dragon was over the tall coliseum wall, it dove down the other side to gain speed and their freefall grew faster.

Tilli was hanging on for dear life, and every muscle in her body tensed up as the ground quickly approached. And then, just before hitting the earth, the dragon arched and lifted back up, scraping treetops as it rose up over the forest before leveling out.

Greyson could feel the rigid body of the Num up against him. "You need to loosen up or you're going to be in pain by the time we're done."

"I'm fine," she said in a clear lie.

Grabbing onto one of her shoulders, he pressed it back down away from her neck. "You have to relax your muscles when riding. Allow your body to be flexible and sway with the dragon instead of fighting against its movements."

She lowered her shoulders as instructed, but her back was still too tight, and her legs continued to press firmly on both sides of the beast to prevent her from sliding off. It was only then that she started noticing her surroundings.

Soaring a dozen yards above the trees, they could see distant mountains and bodies of water. Soft clumpy clouds clung to a few mountain peaks, and smoke rose from settlements within the forests. It was as though one of her maps had come to life and filled in a beautiful palette of colors. It was an amazing experience that she truly loved as well as wanted to end.

It wasn't long before they approached one of the settlements and landed in an open field nearby.

Tilli collapsed on the back of the dragon. Her muscles were killing her after being tense for so long.

Greyson dismounted and reached up for the Num, only to find her hand still shaking from the experience. "We don't have all day."

As Tilli allowed one hand to let go, she reached out to him, only to miss and end up falling off the beast into the short grass. She quickly shook off her moment of embarrassment and popped back up onto her feet like nothing had happened. "Where to?"

Greyson walked toward the structures, most of which were made of stone and sturdy woods. Lush green vines covered many of the walls and produced random orange and yellow leaves. Large vases were scattered about with tall grasses or colorful flowers. "Welcome to the community of Risen."

The people were pleasant as they went about their daily chores. In a lot of ways, it felt more like Eldor'Craft than Stone'Ring. However, there was one main difference; most of these citizens were using magic.

An elderly man slowly moved a folding hand fan back and forth, allowing the item's magic to sweep up the recent snowfall from the street. With slight movements of his wrist, he was performing a task that he normally would not have been able to do with a broom or shovel due to his hunched back.

Two girls ran past while each chanting a tune and slapping two-foot-long sticks together. In doing so, they were herding a few dozen fire logs down the street to deliver firewood. Arriving at their first stop, they changed the speed of the slapping of sticks and tune, causing a half dozen pieces to pile themselves up outside a home. There was no need to carry the heavy logs, because of their enchanted tools.

Several adults noticed Greyson and bowed to him as he walked past. He nodded back but gave no more interaction. His focus was on showing Tilli the value of adding magic to cultures.

Nearing the water well in the center of the community, Tilli noticed there was no bucket and rope, such as the one in Eldor'Craft. Giving Greyson a curious look, she walked over to look over the half-wall, and into the well to see what she was missing. However, nothing seemed out of place except for the missing tools needed to gather water.

Greyson grinned at her challenge to figure out the riddle before her. Playfully, he chose not to help her figure it out.

As she inspected the well, she noticed some writing on the far side of the wall. Curious, she walked over to read it, only to find a small bell built into the half-wall, so she rang the bell. To her surprise, nothing happened. So instead, she read the words engraved on the flat surface of the wall. Again, nothing happened. But once she rang the bell while saying the words, the embedded magic kicked in and a fountain of water rose from deep within the well, up high enough to collect the water.

Not having a container to catch any, she used her hands to collect enough to drink. "Mmm, that's very good. Thank you." And once her final two words were heard, the fountain stopped.

"Now anyone can collect water without needing the strength to pull up a heavy bucket full of water from this deep well."

Tilli was flustered at how well magic had been integrated into everyday life. "You actually embedded magic into a water well."

"Yes," he replied with a chuckle. "This is the future of our people. They can live with less stress and more comfort. It baffles me why O'vette and so many others oppose this."

Tilli turned and leaned back against the small wall of the well as she watched the locals function with ease. No chore was too heavy or too hard for anyone to perform. Strength and skill level no longer mattered. Goods and supplies were made using an assortment of enchanted items along with a physical and verbal command.

"Can you embed magic spells into anything?"

He thought about it for a moment before answering. "Almost. I'm even experimenting with embedding some of my Charm Stone powers into crystals for my close servants, but the effects don't even last for a day before I must add new orders."

The comment struck a nerve with Tilli. "Is that what is mounted on the back of Dwall's head?"

"Very observant. Yes, he has been my test subject. He has free will on most of his activities, but he cannot harm me, nor can he disobey my orders... at least until the crystal loses the charm," he laughed at the idea.

"So, he's your slave."

"Tilli, Dwall was a lost soul that I saved many years ago. He has a life debt to me and was a willing participant when I started these tests. He is not a victim." Glancing to her and then back out at the town. "Let's not get distracted from the bigger picture here. This, before you, is the future of our world. Living with enchanted items will change life for the better for everyone."

She nodded as she gazed in awe at what Greyson had created, regardless of his actions with Dwall.

Just then, one of the girls that had been herding firewood approached them. "Sir, can you make this work again?" she asked while holding her two sticks out for him to take.

He glanced down and graciously took the items from her. "Ah, it appears the enchantment has worn out on your sticks, little one. Go ahead and get a few more that are in stock so all the homes will have plenty of heat tonight."

She nodded and ran off to get more.

"Worn out?" Tilli asked.

Greyson didn't think much of it. "Yes, we continue to improve the process, but spells embedded in items only work so many times before the magic must be implanted again." Seeing her concern, he continued. "It still allows them to have this lifestyle. A snap of their fingers with the right item and they have fire for their home to keep them warm and heat their food. A click of their tongue while releasing an enchanted arrow ensures they hit their target and meat is brought home for a feast without having to be a good shot."

"I can't imagine how easy things could be."

"I know, which is why I wanted to show you the power of my vision for these lands."

Chapter 34
Training

"Close your eyes," Tilli instructed. "Slowly follow the ridges on the Runestone and visualize them rising and holding within a calm body of water. One after another the water lifts to mimic the stone's pattern."

Greyson continued to do as he was told while standing at the edge of Risen, facing his large dragon. A slight glow began to form within the central crystal as he traced the surface of the flat stone.

"Good. Now, once all of the water ridges are in place, start having them move from the center crystal and each of the gems, just like they would if those were dropped into the water. Keep it slow at first."

His concentration was locked in as the raised ripples in the water of his thoughts began to move. And they did so, he could feel the consciousness of his dragon. Each small wave brushed against the creature's thoughts and then bounced back. He was starting to get inside the beast's head and hear its thoughts and feel its emotions.

Excited about the feeling, he rushed to give it a command. "Flap!"

The dragon impulsively started flapping, so much so that it was out of control. Bouncing up a few yards and then landing on its side, it continued to flap uncontrollably as it rolled its way toward them.

"Greyson! Stop!"

Opening his eyes, he could see that his dragon was about to crush both of them as it flopped about. Instinctively, he grabbed the Runestone like he normally would and gave the command, "STOP!"

Flopping one last time near them, the dragon landed on its back, confused and dazed.

"What happened?" Greyson stared at the Runestone as though the object was dysfunctional.

"You can't jump to the final lesson before you understand the basics!" Tilli yelled. Her heart was still racing after thinking they were going to be crushed by his beast.

He continued to glare at the stone. "I could feel it. It was different. It should have worked."

"No, it shouldn't have! This is the same logic you used when you tried to embed life into objects in Eldor'Craft, which cost you everything. Have you learned nothing?" She was visibly emotional. "This time you could have cost us our lives!"

"Don't shout at me!" he ordered. "I'm doing the best I can!"

Tilli took a moment to calm herself down. "That's not the issue. You must learn some patience. You can't get to where you want to be without taking the time to learn what's needed."

Greyson grumbled for a moment before using his old method on the Runestone to calm the dragon and get it back on its feet. "I made a mistake," he said to the Num. "Don't read so much into it."

Chapter 35
Homeward Bound

A fresh foot of slushy snow coated the landscape, making the paths unusable by the wagons. It was just warm enough to prevent the muddy tracks from freezing over, and every step forward was a new opportunity to slip and fall.

Goothr and his two warriors passed yet another wagon stuck in the muddy slush. The driver had given up trying to dig out the wheels and had settled in, crouching down beside the vehicle, out of the wind, and covered with a thick blanket.

Despite this wagon and the ones before it being stalled, Goothr saw the movement of one heading his way with great haste. As it neared, it became apparent that it wasn't a wagon at all. Instead, it was a large sleigh pulled by four faralopes.

Oddly enough, no matter how much the blothruds tried to step out of its path, the sleigh seemed to turn toward them, until it finally arrived and slowed to a stop, blocking the warriors' path.

"Halt!" The driver held out his hand as though he could actually stop the blothruds. He wore a uniform with symbols on it that meant nothing to Goothr. "Enjoying your trek back to the city?"

Goothr shook his head. He'd take the heat over the cold, as would most blothruds. "Goothr not like it here." He glanced over at Dirk who shook his head as well.

"That's unfortunate," he replied with no empathy in his voice. "I have new orders for your leader."

Chaos stared into space as though he didn't notice the man, his companions, or even the faralopes.

Dirk pointed at Goothr. "Leader."

The driver looked Goothr up and down in disgust. "You are hereby informed to stay at the front line and continue to fight with the rest of the army until told differently."

The order immediately concerned Goothr. "On whose orders?"

"Our leader, Lord Greyson himself."

"But why? They told Goothr we could return once we finished our mission."

"It is because of the one called Goothr that you can't return. As leader of your group, your new mission is to keep Goothr from returning to the city."

His brow pulled tight in the middle as he stared down at the man. "I'm Goothr!"

A bit surprised, the driver took a moment to collect himself. The blothrud had referred to Goothr twice during their conversation, implying it was one of the other two. "I was told Worvik was the leader."

"He was. But he's dead. Now I'm leader and I don't like your orders."

The other two men in the sleigh stood up. One was in the military and placed a strong hand on the hilt of his sword. The other was dressed in more comfortable clothes and had dozens of pouches and magical components hanging from his belt and from his shoulders.

"Goothr has to get back to check on Ayva. She is sick."

"I don't think you understand. We aren't asking you; we're giving you a direct order."

A slight growl escaped from his dragon-like head while glaring at the man. "And if Goothr refuses?"

An eyebrow raised above one of the driver's eyes. "You don't want to go down this path. Treason in punishable by death."

"I promised Ayva I'd return. I have to keep my promise." He glanced at the three in the wagon and then his two warriors. "We are heading back to the city."

The swordsman unsheathed his long sword, and the other man grabbed a few magical components as they prepared for a battle, while the driver stood steady. "Even if you could get past us, you'll never get past the main gate. They already have been instructed to kill you upon sight, no questions asked. So you see, I'm doing you a favor by allowing you to head back with your life versus move forward with a death sentence."

Goothr shook his head at the unfortunate situation. "I didn't want to have to do this."

The spellcaster released his magic, sending a massive wave of acid spraying at the lead blothrud, covering him is the sizzling green liquid.

The snow evaporated around Goothr, and a flume of dense moisture so thick they couldn't see the blothrud for several seconds. But when they finally did, they were stunned. The magical acid had no effect on the warrior.

Goothr growled as he held the ring hanging from his neck, which gave off a slight glow. Tilli's gift had come in handy. "Chaos! Wake that beast!"

Snapping out of his trance at the distant trees, Chaos let out a powerful roar that shook the wagon and the team of faralopes that pulled it.

All four of the animals bucked and panicked, jarring the wagon forward before breaking free from it and racing off into the distance.

The unexpected event knocked all three men off their feet. The driver and the soldier fell over, while the spellcaster tumbled out of the back and into the thick snow.

"Dirk! Sleigh!" Goothr ordered.

Wasting no time, Dirk slammed against the sleigh, knocking it all the way over, and trapping the driver and soldier underneath it.

Slapping the magical components out of the spellcaster's hands, Goothr quickly stripped him of all his potions, powders, and enchanted items. By the time he was done, the bony little man had been stripped down to his undergarments and shivered with fear for his life.

"Goothr just wants everyone happy. You leave us alone and we'll all be happy."

Dirk stepped up behind him. "You dropped something," he said as he handed him his spiked club. "Warriors pick up and give back what other warriors drop."

Goothr nodded before pointing the thick wooded club down at the freezing spellcaster. "You come after us, and Goothr will have to release Chaos on you. That won't be good."

With the sharp metal spikes inches from his nose, the man nodded in agreement.

"Good." He then glanced over at the men reaching out from under the sleigh in their attempt to escape. "Leave them there. Time to keep heading to the city."

Chapter 36
Moordok

The arena area was full of noise and crowds as shoppers from local villages arrived to purchase goods and services from the hundreds of vendors available. Wagons of merchandise rested behind many of the shops as families worked together to run the stores, move the inventory, and make runs to the food vendors.

Tilli had started getting used to the hustle and bustle. It was completely different from Eldor'Craft, but it wasn't all that different from the streets she grew up on, outside of the E'rudite temple.

After learning to wave off merchants trying to sell her things she didn't need, she started getting a bit more curious as to what was being sold in each shop.

There was an array of oddities that the Num had never seen before. Nothing was crafted as finely as what she had seen in the village, but they didn't need to be. They functioned just fine without that level of sophistication, and no one seemed to require more.

The most interesting products that caught her eye were the items that weren't necessities. These had been few and far between in her past, but here there were plenty of items for art, music, sports, and other interests.

Tilli made her way to a vendor who supplied paper, canvases, charcoal, ink, paint, brushes, and other art supplies. She had never seen such an assortment of options all in one place. Her imagination went wild with what she could do with all of it. To have the security of living so that she could have the luxury of time to create art was something she never imagined. It was tantalizing and intriguing. But it was not to be.

She knew she couldn't stay, even if she wanted to. Ayva and Goothr were her top priority. They needed to get back to the village. But after that... Her mind wondered at the idea of coming back and living in the city. The idea of not having to worry about whether they would catch food to eat, or be robbed in the woods, was very appealing. Sleeping on a comfortable bed with nice silky sheets in a private room was something she had dearly missed ever since she left the E'rudite temple. And then to have the free time to paint or write; it would be a dream come true.

"You going to pay for that?" the merchant asked.

"What?" Tilli realized she had picked up some paper, ink, and a quill for writing. "Oh, I'm sorry."

"Put them back!"

"Okay," she replied, but the hesitation in her actions made it clear that she didn't want to leave without them.

"How much are these?" Moordok said as he approached the shop with a handful of coins.

Tilli twisted around. "I can't let you buy these for me."

"Nonsense." He grabbed a leather pouch from the merchant's table and placed all the writing supplies within it, along with some paints and brushes. "It will ease your mind about what your friends are going through." Moordok paid the merchant. "Besides, it would lift up Ayva's spirits to see what you come up with for her."

With a slight bow of her head, she thanked him for his generosity. "I truly appreciate this," she added once they began slowly walking down the aisle between the rows of vendors.

"Well, we Alchemists aren't all driven by the need for power."

She chuckled, before adding, "You mean you're not all like Greyson?"

He gave her a scornful eye. "Greyson is no Alchemist."

"What do you mean? I thought he was the head one."

Scoffing at the thought, he felt he needed to set the story straight. "It is true that he coordinated the idea of pulling all of the Alchemists together into one location so we could learn from each other and improve our techniques and abilities. In doing so, he profited from what we made, as well as the commerce that grew around this new city which he had established, based on the idea of embracing competition and new methods of business. Let's call the man what he is. He is a visionary and a business leader, and we must give him credit for creating a successful and progressive society that has enriched many lives."

"Am I hearing you correctly? Are you saying he never learned to cast spells?"

"Oh, perhaps a few minor ones at first. But Greyson doesn't have the patience to learn the art and study the mechanics of what it takes to create spells. Instead, he uses enchanted items and that mind control stone."

Tilli smiled. "The Charm Runestone?"

"Yes. It's been the seed to his power."

Tilli found that odd. "He's not skilled enough to use it on most people."

"No. But he uses it on those mutants, which are leftover beasts from the ancient Alchemist and E'rudite War. If they weren't at his beckon call, most of us Alchemists would have taken over long ago."

Tilli felt it was worth seeing how deep the friction was between Greyson and the Alchemists. "Are you saying that if he ever lost his ability to control them, that you and the others would stand up to Greyson?"

"It's been tried, but each time one of my brothers or sisters in the art betrayed us before we could contain him and prevent him from using the mutants." Moordok's stern facial expression softened as he thought about his future. "It doesn't really matter. There is a new city for Alchemists in the south being established called 'EverSpring' where most of us are planning on heading this spring. It will be nice to get away from these senseless wars."

"Sounds wonderful," Tilli replied. "Speaking of war. Have you heard any news on Goothr?"

"I hear a lot of news from the battles, and I don't know how much of it is true."

"I'll take what I can get."

Moordok nodded. "There are two stories being circulated. The first is that Goothr has lost his mind, gone rogue, and refuses to be escorted back to the city. Instead, he is heading back on his own while killing all in his wake, including everyone in small villages along the way."

Tilli stood in shock. "That can't be right. What's the other story?"

"A less publicized version is that he has become a war hero to the troops and he is bringing them back to Stone'Ring to take over the city."

"Hmm. Neither sound like something my friend would do. But they both imply he's heading back to the city. Any idea how close he is?"

"Unless something changes, it wouldn't surprise me if he arrived tonight."

"Tonight? That's wonderful news."

Moordok shook his head. "If either of the stories are remotely true, Greyson will surely have an army blocking his path to get here."

"No. I was assured by Greyson that he would bring Goothr back here. In return, I would continue to help him learn more about the Charm Stone."

Stopping in his tracks, he glared down at her. "Why on this earth would you want to give him more power with that stone?"

Tilli held up a calming hand. "I understand your concern. But if all goes well, once Goothr arrives, I will be leaving with him and Ayva, as well as his Charm Stone."

Stroking his beard, he pondered the thought. "Greyson without his mind controls over his mutant army. Now that would be a change I'd like to see."

Chapter 37
Blockade

Goothr and Dirk left of the highlands and no longer were walking through the thick, slushy snow. Instead, they had returned to the windy forest path that was wet from the recent rain and melting snowfall.

It felt good to be on a path that he remembered, even though it was from when he was being taken away from his friends and sent to war. They were on the home stretch, and he couldn't wait to see Ayva.

Although Goothr was starting to relax while thinking of the end of their trek, Dirk stayed on high alert, as usual. Chaos, on the other hand, was not there with them. Goothr had sent him off on a special mission.

In spite of them nearing the end, they encountered a problem as they made a wide turn. Blocking their way, stood the driver of the sleigh they had topped over in the snow. This time he had brought several dozen fighters with him.

The blothruds didn't slow their pace as they continued down the way, as though there was nothing wrong or concerning. Although Dirk gave off a low growl at the mob blocking the path. He was ready for an order from his leader to attack.

Greyson's men had three faralope-pulled wagons, each with a few archers, along with nearly thirty sword and shield-carrying soldiers straddling the passage.

The driver, now leader of a small army, stepped forward, far too confident for his own good. "Surprised to see me again?" he yelled down the path.

Goothr shook his head while approaching. "No. Goothr smelled you from a long way back. Goothr learned from Santorray and Worvik to stay downstream of opponents. Your odor gives you away."

He tried to ignore the insult. "We don't need to hide. Your attempt to return to the city ends here. This is no longer a request. It's your last chance to stay alive. If you even utter the word 'no' we will attack and kill you all... wait, wasn't there a third blothrud?"

"No" Goothr said as he continued to casually walk toward him.

Confused, the man asked for clarification. "Was that a 'no' as in there wasn't a third blothrud, or 'no' you won't stop?"

"Yes," Goothr said with a nod. "Goothr not want to hurt you, but nothing will stop me from reaching Ayva."

The leader wasn't willing to take any chances. "Archers! Prepare to fire!"

"Goothr sorry that I have to do this."

"Aim!" the leader ordered.

"Chaos! Create Chaos!"

A roar bellowed from behind the blockade, startling all of the military personnel. But before they could react, it was already too late.

Chaos snapped, going from a docile spaced-out blothrud to an uncontrolled berserk. Rushing, spinning around, jumping on and off wagons, he was out of control as he began slaughtering the army.

By the time the leader turned back to Goothr, the spiked club of the warrior was slapping against the man's head, snapping his neck while crushing his skull.

Goothr and Dirk attacked, and the warriors split up to cover more ground.

Archers' arrows flew through the crowd, missing often as their targets were in fast moving hand-to-hand combat. Those arrow heads that hit often impaled their own fighters, helping the blothruds.

Chaos was ferocious in his attacks and released his uncontrolled brutality on anything in his way, as though a tornado filled with blades was wreaking havoc along the path. Nothing was safe as wooden splinters exploded in all directions when Chaos approached a wagon. Bodies flew from the area after being struck by the madness.

Goothr fought his way to a wagon and swung his mighty club, shattering the legs of all three archers who stood upon it. He then used the spikes on the back of his arm to slap against the chest of an oncoming attacker, piercing his leather armor and puncturing his heart.

Dirk grabbed the side of another wagon and flipped it over on its side. The occupants were tossed onto the ground, near Chaos, who quickly shredded their bodies into unrecognizable chunks of flesh.

It was a bloodbath, and by the time the three stopped, not a single one of Greyson's men was still alive.

"Chaos! Stop!"

Immediately upon hearing Goothr's words, Chaos stopped his insanely out-of-control swinging and twisting and then returned to his blank staring. Aside from the blood splatter covering his body and a few arrows sticking out of him, he seemed oddly normal.

Goothr shook his head. "Goothr not like killing. I promised Tilli I would be happy, but this did not make me happy."

Dirk stepped near his warrior leader and waited for the next order. There was no sense of regret or dismay in him. In fact, he seemed to enjoy the fighting.

Lifting his nose up, Goothr inhaled slowly. "There is water nearby. I don't want Ayva to see us like this. We need to rinse off before we go into the city."

Chapter 38
Reunited

After visiting Ayva in the infirmary again, Tilli returned to her room and opened her window so she could hear the light rain slapping against the stone walls. Flopping on the fluffy mattress, the soft linens felt silky on her bare skin and the smell of lavender filled the air each time she brushed her arms across them. Most importantly, it was quiet, which allowed her to relax and think about the day.

Once again, it reminded her of when she lived in the E'rudite temple. The smells and views were different, but it gave her the same sense of comfort and security she loved after living on the streets in poverty.

She took a deep breath and let it out slowly.

Tilli had a lot to think about. She was doing what she needed to ensure Ayva was being healed and Goothr was returning from the front line. Sending them back to the village was her top priority. But then there was still the stealing of the Charm Runestone, and then getting her own Runestones back as well.

She took in and released a second cleansing breath.

Closing her eyes, she stretched out and took in the lavender scent from the sheets one more time to help her relax.

"Comfortable?" Pheosco asked.

Tilli sat up in a state of panic. "Where have you been?"

"I'm fine, thank you so very much for asking," the green dragon replied, while perched on the windowsill.

"Did you find him? Did you get it back?"

"Your concern for me is overwhelming." Pheosco flew into the room and landed on her bed."

"Be careful with your claws. These are fine linens."

Pheosco clenched one of his claws, ripping into the sheet.

"What are you doing?"

"ME? What are you doing?" he barked back at her. "I risked my life fighting Mel'tayn for your Runestones, which ended with me breaking his leg just before I got knocked out. By the time I woke up, he was gone. I returned to the village and O'vette told me you stowed away with Goothr and Ayva in the shipment to Greyson!"

"That's not exactly how it happened," she started feeling on the defensive.

"Then what did happen? Where are they right now?"

"Right now?"

"YES! At this very moment."

"Well, Ayva is in the infirmary."

"You left her alone?"

"No!" Tilli raised her arms up to calm the dragon down. "They are treating her. They are going to cure her."

"There is no cure for her! Why can't you accept that?"

"That's not true! I know some of the E'rudites have cured this disease."

"The disease wasn't this far along."

Tilli didn't want to hear that. "How far along was I?"

"You don't know what you're talking about."

"Look me in the eye and tell me that you didn't help cure me of this same disease."

Pheosco squinted as he glared at her. "I did."

"Then do the same thing you did for me."

Pheosco straightened up. "I will not."

"Why?"

Growling, he finally told her the truth. "It required taking the life of my best friend, Chug."

"What?"

"Your grandmother asked us to do whatever it took to keep you alive." He turned away in the first show of emotions that Tilli had ever seen. "It broke my heart when Chug made the decision, and it was up to me to carry it out. I would have followed him to the ends of the world, but instead he asked me to take his life for yours. I never told your grandparents how I was able to save you. They only knew that Chug was lost in our search to do so."

Tilli was shocked. "I don't understand. How? Why did it cost his life?"

"I'm not going to relive this!" he spit back as tears flowed from his eyes.

"I'm sorry."

"Sorry? You should be thankful we all loved you more than our own lives. And you should make sure you're making the most of your life that Chug gave you."

"I'm trying to," she said as she wiped her own tears away. "These Alchemists will be able to help. Are you saying they would have to kill someone to do so?"

"No, it's too late. Ayva is in the final stages of this. There is no cure for her, even if O'vette agreed, it's too late."

"How do you know that?"

"You have to trust me. You have to stop trying to change events and just let her die in peace."

"No! He said they were healing her, and she would overcome this."

"He? He, who?" Pheosco leaned forward as she leaned back.

"Greyson."

"Greyson?!"

"And his Alchemists. They are treating her. We almost lost her but she is doing better."

"You made a deal with Greyson in order to save her?"

"I had to do something. She was going to die!"

"You could have not taken her from her mother!"

"I didn't know she was in the crate."

"What? The crate was less than half the size of this room. How can a blothrud and a child be in this room without you knowing it?"

Biting her lip, she needed to get a hold of the conversation. "I didn't do anything wrong. It was only supposed to be Goothr and I in the crate. By the time I found out she was there, we were already in the air."

Pheosco shook his feathers, shedding a layer of water that he had collected during his recent flight. "Is your blothrud friend in the infirmary with Ayva?"

"No. He went into battle," Tilli said, while brushing the water off the nice sheets.

"Why would he do that?"

"He didn't have a choice," she spit back. "A lot has happened here. You don't understand how hard it's been."

Pheosco looked around the room and then stroked the fine linen with one claw. "Yes, this is torture. How can you stand this horrific dungeon? Do they cater meals to you, or do they force you to walk downstairs to eat?"

"You know, you weren't successful on your mission either! You had one job, and that was to get my satchel of Runestones. I could drill you with questions as well."

They both grumbled under their breaths for a few moments before the green dragon finally spoke up.

"You have to understand that Greyson won't honor his agreement with you. He's using you."

Tilli knew he could be right. "I had to try something. Once I can earn his trust, I'll grab the Charm Runestone and head home with Goothr and Ayva. It's the only way I can fix everything."

"You can't fix everything, nor should you be trying to do so. You have to focus on what was introduced to this time and remove it before history is changed. Changing anything else because of your emotional attachments will most likely cause a rift through time. Haven't you been listening?"

"You're suggesting I just let Ayva die!"

"Yes! That is exactly what is supposed to happen in this line of history."

"Why are you so opposed to me helping others? Gluic sent me here to help Pruva fix history, but all you're doing is trying to have me leave history alone."

"Gluic? That bird is crazy!" he squawked. "Even if she's right about you helping Pruva, your grandparents sent me here to prevent you from changing anything more than what contaminated this time, such as the Runestones."

Pheosco shook his head as he paced on the bed. "You may think helping someone here feels right, but their actions or even great grandchildren's actions could cause have ramifications that would lead to the Mountain King never saving our world."

"How could you possibly know this?"

The green dragon turned and glared into her eyes. "Because at some point in your future, you will meet your grandparents and you will tell them to send me here to stop you from making changes at this point in history. To be blunt, you are the one who asked for me to stop you."

Confused, she shook off the entire conversation. "I don't have to listen to you. In fact, I don't have time for any of this. I need to meet Greyson so I can ensure he continues to trust me until my friends are safe." Leaving the dragon on her bed, she headed for the door. "If you loved my grandparents as much as you say, then you'll do what you can to help me complete my mission."

And with that, she left the room and slammed the door behind her.

Chapter 39
Confrontation

Tilli sat on the bench in the hallway, just outside of Greyson's quarters. Her mind raced between priorities as there were so many items at play that all hinged on her actions.

As she sat there, she could overhear the arguments on the far side of the doors. Greyson was upset about several events that weren't going as planned. Updates from his team became heated and loud enough to escape his private chambers.

Leaning forward, Tilli rested her elbows on her knees and her head on her palms. It allowed her to inch closer to the door without it being obvious to the guards on either side of the entrance.

She overheard that something about funding the war was causing issues and supplies were sparse. Her ears perked up when the topic of the community of Risen was addressed, and Greyson made it clear that if they didn't produce more for him then he would charge more for the enchanted items that they had become reliant upon.

The Num leaned a bit further, to the point of exposing her actions if the guards were interested in looking at her.

After a few more topics, she overheard a conversation about keeping the girl with oma'haige. She nearly fell off the bench as she leaned forward even more. Moordok explained to Greyson that their attempts to keep her alive would not last much longer.

Tilli slipped off the bench and fell to the floor after hearing the news. In doing so, one of the guards approached her and ordered her to sit back on the bench until he allowed her to leave. By the time he had finished lecturing her about sitting appropriately, the conversation in the other room had moved on.

Additional topics were discussed and the occasional word or two leaked out into the hallway so Tilli could hear, but not enough to piece together anything valuable.

After the meeting was adjourned, both doors to Greyson's room were opened and eight of his leaders slowly walked out while still arguing about various topics. Moordok was one of the many leaving, and he gave Tilli a nod of his head while passing. Once the room was empty of guests, Tilli was allowed to enter.

Standing up from the bench, she marched in with an agenda of her own. She was boiling mad from what she had overheard, and she would call him on it. The table used for the earlier discussion still had papers and books scattered about, but her focus was on Greyson, who had his back to her as he gazed out his window.

"You have no idea the responsibility I have upon my shoulders," Greyson told her without looking back at her.

"It must be difficult keeping all those lies straight," she fired back to get his attention.

He slowly turned to face her. "Excuse me?"

"You lied to me!"

"We all lie from time to time. What specific topic are you accusing me of lying about?"

"The community of Risen as well as my friend, Ayva!"

"First of all, I don't answer to you, so calm your voice down before I have you removed."

Taking an emotional step back, she nodded as she glared at him. "Risen isn't the paradise you painted it to be. It's a slave labor camp. You were able to get them addicted to your enchanted items and now force them to pay you to continue to get more. It won't be long before a generation goes by without learning how to live without your items and they won't have any option but to pay you."

"There is a price to be paid for the luxury I have given them," he replied with a shrug of his shoulders.

His arrogance reminded her of how she originally felt about him when they had met in Eldor'Craft.

"What about Ayva? You promised to heal her, only to lead me on to train you how to use the Runestone better. You never had any intention of keeping your side of the bargain, because you knew all along that your Alchemist couldn't cure her. You planned to keep lying to me as long as they could use their magic to keep her alive."

"Is that what has you all fired up? I lied to you? Isn't that the basis of our relationship?"

Tilli was taken back by the comment, but continued to scowl at him. "It clearly has been on your end."

"Really? You truly came to my city to save your friend?"

Stiffening slightly, Tilli kept her composure. "Yes."

"Interesting," he said with a grin. "And you still stand by your answer that there is only one Runestone design, and it is for the use of controlling other's thoughts?"

"What other uses would Runestones have?"

Greyson walked over and opened a drawer of a large cabinet. "Therefore, you'd be surprised to find out that there are many different Runestones, all with their own unique powers?"

A tingle of nerves raced up her spine. She didn't know what he had discovered that could lead him to believe differently.

Reaching into the drawer, Greyson pulled out a leather satchel. Not just any leather bag, but it was in fact Tilli's own that had been stolen from her. He tossed it onto the table, and the Runestones clanked against one another as a few of them spilled out.

Neither of them said a word. Greyson's eyes glared at Tilli, while her focus was on her family's Runestones. The sight of her satchel made her heart hurt. She was so very pleased to see it, and yet she dreaded the fact that Greyson now had knowledge of and access to all her Runestones.

"Where did you get those?" she asked with an innocent tone.

He knew he was driving the conversation and was simply playing with her. "A friend of yours gave them to me."

"A friend of mine?"

"Yes. He gave me a completely different story as to why you are here."

She wanted to continue to avoid answering questions. She didn't want to give away anything that he was simply guessing at. Replying with additional questions was her best strategy. "Who? What is the name of the one who claims to be my friend?"

Greyson stepped back and gave a slight wave of his arm to invite someone in from the next room.

In doing so, Tilli froze with fear as she watched them appear from the side room. It was her greatest concern. She hadn't expected to see a small black dragon enter the room. Mel'tayn had survived Pheosco's attack and teamed up with Greyson. "You low-life little…" She trailed off and never finished her sentence.

"Greetings, friend," the dragon said.

Tilli held herself back from pouncing on him and ripping his wings from his body. "You're no friend of mine!"

"Ah!" Greyson stepped in to moderate the conversation. "I always enjoy seeing the reuniting of old acquaintances. In doing so, I can often get what I need out of one of them."

"You'll get nothing out of that viper's mouth except lies and tricks," Tilli said out of spite for the creature. "He only cares about getting what he wants. He'll do whatever he has to when it comes to serving his master, Irluk."

Greyson stepped back to the table and dumped a few more of the flat Runestones on it. "Actually, I find his honesty about what his desires are to be very refreshing. No games. We simply got down to business and made a trade that benefits us both. My Alchemists healed his broken leg, and I provided him with a position at my side. In exchange, he supplies me with the rest of the E'rudite Runestones to increase my power and he tells me the truth about your mission."

Tilli's glare at the dragon never wavered. She hated him with a passion, and his arrival had completely unraveled her plans. "What did he promise you?"

"It was more of a trade than a promise. He provided me with this satchel of Runestones along with the facts about your true mission to steal my Charm Stone."

"He's not good for it. He wants all of the Runestones for himself. Don't trust him."

"Oh, dear Num, I don't trust anyone." Greyson stood confidently as he leaned against a chair. "Mel'tayn has lived up to his word so far, and I respect that. Therefore, I have lived up to my end of the bargain."

Pulling her gaze away from the black dragon, she looked Greyson in the eyes. "What's your next move, send me to your prison? Behead me? What shall it be?"

His facial expression gave away his amusement of her comments. "No. I expect you to continue to train me, but now we will focus on the other Runestones as well."

"Absolutely not! Why would I do that?"

"Because if you don't, I can make life very unpleasant for you and your friends.

"You already have. My guess is that you never sent anyone to escort Goothr back. Otherwise, he would have been here by now."

"Oh, I did send someone for him. That you can be assured of."

"You want me to provide you training or you'll keep Goothr in your military until he dies on the battlefield? And what of Ayva? Is O'vette's daughter to simply die in your infirmary?"

"This is a game you created," Greyson said with a calculatedly forceful voice. "I didn't bring either of them here. You did. You came into my city without permission with the intent to steal my most valuable prize. Then you stand before me complaining that I'm not doing enough to help your friends. Just who do you think you are?"

She calmed herself a bit before continuing. "Please, send Ayva and Goothr back to Eldor'Craft… and I'll stay here and continue your training. If you truly wish to show O'vette that you have a heart, you'll return her daughter to her before it's too late."

Greyson looked down in disgust at the girl while considering her proposal. Moving a few of the Runestones around, he considered his options. "Guards!" he called out for them to come in. "Take the Num back to her room."

Tilli was getting desperate. Her plans had failed, and she didn't know what to do. "Greyson, I beg you. Please send Ayva home to her mother."

"It was a pleasure seeing you again," Mel'tayn hissed as she was escorted away.

Chapter 40
No Way In

The three blothruds stood near the edge of the forest. The clearing before them would leave them completely exposed to Greyson's army protecting the city of Stone'Ring. Archers flanked the upper levels while nearly a hundred swordsmen were stationed outside of the city's main entrance waiting for Goothr's return. In addition, bands of Greyson's mutants were wandering about and searching the edges of the forest for any intruders.

The warriors had made it so far and yet the last hundred yards appeared to be the end of their journey. There was no way they could survive a straight-on attack in order to enter the city.

"Goothr not know how to get inside," he mumbled to himself. He had pulled off a sneak attack from the rear at their prior encounter, but that was the most military planning he had ever done. This was over his head.

Dirk waited patiently for orders. He would attack head-on to a certain death, if Goothr should order it. He was there to serve his leader. "We are warriors."

"True," Goothr replied. "But we will be dead warriors if we attack now." He glanced around, searching for options. "We will walk around the city to see if all gates are blocked."

Fading back into the forest a bit, Dirk and Chaos followed Goothr as he started his long slow walk in their pursuit of a better option to get inside. Stopping periodically to prevent being detected caused the inspection to take many hours.

Chapter 41
The Plan

Tilli paced in her room as she considered the extent of her options. Seeing Mel'tayn working with Greyson was unexpected and added another level of challenge. "I could strangle that little neck of his!"

Standing on her bed, Pheosco smirked at the sight. "You remind me of Thorik when he would pace back and forth while thinking of a way out of his messes."

"I doubt he put himself into anything that endangered his friends this bad."

"Oh, you'd be surprised at the situations he found himself in, mostly of his own doing. But he always figured a way out."

She stopped pacing long enough to size up the dragon's words. "And how did he get out of them? What was his secret to success?"

"Secret?" the green dragon coughed. "No secret. Thorik and Avanda never gave up on themselves, each other, or their friends. They fought for what was right and allowed their friends to be a part of the solution. They turned bad situations around to their benefit, when possible. It didn't always paint a colorful portrait of himself, but he never let his ego get in the way of his success."

Tilli froze in thought as she considered his words.

"Okay, I can see the wheels spinning. I've seen that look before from your grandparents."

Snapping out of her moment in thought, she ran over to her pack and pulled a few items out before moving to her art supplies. Spinning around she smirked at Pheosco.

Unsure what was rolling around in her head, he was slightly uneasy about seeing her staring at him while holding a thin black crystal, a Runestone, and a jar of black paint. "What do you plan on doing with those?"

"I'm enlisting the help of a friend."

Pheosco took a few steps back. "Just what friend and what do you expect them to do?"

"I'll take care of most of my plan. We can use Mel'tayn's arrival to our benefit."

Squinting, he glared at her. "Why do I get a feeling you're expecting me to do something I don't want to do?"

She gave him a clever grin. "Because that's exactly what I'm doing. You are going to be Mel'tayn."

"Absolutely not!"

"You're both about the same size. If I coat you with this black paint, you should look similar enough to fool others. This should work."

Standing proud of his heritage, he boasted, "I'm a green dragon! We would never lower ourselves to impersonate a black dragon." He glared at her, waiting for her to back down. "And even if I would, how would that help?"

Tilli's shoulders fell a bit as she relaxed her body. "I haven't always fully trusted you, but I am now open to changing that." Sitting next to him on the bed, she held out the thin, black crystal. "This is an E'rudite portal crystal. If we give it a specific harmonic tone and then break it in half, we can use the other half to open a portal back to the first half."

Skeptical, Pheosco studied the normal looking stone. "How does that help us?"

"If you can get inside Greyson's quarters, you can plant half of this crystal in his room. Then at night, when everyone is sleeping, we can open the portal from my room into his. I'll step in and swap the fake Charm Runestone O'vette made for me with the real one. Now that Mel'tayn has delivered my satchel, I can grab it as well before I step back through the portal into this room."

Pheosco shook his head at the proud Num, as she stood there beaming with delight that she had come up with a plan to resolve the issue. "It won't be that easy."

"This is perfect. We will no longer need to hunt down Mel'tayn to recover my satchel. Plus, Greyson will assume the Charm Runestone no longer works. But even if he recognizes the Runestone is fake, it will be too late. Hopefully we'll be home by that point."

"Do you think Greyson is just going to let you take one of his wagons out the front gate to haul Ayva home to Eldor'Craft?"

"No need. I planted one of these portal crystals at the village, so once I return from Greyson's room, we can open the second portal and step back near the town hall." She was very pleased with herself and waited for Pheosco to congratulate her.

Grumbling, he finally replied. "It won't work."

Confused, she tried to determine what she could have missed. "Why?"

Pheosco gave off a low growl. "First of all, I'm not interested in you pouring paint all over me. And even if I was, the moment I fly in Greyson's window, I'll be in another life-or-death battle with the real Mel'tayn."

"Good point. That would be awkward."

"Awkward?" Pheosco was shocked at the choice of words. "It could mean my death!"

Tilli discarded his emotions and continued to plan. "We need to wait until Mel'tayn leaves the room before you go in."

"I still haven't agreed to do this."

Dismissing his comment, she walked through the steps. "While you're perched on a nearby ledge, waiting for Mel'tayn to fly out of Greyson's window, I'll find out where Goothr is. Once he arrives, he can bring Ayva up here and we'll meet you in this room. Then we can execute the plan."

"We don't know when, or if, Goothr is returning. Even if he does, how would he get past all the guards and mutant creatures? Assuming he can fight his way past, what makes you think they will allow him to remove Ayva from the infirmary filled with Alchemists? Greyson controls all of these factors, not you!" Standing defiantly on the bed, he glared at her to intensify his statements.

"Perfect! That's what we want him to think. That's going to be his downfall."

"Wait! I still have not agreed to you coating me with black paint!"

Tilli then turned and leaned down to place her nose at the end of his muzzle. "You came here at the request of my grandparents to help me prevent changes to our future. Removing my Runestones and Irluk's Charm Stone from Greyson is what's needed to make that happen. All I need you to do is deliver portal crystals." She paused as she gave him a kind look into his eyes. "Can my family count on you to help?"

Pheosco growled, as the end of his nose continued to touch hers. "Don't you try to manipulate me because of my history with your family."

"I'm only trying to persuade you to work with me and my friends to save the future." She smiled, waiting for him to give in.

Another growl escaped the green dragon. "Fine!"

"YES!" She felt victorious for the moment.

"But you better take care of the rest, because I'm not always going to be there to save you when your plans go awry."

"Yes, you will," she replied with a grin. "Because under that rough exterior, you'll always do what's right for our family."

Pheosco backed away and stretched his neck. "What makes you so sure of that?"

"I've had some time to read some of my grandfather's notes. You're as much a family member to me as they are, and you'd never let us down."

"Clearly, Thorik had some wishful thinking."

She smiled at him as she grabbed a second portal crystal out of her pack and prepared to tap it with her tuning fork.

Pheosco was confused. "What's the second one for?"

Tilli gave him a smirk. "Just a delivery I need you to make before we get you ready for Greyson's room."

***

Returning to the infirmary, Tilli kneeled by Ayva's cot and held her hand. The guard that Greyson had assigned to her stood at the doorway to ensure she stayed within the city's walls. Aside from limited restrictions, Tilli was still free to roam about. Greyson was confident that she was at his mercy to comply with his demands. He also knew she wouldn't leave Goothr and Ayva.

"How are you feeling?"

Ayva skin and lips had turned a light shade with a gray hue. Dark circles under her slightly yellowing eyes gave away her health without having to answer. "I'm done with my adventure. I want to go home."

Her words broke Tilli's heart. She had pledged to cure her, and instead she had allowed her to slowly die away from her mother and those that loved her. "Tonight," she said softly. "We leave tonight."

"I want my mother."

Trying not to allow Ayva to see her emotions, the Num tightened every muscle in her face. Her heart was breaking as she watched her wither away before her very eyes. "You will see her by morning."

"You're back," Moordok said as he walked over to them. "I'm not sure how much longer I can keep her alive. I can't even guarantee she'll survive the night."

"She's stronger than you think." Nodding, she took a moment to kiss Ayva's forehead before standing and addressing the Alchemist. "Do you have any word on Goothr?"

"It's not good. Word has spread of his little rebellion, and reinforcements have been established at the city's gates, as expected. He would need an army to get in here tonight."

Tilli was worried about Goothr, but she knew if he didn't make it, she would have to leave with Ayva without him. She couldn't risk Ayva's health by staying another day, so a plan to return for him would have to be created. "What if he had help from within?"

Moordok lowered his brow and glared down at her. "I've gone beyond what I should have with you already. I'm not going to lead a rebellion against Greyson and his mutants."

She studied his face to see his conviction. "If Goothr could arrive tonight, without anyone knowing, would you be willing to let him take Ayva to my room?"

"You're not listening. They know he's coming. They are moving all available military to strengthen all entrances. He couldn't get through with an army."

"I understand and having the all of the military outside these walls works to our favor." She could see he was confused. "You have been so very helpful to me, but I need one last request."

He glanced around to make sure no one was close enough to hear them. "What is this final request?"

She handed him the leather pouch that he had purchased for her, which had originally held writing supplies. "The instructions are inside."

Chapter 42
Plan Execution

Perched outside on a tower, Pheosco continued to complain to himself about his mission. Armed with nothing more than a half of a black crystal, he waited to see Mel'tayn leave Greyson's room.

"So nasty," he hissed as the black paint slowly dried on his face, neck, and body. A trail of claw prints identified every step he had taken since he landed there, and a spattering of black droplets had coated the area each time he shook from discomfort.

He rubbed a talon across the stone wall to see how dry the paint was, only to find it left little to no mark. "Still tacky, but as long as it doesn't rain, the paint should be dry enough."

Pheosco returned to watching the ruler's window. "Why do I tolerate Nums in the first place? I had a simple life until they came into it." His mumbling and grumbling served no purpose aside from passing the time as he impatiently waited for his opportunity to deliver the crystal.

He finally spotted what he was looking for; Mel'tayn eventually flew out of Greyson's window.

"It's showtime," he told himself. Grabbing the thin crystal, he spread his wings and lifted off like he had done thousands of times before. The difference was that this time he held a smooth crystal covered in paint that had not completely dried. It was slick. It was hard to grasp. And before he knew it, it was gone.

The second half of the portal crystal, which Tilli had given him, was tumbling through the air, increasing speed as it went.

Pheosco's normal agility in the air was hampered by the coating of paint, which ever-so-lightly sprayed in every direction as he twisted his body to go after the crystal. Plummeting down, the crystal spun around, making it even more difficult to grab as the dragon streamlined his body in an attempt to catch it before hitting the ground.

Below was a courtyard, filled with walkways outlined with various bushes, and intersections that boasted large fountains to marvel at. But the vast beauty of the architecture and landscaping was not apparent to Pheosco as he quickly drew near them.

His middle talon on one leg touched the crystal, but wasn't able to pull it in. A second attempt only caused the stone to be pushed away and twist faster. He had one last chance before he and the crystal would crash, and it was on this attempt that he was able to grip it between his first and third digits.

Feeling the firmness within his grasp, he pulled up just as he grazed one of the fountains, splashing water out across the walkway as he regained control. Without taking the time to regrip the item, he headed back up to Greyson's window to perform his task before it was too late.

Flapping hard to gain altitude, he kept his eyes open for the returning black dragon. He had no idea how long he would have, so time was of the essence.

The windowsill was unattended and provided a good vantage point into the room to ensure it was safe before entering. Once he landed, he took a breath and scanned his surroundings.

The main room was large and held many heavy pieces of furniture, including a large table with a half dozen chairs around it. A large desk, shelves, several mirrors, and an area that Greyson used to display his trophies were all visible, including Tilli's satchel of Runestones. What wasn't known was within the rooms to either side that most likely held his sleeping quarters and maybe even a room for staff, personal attendants, or a bodyguard.

Pheosco leaped down off the sill and onto the floor to minimize the chance of being spotted. He needed to find a location to place the crystal that wouldn't be seen, but also in a location Tilli could step out into without knocking things over in the middle of the night.

There it was. A crack in the floor, between two large stones was just large enough to tuck the black crystal inside. The lighting was poor, due to the large table casting a shadow over it, making the crystal nearly invisible.

Pressing it firmly into the crack, he heard someone coming from the other room. He wanted to leave quickly before being noticed, but it was too late, so he leaped under the thick table.

Greyson walked out from his bedchamber while dressing himself. "Mel'tayn?" he asked, looking about. Not receiving an answer, he asked again while doing a quick visual search. "Oh, there you are. What are you doing under the table?"

Pheosco did his best to impersonate the black dragon. "Nothing." He realized that was a stupid answer, so he added, "Just thinking."

"Really?" He adjusted his shirt as he looked at himself in one of the many mirrors in the room. "What about?"

He really didn't want to have a conversation. "Tilli."

"Ah, yes. Well, don't worry about her. She's not going anywhere. Her friends will soon be dead, and she will lose her fight. Then her instincts will kick in. She desires security and access to good food and clothes. With no reason to leave, she will become a fine puppet to control."

Pheosco gritted his teeth. "Yes. I'm sure you're right."

Greyson stopped and cocked his head to look under the table. "Do you think otherwise?"

It was then that the dragon noticed that the water from the fountain had washed off some of the paint, exposing some of his green scales. "No. You know exactly what she wants."

"Good. I expect you to join her and I at dinner tonight. It's time you two start getting along if you're both going to be working for me."

"That will be the day," Pheosco said, forgetting he was supposed to be Mel'tayn.

Greyson stopped and turned to glare at the dragon still under the table. "Excuse me?"

Pulling back into the table's shadow, he didn't want to be exposed. Pheosco put aside his feelings and returned to pretending he was the black dragon. "That will be quite the day when Tilli and I work together after what we've been through."

"Ah, yes." Greyson returned to his mirror and tucked in his shirt. "You know, now that you have given me all of these Runestones, I can see my empire growing farther across these lands. I'll be unstoppable."

While Greyson continued his speech about how powerful he hoped to become, Pheosco snuck out from under the table, and flew out the window before being spotted.

"Of course, I'll make sure you and Tilli are rewarded properly. Perhaps you can discuss which of the Runestones I should be taught first. It will make for an interesting topic over dinner."

"Dinner with Tilli?" Mel'tayn hissed as he landed on the windowsill. "She's a thief. A low-life bandit that stole Irluk's Runestones. She doesn't deserve the right to dine with us."

Confused, Greyson stopped dressing and turned to the dragon. "You've already agreed to dinner. Don't start playing games with me by changing your mind."

Mel'tayn was about to rebut the comment but held back as he noticed something odd. "What's this?"

"What's what?" Greyson said with little interest.

"There are black footprints on this ledge."

The man nonchalantly glanced over. "I'm not cleaning up after you."

"They aren't mine."

"Of course they are. They are dragon footprints."

"True, but they are not mine."

Greyson and Mel'tayn both stared at the black specks across the windowsill and onto the floor before their brows lowered. They knew something was wrong.

Chapter 43
Lost in One's Mind

"Where am I?!" Pruva shouted at a few of the villagers. His head was pounding, and his voice was raised. He didn't recognize the room he was in, nor the symbols upon the walls of various skilled trades. "Someone has stolen my supplies!"

A couple of the Eldor'Craft villagers had been trying to calm the giant sloth-like creature ever since he woke up in a panic from his nap within the town hall.

Seeing a large bag filled with a diverse set of materials, with some of the items poking out, Pruva snatched his backpack off the table and wrapped his arms around it to prevent anyone from taking it away. "Mine!"

Neither of the villagers had indicated they wanted it, but one had decided that O'vette needed to be notified that their visitor was having another episode of confusion and was starting to act unruly. "Keep an eye on him. I'll be back with help."

Standing up, Pruva found himself struggling as vertigo swept in and spun his world around. He quickly fell back to the stone floor, taking a few chairs and a table with him.

"Hurry!" the other villager yelled to her friend leaving with a slam of the door.

Pruva opened his eyes and glared at the remaining human. "You can't have these. They are small treasures from across these lands and across thousands of years."

He then reached in and started yanking items out of the large bag before inspecting them and then tossing them to the floor. An odd assortment of stone, leather, glass, and metal items began piling up. Vials of liquid were flung onto the growing heap of random objects with far too little care as Pruva diverted his attention to the next handful from within.

After nearly half of the bag's contents sprawled out near him, he grabbed an item that made him stop and focus. It was the gyroscope he had designed and built after a decade of studying the patterns of the magical orbs within the Govi Glade. It allowed him to do what no one else had; he could navigate his way through history and the future by stepping into the proper orb at the correct time.

Pruva held the mapping device before him in a blank stare until he tapped one of the rings with a claw to watch it spin. The movement within that one ring created a cascade of motion throughout the rest of them, all moving at various speeds. Rings within rings within rings, each with a small, weighted metal ball to represent an orb within the glade.

The long metal post handle was comprised of various independent moving parts that allowed the user to calibrate the tool to a specific time in history. It was Pruva's greatest invention.

The front door swung open, allowing a cool wind to follow O'vette into the town hall. As usual, she stood with great composure, regardless of the stressful situation. Removing her winter coat, she handed it to the villager watching the gathler and waved for her to step aside. "I will deal with this."

Studying the gyroscope device, Pruva rotated a few tubes on the handle to see how it affected the spinning of all the rings. Confused, he turned them the opposite way to watch how they reacted.

His brow lowered as he became frustrated with the device. It simply was not doing what he expected. His tolerance eventually reached its limits, and he slapped the device hard onto the floor, bending many of the rings.

"Pruva?" O'vette stepped near him and spoke with a calm voice. "Do you know who I am?"

He lowered his head and glanced at her off to his side. "They are mine."

She scanned the assorted treasures in disarray near him. "Yes, they are. No one will take them from you." She stepped closer to him and softly placed a hand upon his back.

He initially retracted from the touch but then allowed it to continue. "I don't understand."

"What is it that troubles you?"

Pruva wasn't sure where to begin. "Everything. This place, these items, my past. They are all mixing and fading. I can't tell what's real and I can't recall what things do or how to use them."

O'vette picked up the damaged gyroscope and inspected it. "This looks special. It's unfortunate that you've bent it."

He couldn't make eye contact with her. "It doesn't make sense. I don't know how to use it." He scanned the rest of his items on the floor. "I'm unsure of so many things. I feel lost and afraid."

"There is no reason to fear me. I am here to help." Her confident yet soothing tone caught his attention. "Your name is Pruva. You came here with Tilli and Goothr to help our village and remove the Charm Stone from Greyson. Do you recall any of that?"

Pruva began to relax as he listened to her. As he did, the turmoil within his mind began to dissipate and he was able to focus. "I am Pruva," he said to himself. His voice was slow as he searched for the right words. "I am here to prevent a disaster. The Charm Runestone was not meant to be here."

She smiled. "Yes. But you have been having odd episodes of forgetfulness and dizziness, and we yet to determine how to stop them."

Glancing at the gyroscope she still held, his eyes lowered with shame over his anger being released upon it. "Something major is at risk of changing all my history.

Waves of variations crash against my head, causing me to act inappropriately. I apologize."

"No need to. I am just concerned about your well-being." Her light touch upon his shoulder was now a strong comforting grip. "What can we do to help?"

"Nothing," he replied as he rubbed his forehead. "The only way to make this end is for the turning point to be resolved and a final path for history to be chosen."

"And that will stop your pain and allow you to return to normal?"

"Yes, or it will be my death."

Chapter 44
Returning

Night had settled in over the city and most of the excitement had faded off as well. Merchants had closed and shoppers had left with wagons and arms full of goods. Aside from the occasional stocking of military gear and rations, the infirmary was once again the only busy room in the entire city.

Hiding in the shadows of the partial moon, within the arena, Moordok dug a small hole into the sand before pressing one half of a portal crystal into it. He glanced back and forth constantly; he needed the area to stay as empty as possible. He then tucked Tilli's leather pouch away.

Each time someone entered the area, he slipped behind a statue to stay out of sight until they moved on. It was nerve-racking.

"Come on..." he mumbled softly.

Then, without warning, a spiral of deeper blackness began to spin above where he had planted the thin crystal that Tilli had given him. It spun faster as it increased in size, and then, once it was nearly three yards tall, a sideways vortex formed.

Moordok glanced around to make sure no one else was around while the portal pulsed with spinning shades of gray. A slight bit of anxiousness teased him while waiting to see who all would step through.

The first sign of life coming through was a large wolf-like leg, followed by a large red human torso and dragon head. It was Goothr. But it didn't stop there. Another blothrud followed, and then another before the vortex faded away.

All three warriors searched their surroundings. Dirk was mesmerized by the fact they had just been standing in the forest a few seconds ago, and now they stood in the center of the city, near the marketplace. It took a few moments for the disorientation to wear off.

Goothr had no issue with the radical change in scenery. He had traveled through these before and knew what to expect, normally. However, this time he was a bit hesitant to greet the one waiting for them. "Where's Tilli? Pheosco gave us the vortex crystal with instructions to bring Ayva to Tilli."

Moordok stepped out of the shadows. "She's in her room, under the watchful eyes of Greyson's guards."

Dirk stepped over and grabbed the Alchemist. Lifting him up to his eye level, his heavy breath blew across Moordok's face and beard. "What did you do to her? Why have you imprisoned her? She just a sick child!" His voice was far too loud for them to stay covert.

Goothr placed a hand upon Dirk's shoulder. "Ayva's the sick one. Tilli is the other one."

"Oh," Dirk said, slightly confused. "Where's the sick one?" he asked, still only inches from Moordok's face. "Ayva!" he said sternly before glancing over to Goothr for confirmation.

"That's why I'm here. Tilli sent me to take you to Ayva in the infirmary. Once there, I'll release Ayva into your care. From there, you'll take her to Tilli's room."

Dirk attempted to give the man an evil eye. "Is this a trap? Ayva has a guard outside her room."

"No, Tilli's room is being guarded." Moordok sighed as he hung in the blothrud's hands. "Is there someone else I can discuss this plan with?" he asked, glancing over to the other blothruds.

Goothr patted Dirk's shoulder to have him release the man. "Goothr will handle this, Dirk."

Catching his balance after the abrupt release, the Alchemist stood up straight to address them all. "I'm sticking my neck out here for Tilli and Ayva, not for you. So let me explain just how far I'm willing to go on this mission to save them. Once I get you out of the infirmary, you're on your own." Pulling a rolled-up paper out of a pocket, he handed it to Goothr. "Here is a map from the infirmary to Tilli's room. It's just down the hall from Greyson's, so you'll want to remove Tilli's guard in a very quiet manner to ensure the guards outside of Greyson's quarters aren't alerted."

Dirk and Chaos loudly grunted and slapped each other's weapons together over their heads in a sign that they were ready for the challenge.

"Well, that doesn't give me much comfort." He shook his head; it was hard to believe that Tilli was betting her and her friend's life and safety on these three half-brained warriors to sneak into her room and save her. "Put the weapons away and follow me inside. Don't engage with others. I'll do the talking."

Moordok turned and calmly marched out of the arena and into the surrounding building. He didn't look back, as the action would look suspicious, at least until he reached the infirmary doorway. It was then that he noticed Dirk was glaring at any passerby as though he was ready to pick a fight. Goothr was trying not to make eye contact and would snap his head away whenever anyone looked his way. Chaos stared into space the entire time.

In spite of the ridiculous antics of the three blothruds, they made it into the room and over to Ayva's cot, where she slept.

Goothr fell to one knee and softly cradled her head in his massive hands. "Ayva, I'm back. I promised I'd be here for you."

Her eyes slowly opened. "Goothr," she said with great strain. "You said you wouldn't leave me."

"I know. Goothr sorry." Tears flooded his eyes. "Goothr fought hard to come back for you, to save you."

She reached up and touched his arm. "You're too late. I'm not going to make it home."

"No!" The blothrud looked at Moordok who gave the confirmation that she was telling the truth. "No! Goothr take you home right now!" He gently picked her up into his arms. "We go get Tilli and go to village. Goothr not want to be here anymore. I'm taking you home."

With that, he turned and headed to the door, while several nurses attempted to stop him. But it was Moordok that gained control of the infirmary workers as the three blothruds exited and turned the corner.

Nearly lifeless, Ayva's frail body bared little burden to Goothr as he cradled her in his arms. She drifted in and out of consciousness, often to just look up at her friend with a soft smile, knowing she was in the arms of someone that loved her.

"Adventure is over, Ayva. Goothr get you back to your own bed now." His voice was soft and compassionate, but provided the air of finality that she was looking for to get home and see her mother.

Goothr handed the map to Dirk. "Which way do we need to go?"

Dirk unrolled the map and reviewed it for a few moments. Nodding, he stroked his chin in deep thought before glancing up and down the hallway to get his bearings. "It's this way," he said, pointing down the hall in front of them, "or this way," he finished while pointing down the opposite direction.

Chaos stared into space and was no help, as usual.

Goothr was confused. Could both paths lead to his friend?

"Map," Ayva said softly as she reached out her hand.

Dirk and Goothr looked at each other for a moment before Goothr nodded his head to Dirk for him to give the girl the paper, which he did in the most delicate way a blothrud could.

With map in hand, Ayva took a deep breath and then coughed before studying it. "Go up two flights…" she had to catch her breath before finishing her sentence, "…to the third floor." It was all she could say at this point, as the few words had already winded her.

All three blothruds nodded simultaneously, and then headed back to the last staircase they had seen. Passing a few locals in the hall, Dirk glared at them until they looked away. No one was curious enough to engage with the warriors.

Marching up to the third floor, they came to a wide hallway which was still about a fourth the size of the one on the first floor. As with all the main hallways in the city, they curved around the ancient coliseum structure and only allowed them to see so far down the way. In this case, they could view about a dozen yards.

Once there, they looked down both ways, unsure which way to proceed.

Dirk scratched his brow. "Ask Tilli how to get to Ayva's room."

Ayva heard her name and opened her eyes to see they had made it to the third floor. She then pointed to the right.

Dirk nodded. "Tilli is good."

Goothr shook his head as he started down the hall.

"Tilli is not good?"

"No, well, yes, but it's not Tilli."

Dirk's eyes widened as he gazed at the girl. "Then, who is it?"

"Ayva."

"Ayva and Tilli are the same person? Why the disguise?"

"No," Goothr was getting confused. "Never mind."

They continued past many doorways before they noticed one with a guard standing out front, leaning against the wall trying to stay awake on the night shift. His head kept nodding as he fought off the temptation to sleep. By the time he heard something, he opened his eyes to see three blothruds standing around him.

"What were we supposed to do with him?" Dirk asked.

Goothr tried to remember what Moordok had said. "We need to keep him quiet."

The guard stood frozen with fear as the three massive blothruds discussed their plans. He raised his hands to signal he wasn't going to cause any issues.

"But he is quiet." Dirk tried to give him his evil eye. "Do we let him go if he stays quiet?"

The guard nodded. "Yes, I'll say quiet."

Dirk's fist swiftly struck the guard on the head, knocking him out. "He didn't stay quiet."

"Drag him in," Goothr said as he opened the door and began entering the room. "Tilli?"

"Ayva?" Dirk said to correct him as he dragged the guard in.

"Goothr!" Tilli's excitement was clear even in her hushed tone to prevent being overheard down the hall. "You brought friends."

"No, we are warriors," Dirk corrected.

Tilli waved them in. "Hurry inside and close the door."

Once everyone was in, the room seemed smaller than it did before. The wide shoulders and height of the three warriors quickly filled up a lot of the room.

Gently setting Ayva onto the bed, Goothr's entire focus was on the ill child. Pulling his hand out from under her head, he made sure the pillow was properly situated for her comfort.

Tilli couldn't wait for her friend to stand back up, so she took the opportunity of him kneeling next to the bed to give him a warm and loving hug. "I'm so glad you're safe." She then noticed the tears in his eyes.

"Ayva not safe yet. We need to get her home right now."

"We will. I promise."

Goothr grunted at the word. "No more promises."

"Why? What do you mean?"

"Goothr promised you and Ayva, but broke both." He turned his long muzzle toward her. "Goothr promised Ayva I wouldn't leave her, and then I did."

"You had no choice."

"Goothr also promised to you that I would always be happy, but I didn't. I got mad. I did things that did not make others happy."

She reached around his neck and hugged him again. "You did what you had to in order to come back and save us. We both understand."

"Goothr never make promise again."

"I've made my share of promises that I couldn't keep either. I wanted to, and I did my best, but I failed. But that doesn't mean I'll fail at everything. We may need to start promising to do our best instead of promising an outcome. The world tends to throw more at us at times than we are expecting. Sometimes the right answer isn't keeping the promise, but instead keeping the intent of it."

"But Goothr hurt others," he added.

"I did worse. I forgot about my friendships and how much better I am to have them. No matter where we live, as long as we're together, it's the best place in the world."

A moment of silence was broken by an unexpected voice. "Enough of the emotional sharing," Pheosco said. "We have a mission to finish!"

Goothr snapped his head toward the black dragon. "Mel'tayn!"

"What?" Pheosco hadn't been able to wash the paint off his scales, and realized he still looked like his enemy. "No!"

Goothr pointed. "Get him!"

Chaos and Dirk both reached for the little dragon at the same time, slapping each other's hands out of the way, and giving Pheosco time to retreat under the wardrobe cabinet.

Chaos quickly picked the cabinet up over his head, and doors and drawers opened, emptying Tilli's items onto the rug.

Dirk used the opportunity to snatch the dragon off the floor before he could escape. But Pheosco was quick and raced under the blothrud's legs. Dirk reached between his legs to grab the dragon's tail, only to flip over and land on his back just as Chaos set the cabinet back down on top of him.

Pheosco bolted across the room and landed on the windowsill. "Idiots!"

"It's not Mel'tayn. I painted Pheosco black in order to make him look like a black dragon," Tilli stated before anyone tried to attack him again. "We've just had some difficulty getting the paint to completely wash off."

"I was assured that it wouldn't be an issue," Pheosco hissed. Green scales were seen in the better light, although a random spattering of black still covered most of him.

Tilli had no interest in having that argument with the dragon again, so she changed the subject while digging for something in her pack. "We need to get Ayva home. Step back so I can open the portal to Greyson's room."

Once the two new blothruds moved away from the wardrobe cabinet, Tilli tossed a portal crystal into the air. As the two newcomers had seen once before while in the forest, the crystal spun in midair before releasing the black color from within the crystal into the surrounding swirling vortex.

Tilli stepped up and looked through the center of the vortex, where she could see a section of Greyson's quarters completely deserted. Dropping her pack on the floor, she took a deep breath and let it out slowly. "Stay quiet. Loud noises travel through the vortex," she said softly before stepping through.

Recalling how Goothr had instructed them to walk through the portal while in the forest, Dirk picked up her pack, stepped forward, and followed Tilli through the vortex. "You dropped something."

Goothr and Pheosco couldn't believe their eyes at what had just happened. In addition to the unexpected move by Dirk, they heard a loud roar and scream from the other side of the sideways tornado.

Jumping to his feet, Goothr leaped for the vortex, only to hear Tilli scream, "It's a trap!" from the other side before the portal closed. Still in midair, Goothr crashed into the cabinet, sending pieces of wood in every direction.

Chapter 45
Greyson's Forces

"We need to get down the hall into Greyson's quarters!" Pheosco shouted.

Shaking off his head-on attack of the wardrobe furniture, Goothr stood back up and headed for the door. "Chaos, you're in charge of protecting Ayva!" he ordered as he opened the door and then raced out of the room and down the hallway.

Goothr charged forward with Pheosco flying over his shoulder as they both rounded the hallway to Greyson's quarters. But instead of seeing a couple guards protecting his room, there were a dozen mutant creatures waiting for them to arrive.

The group of hideous beasts growled and barked at the two as they approached without wavering their speed, but the creatures knew they had them outnumbered.

Moments before Goothr plowed into the mutants, one of the wooden double doors to Greyson's room exploded into the hallway as Dirk was thrown through it and landed hard against the far wall.

Splinters from the door impaled many of the creatures, who screeched and cowered from the pain. However, even with their injuries, they were under the Charm Runestone's power and went on the attack.

Tilli's friends rushed in on the creatures as they questioned what could be in the room that had shot the warrior, Dirk, through the air at such a speed.

Swinging his mighty club, Goothr sent the first few beasts sailing down the hall. "Help Tilli!" he yelled to his flying friend. He then followed it up with the smashing of one of the creatures against the stone floor before the others started to overtake him.

Pheosco never slowed down; he zipped around the corner into the room to save the Num. But what he found was more than expected.

Greyson stood tall, clutching the Charm Runestone in his hands as he focused on summoning all of his minions to his aid. Perched upon his shoulder was Mel'tayn, reveling in Tilli's defeated plans. Next to them stood the bodyguard, Dwall, who had just finished slapping Dirk with his hammer, knocking him out through the doorway. The mognin was ready to take on his next opponent.

Pheosco's keen eyes spotted Tilli on the far side of the room, where she had been tossed by Dwall after stepping through the portal. Her lack of being tied up or hurt any further was due to the giant's attention on Dirk.

"My satchel!" she yelled to Pheosco as she headed for her pack.

"I'm on it!" Pheosco swerved under Dwall's swing of his massive arm. However, the dragon was way too fast for the big clumsy giant.

"No, you don't!" Mel'tayn yelled as he leaped up and met Pheosco just as he yanked the satchel from the shelf.

The two dragons locked themselves into another battle, but this time it was hard to see which one was which in the room's dim lantern light. Biting and scratching, the two fell to the ground and rolled about, each with the same strength and desire to stop their opponent.

Bodies of mutant creatures were still being knocked down the hall and into the room as Goothr continued swinging his spiked club. He tried to ignore the little beasts the best he could while they climbed upon him. Covered in mutants biting and scratching hiss flesh, he used his free hand to try to pull them off, but he eventually found them overwhelming. Another swing of his club, and he lost balance and tripped, falling backward upon several of his enemies as the mob of creatures piled upon him.

Greyson smiled as he controlled his army with more strength than ever before. With Tilli's training, he had the ability to not only give them general commands, such as 'attack', but could now control the very moves they made. They were now an extension of his body.

Tilli found her backpack and reached down to grab it before anyone noticed. But it was too late. A familiar acquaintance with facial tattoos and a black mohawk grabbed her wrist and yanked her away. Durren had been in the side room, along with two of his friends, and they had arrived to assist Greyson.

"What's this gift?" He pulled the pack away from her. The leader of the thugs was far too arrogant for the little he brought to help Greyson, but it was enough for him and his team. "What, no blothrud to help you this time?"

Still in the hallway, Goothr attempted to fight off the mound of mutants while also protecting himself as they bit and scratched his flesh near his eyes. Unsure how he was going to get out of the bottom of the pile, he decided to roll sideways and start squishing them.

The plan worked to a degree, and it removed enough of the creatures for him to stand up, even though they were still clinging onto him while he started swinging his club again with one arm and protecting his eyes with the other. But, before he knew it, his club was yanked out of his hand.

The screeching of mutants echoed through the hallway. It was louder than before and more terrifying than ever. Goothr no longer had a weapon, but he had his muscular body covered in sharp spikes, and that would have to be enough.

Pheosco and Mel'tayn rolled around the floor, attacking each another in a life-or-death battle for the satchel. Landing on top of Mel'tayn, Pheosco started raking his claws through the other dragon's wings, tearing them up so he wouldn't be able to fly away.

Screaming from the pain of his wings being shredded, Mel'tayn grabbed the leather tie string of the satchel, looped it around Pheosco's neck and pulled it tight, cutting off his air.

Tilli grabbed her pack in an attempt to pull it away from Durren, which resulted in a tug-of-war over the item as they spun around the room, knocking over furniture and breaking chairs.

"Stop her!" he yelled at his friends.

Letting go of the pack with one hand, she scooped up a broken chair leg and began swinging it at him, cutting him on the arm twice before slicing him across the bridge of his nose.

Durren wasn't expecting the Num to fight back with such ferocity. "Kill her!"

One of Durren's friends, Logy, finally got behind her, and wrapped his arm around her neck to stop her from fighting their thug leader.

Tilli released the pack and pushed all of her weight backward, landing on her assailant and knocking the wind out of him. She then seized Logy's hand that was still on her neck with both of hers. Gripping a few of his fingers in each hand, she pulled opposite ways, breaking one of his fingers.

Making headway in ripping the mutants off his upper body, Goothr glanced down the hall only to see hundreds of the little creatures heading his way. He was cut up and bleeding, and he had no weapon to help him. But somehow, he had to prevent them from getting into the room with Tilli and Pheosco.

From behind him, over his shoulder, several creatures flew past Goothr toward the oncoming hoard. They landed with thuds as their bodies had been crushed. Dirk had been using the spiked club to wipe out the rest of the original crowd of creatures and was finishing them off.

After one final smack with the club, Dirk handed the weapon back to Goothr before noticing the hoard heading their way. "You dropped this."

Goothr knew Dirk would charge at the oncoming assault, but determined it was not a smart move. "Inside the room!" Pushing his friend, they both bolted out of the hallway and into Greyson's quarters. But when they entered, they were standing in front of Dwall, who was ready to attack with his oversized war hammer.

Durren's second friend, Miv, raced at Tilli, who was still on her back, lying on top of Logy, as he gasped for air and clutched his broken hand. Grabbing a chair on his way, Miv pulled it over his head to smash it down on the Num.

On her back, with no weapons, Tilli could roll either way to avoid the attack, but she didn't have the time to be on the defensive. With her knees bent, she waited until the young man was close enough to strike her. She then straightened her legs with all the force she could, hitting his knees and bending them both backward.

Miv hollered in pain and in disbelief as he fell forward onto his friend, Logy, and Tilli moved out of the way.

Rolling to her feet, she glared at Durren. "Give me my pack!" she ordered.

Greyson moved back behind his bodyguard, away from all the fighting as he focused on using the Charm Stone, which he grasped in both hands. Tilli's lessons allowed him more power, but also required more concentration. However, when he attempted to use it on Goothr, he once again found the blothrud couldn't be controlled.

"Block the doorway with that table!" Goothr ordered Dirk as he prepared to fight Dwall. Once again, Tilli's ring, which he wore around his neck, shielded him from Greyson's Runestone, but it wouldn't protect him from the impact of the giant's hammer if he was struck. "I'll keep the mognin busy until you're done!"

Slapping the chairs out of the way with a few swipes of his arms, Dirk picked up the heavy wooden table. He propped it up in the doorway to cover up the door he had broken when knocked out of the room by the giant. Dirk then tossed a heavy cabinet in front of it to prevent the table from getting pushed inside. The doorway was blocked, at least until the table fell into the hallway, leaving only the cabinet as an obstacle to enter.

Unconcerned, Dirk shrugged. He had followed his orders.

By this time, Goothr was swinging his spiked club at Dwall, and avoiding the giant's attempt to slap him with his mighty hammer. On the third attempt, the club's spikes raked across the giant's chest, but the small victory was short-lived.

Dwall grabbed the club within his fist. Blood squeezed out between his fingers as the weapon's spikes dug into his palm. Lifting the item, Goothr hung on as his feet began to lift off the ground.

"Dirk! Stomach slam!" Goothr yelled.

As always, Dirk did as he was told. Putting his head down, he raced across the room and smashed his head and shoulders into the stomach of the giant.

Dwall buckled forward and then fell back, tossing the spiked club as his towering body slowly crushed everything he landed on.

Pheosco and Mel'tayn were under one of the tables the giant smashed on his way down. Still hanging onto his club, Goothr was thrown to a far wall. Tilli leaped out of the way to avoid being flattened, only to land at Durren's feet, while both of his friends were crushed. The impact caught Greyson unprepared, and he was knocked off his feet and tumbled across the room. His necklace broke and the Charm Stone was sent sliding across the floor.

It was at that moment that the second of the double doors to Greyson's quarters swung open and the cabinet blocking the doorway was pushed aside. The wave of mutant creatures had arrived.

Baring teeth and claws, they drooled with excitement for the attack. And yet suddenly, without the Charm Stone controlling them, they didn't know who their enemy was, therefore, everyone was. The wave of beasts flowed in the door, swarming up on the blothruds and giant first.

Avoiding being kicked by Durren, Tilli rolled to her feet and grabbed the pack he was still clutching onto. The two were back into a tug-of-war over the leather backpack. Knowing he was stronger, she couldn't rip it out of his hands, so instead, she spun herself around until she had his back where she needed it.

"You can't win," he taunted her as he kept pulling the pack. "And when this is over, I'll have my way with you before disposing you on the streets like the rat you are."

"You want this pack so bad?" Pulling the pack, she spun it upside down, dumping out the contents before shifting her weight and pushing the empty pack toward him.

The change in motion caught Durren off guard and he fell back, hitting the windowsill with his hips and then tumbling outside. He fell head-over-feet down the outside of the city wall while screaming in horror. Moments later, his cry for help ended with a loud thud.

Tilli had just let out a sigh of relief when a deep unexpected roar rocked the room. It came from the hallway as though the lord of dragons, Rummon, was about to approach. With that, the mutants cried out in terror and raced out of the chamber and down the hall, the opposite way from which they came.

As the final few sprinted out, another massive roar rocked the area. The new beast was closing on the room. The tense moment struck everyone as most had just started to recover from the giant's fall. It was then that it was revealed as Chaos walked through the doorway carrying the ill girl.

"Ayva!" Tilli yelled out of concern for her frail girl being in the middle of a battle, but she quickly adjusted her plans as she glanced down at the pile of items that were previously in her pack. Grabbing the half portal crystal, she tossed it in the air. "We're going home, right now!"

The crystal spun and the black leached out, leaving the crystal clear once a vortex emerged.

By this time, Greyson was crawling toward the Charm Stone. The impact of Dwall's fall had injured him more than he originally thought. One of the giant's arms had struck him and broken several of his ribs. Despite the pain, his anger and drive were enough to keep him moving. Finally, within feet of it, he reached out to grab the chain and pull it back in. Once he had it, he could recall his mutant army.

A large wolf paw with long arched toes slapped down on Greyson's hand. Goothr towered over him, reaching down and grabbing the necklace off the floor. "Goothr take that." Seeing Tilli quickly collecting her other items that she had dumped out of her pack, he noticed Chaos move next to the vortex, so he tossed it to him. "Catch!"

The Charm Stone sailed across the room, just over Dwall's arm as he started sitting back up, and right to the warrior who watched it fly past him into and through the vortex.

Tilli noticed the last moment of the Runestone's journey into the portal. Not pleased about how it had been removed from Greyson, she was at least relieved that it was. She would have to collect it once she jumped through, back to the village.

"NO!" Greyson was furious at the sight of his Charm Stone sailing into the vortex. Defenseless, he raced over to his enchanted items in hopes of killing his enemies and regaining his control.

Seeing a webbed wing, Goothr lifted the furniture off it to free the dragon as it clutched onto Tilli's satchel. Glaring down at the little beast, he wasn't sure which dragon he was saving. "You Pheosco?"

The dragon limped out, dragging the leather bag. "You idiot! What took you so long?"

Goothr nodded. "You Pheosco." Picking him up, he headed toward the portal.

Tilli finished scooping up the items from her pack, and she met Goothr at the vortex just as Greyson regained his composure and Dwall stood back up. Before the Num and blothrud could discuss the next steps, Dwall attacked.

A swing of the mognin's large arm released the oversized hammer at Goothr. The impact would crush the blothrud, or anyone else in its path.

Goothr and Tilli ducked out of the way of the incoming slab of metal that flew past them and through the open portal. At that speed, Tilli hoped it wouldn't destroy any villagers' homes.

Turning, she glanced through the center of the vortex only to see a few magical spheres floating in the distance over a field of grass. "It's the wrong one!" She shot a look at her dying friend. "Ayva won't make the walk from the Govi Glade to the village." She then quickly started searching for the correct portal crystal in her armful of items.

"This isn't over yet!" Greyson yelled as he grabbed a few enchanted items off his shelf. "Dwall, Attack!"

The giant had lost his war hammer, but he was still a powerful fighter. He stepped forward with his arms spread out so wide they nearly could reach both sides of the room. Assessing his biggest threat, he realized it was Goothr.

Finding the other half crystal in her mess, Tilli tossed it in the air as quickly as she could, just as she noticed her blothrud friend doing the same thing on the other side of the Govi Glade entrance. "Goothr?"

Proud of himself, he had activated the portal he had placed with Ayva in order to bring her home if she got sick.

Dwall stomped forward to grab Goothr, who was still carrying Pheosco, who was trying to free himself from the blothrud's grasp.

Leaping next to the edge of his vortex, Goothr prepared to jump in upon Dwall's next strike. "Save Ayva! Run into portal!" Goothr yelled to Chaos.

With three options, Chaos stepped toward the closest one, in the center.

"Not that one!" Goothr said as he leaped away from Dwall's grasp and disappeared into the vortex he had created. Dwall dove in after the blothrud to complete his master's orders.

Not wanting to follow the giant mognin while carrying Ayva, Chaos jumped through the third one, which Tilli had created.

Greyson summoned the powers of his enchanted beads, and a storm of flaming embers began raining down upon Tilli, burning her skin and clothes upon impact. Her priority was her friends, who no longer were in Greyson's quarters, so she took the obvious exit. It was time to focus on getting Ayva to her mother.

Once she disappeared, Greyson ended his spell and turned to see five Alchemists standing at his doorway. "Stop them!" he ordered.

Moordok stepped forward. "We aren't here to help. Your reign of terror is over."

Two Alchemists flanking each side of the old man lifted their arms up to cast their own spell on the prior ruler.

Greyson had lost everything. His Charm Stone, his army of mutants, his bodyguard, and his power over the Alchemists. It was over, and yet he felt he had one last chance. Diving into the center vortex, he disappeared from his quarters, moments before the three portals faded away.

Chapter 46
On the Other Side

In the early morning hours of Eldor'Craft, most of the villagers were sound asleep as a fresh layer of snow coated the roofs and streets. The blanket of white that reflected the moonlight was enough to easily navigate around.

The peaceful environment was interrupted with a blast of noise as Goothr and Dwall crashed out of Ayva's bedroom, sending the newly rebuilt window and wall exploding into the street.

Goothr tumbled away, releasing Pheosco and his club by the time he landed on his back.

Half the roof blew apart as Dwall stood up upon exiting the portal's vortex. A moment of disorientation slowed his attack as he assessed his surroundings. But once he spotted Goothr, he focused his efforts.

Pheosco's grip on Tilli's satchel was tight as he quickly flew off to hide the Runestones in case Mel'tayn arrived.

Stepping out of Ayva's bedroom and into the street, Dwall picked up Goothr by his legs. The giant twisted his body and spun before releasing Goothr through the air.

The blothrud crashed into a roof and then out the other side, flying across the street and destroying a wagon of timbers before coming to a stop.

"Seriously?" Pheosco yelled as he pulled out from under the wagon, where he had been looking to hide the satchel. "What are the odds?" Not giving the blothrud time to respond, he leaped up and landed on Goothr's chest as the giant made his way around the homes toward them. "Get up! Your fight isn't over yet."

Goothr shook his head to clear his thoughts. He was used to being the one doing the tossing of others, not the other way around. "Goothr not like that," he mumbled as he rolled off the timbers and back onto his legs and one arm.

Dwall approached. There was nowhere for Goothr to run.

***

Meanwhile, Tilli leaped out of her vortex and landed just outside of the village, exactly as she had planned. There before her was Chaos, waiting for instructions while holding Ayva.

Smoke rose from parts of the Num's clothes that had been hit by Greyson's magic. "Run!" she told the warrior as she pointed the way into the village. And without another word, they ran. "We need to get Ayva to her mother!"

***

Goothr used the spikes on the backs of his arms to pierce and slice the arms of Dwall as the giant held the blothrud in his hands.

Dwall squeezed harder to kill the warrior, end his battle, and stop his pain. He then slapped Goothr against the street to terminate the blothruds attack. In doing so, Goothr's necklace flew off his neck and landed a dozen yards away.

A growl was heard from behind the giant just as a large, spiked club slammed into his side before raking downward, slicing large gashes within his flesh.

Dwall screamed in pain and twisted around to slap the attacker away.

Dirk had followed them through the portal and had collected the club. "I like your weapon," he called up to Goothr who was still in the massive palms. "It swings good."

"Then keep swinging!" Goothr yelled as he continued to slice into Dwall's arms.

By this point, locals were coming out of their homes to see what all the commotion was about. A circle of yellow light, given off by their lanterns and torches, eventually surrounded the two blothruds and the giant as they fought.

Bishhall noticed and collected the necklace and ring as he approached with the others. He pocketed the item for further inspection later.

Swinging again, Dirk slapped the club into his opponent's leg, causing the giant to fall to one knee. But as a result, Dwall was able to capture his attacker.

Dwall now had both blothruds, one in each hand as he continued to inflict his death grip.

Goothr continued cutting into the giant's hand with the spike extending from his arms. "Did Ayva make it through the vortex?"

Dirk attempted to swing at the mognin's other arm. "Don't know. I left before they did."

The villagers knew Goothr, and anger grew upon their faces as they watched their friend be crushed by Greyson's bodyguard.

"Not in our village! Not to one of our residents!" Bishhall yelled. The metal master who had originally argued against Goothr staying in their community was now the one who would inspire others to save the blothrud. "Attack!"

As trained by O'vette, they had gotten in the habit of always having weapons handy when a potential threat arrived, and this was no exception. Just like when they originally attacked Goothr, they quickly started stabbing and poking the unexpected intruder.

As the villagers clashed with Dwall, Bishhall spotted a glowing gem mounted on the back of the giant's head. Upon this sighting, he turned and ran back into his home.

The locals were enough to distract Dwall and cause the giant to reassess where his biggest threats were.

That was all that Goothr needed to free his arms. "Dirk! My club!" he yelled before pursing his lips and spitting into the giant's eyes, blinding him long enough to not see what was coming.

The toss was made and once Goothr had his weapon in hand, he landed the hardest swing of his club possible across the bridge of Dwall's nose.

The giant yelled and slammed both blothruds onto the ground, knocking the wind out of them both, before he grabbed the spiked weapon attached to his face. The spikes had penetrated one of his eyes, which was ripped out of his eye socket as the club was yanked from his face.

Dwall used his remaining eye to see Goothr and Dirk piled on top of each other, gasping for air. Raising the club overhead, he swung the final blow of the battle.

It was then that a beam of blue light shined against Dwall's face, making the giant stop his swing at the last moment. Confusion crossed his face as he searched his surroundings before tossing the club to the side and falling to his knees.

Bishhall held Pruva's lantern up high and continued the focus on the giant's head. The ring lantern, that had been designed and built by Pruva, had worked and the giant was no longer under the enchanted gem embedded in his head.

Dwall collapsed from exhaustion as the blue lantern light continued to bathe his head.

***

O'vette stood up from her chair and hurried through the town hall to see what the commotion was all about. She hadn't been able to sleep well ever since her daughter had left, leaving endless hours contemplating her options, and blaming herself for not protecting her daughter better. An array of feelings had been flowing through her and they all vanished as she reached the doorway.

Tilli led Chaos up the stairs into the town hall so he could set Ayva upon one of the tables. She focused on the ill child and avoided eye contact with the mother, who was surely blaming the Num for everything.

Shallow coughs escaped Ayva's mouth as she attempted to speak. It was everything she could do to keep her eyes open before she mumbled, "Mother, I'm sorry."

Tears raced down the face of the once stoic O'vette. Years of not showing the emotional trauma she endured finally was released. An emotional dam had held back her feelings as she watched her child die a little bit each day, and now that obstruction had just been destroyed by the flood of love for her only offspring.

A small gathering stood around Ayva and her grieving mother while the ill child fought for each breath, as the final one was soon to come.

Goothr raced up to the town hall, taking all six steps in one stride. But upon reaching the doorway, he froze and then fell to his knees, lowering his head at the sight before him.

Chapter 47
The Journey's End

A light dusting of fresh snowflakes fell upon the peaceful common area in the wee hours of the morning, as every member of Eldor'Craft was there. Each stood in the darkness with a single lit candle, silent and reserved, even the children. Dirk and Chaos too stood in silence, each with their own candle.

At the far end, Pruva had been talking to the villagers. The haunting overlapping memories were fading away as the fractures in history were being repaired. The Charm Stone and Tilli's Runestones were being removed, and most of the other factors were being left alone. Small variances continued to spark in the gathler's mind, but not enough to cause him to suffer.

Words of wisdom had given the crowd humble thoughts of how precious life was for Ayva, and her desire to never be looked at as a victim despite her challenges. Instead, she simply wanted to live life as much as possible.

A low humming grew from many of the villagers as several of the men began slowly chanting a deep folk song of past generations. It was time.

O'vette and Tilli stepped into the common area, the Num consoling the leader as her hands shook. They were followed by Goothr, who proudly cradled Ayva in his arms, as they slowly walked through the middle of the crowd.

Tears flowed at the sight of the limp body of a good friend and neighbor that they would never see grow up. It was clear just how many people's lives Ayva had touched.

Reaching Pruva, Goothr lowered himself onto one knee and bowed his head.

Pruva raised a hand to end the humming and chanting, and as it faded, he began to speak. "O'vette, mother of Ayva, and leader of Eldor'Craft. What is your dying wish to your daughter here and now and the hereafter?"

O'vette took a moment before speaking. What normally came quite fluidly, suddenly became stuck in her throat twice before she could utter a recognizable word. "I wish her the freedom from feeling pain, which she has endured for so many years."

Pruva nodded. "Truth be said." He then looked upon Tilli and asked her the same question.

"I wish her limitless adventures in the afterlife to the ends of our lands."

"Truth be heard," the gathler added before addressing Goothr. "And what wish do you have for our loved one?"

Goothr gazed down at the frail body in his arms. The morning light was starting to shine against the clouds across the sky. "Ayva, open your eyes one last time."

A weak cough seeped out of the nearly lifeless girl, who had but moments left to live. Her breathing was shallow, and her motor skills were limited to her lips and eyes, which she slowly opened.

Goothr smiled as tears ran down his face. "You went on your adventure, and there is only one request left that Goothr can fulfill for you before you go."

He could tell from her eyes that she didn't understand.

He glanced at O'vette before returning his attention to Ayva. "My wish is to give you this wedding. My wish is to be your husband. Will you be my bride?"

The silence of the crowd was deafening as they all waited to see her response, or even if she was capable of responding. Was it too late?

Her facial muscles twitched and allowed a slight smile to form. "Yes," she uttered.

"Then let it be so," Pruva said as he watched the blothrud carefully lean in and hug her.

A range of emotions flooded the villagers at the wedding funeral.

"It is now time." Pruva motioned for O'vette and Tilli to step in closer and place a hand upon Ayva. "You have lived your life your way. In doing so, you have changed us for the better. You have given us a chance to reflect on our own lives in order to grow and improve. Truth be said, truth be heard."

As he finished, the morning sun peaked between the clouds and trees, shining upon Ayva's face. And it was at that moment that she took her final breath of that precious life that she fought so hard to enjoy.

As quickly as the light appeared, it faded away, as did Ayva.

Chapter 48
Saying Goodbye

In the busy morning street, raw materials were being moved about while finished goods were being prepared for shipping. Preparations for departure were being completed by Pheosco, and Pruva stood at the far end of the street, waiting for his companions. He had fully recovered from his episodes once the battle had been completed and Ayva had passed.

The crisp chill of the morning made Tilli shiver as she tossed a cloak over the fine garments that O'vette had provided. They had spent time grieving, consoling, and enjoying memories of Ayva's life. A small gathering had also been held to celebrate the end of Greyson's tyranny. But, by the time Tilli was ready to leave, Eldor'Craft was getting back to normal.

Goothr lifted a bucket of water out of the well to prep for their journey back to the Glade. "This is where I first saw Ayva." He leaned over the short wall and looked at the water far below. "It's where I tossed Tilli in to save her."

Tilli smiled at the memory that seemed so distant and yet far too recent. "Yes, if you hadn't done that, we would have never met any of our new friends or accomplished what we did."

Goothr was pleased with himself and headed over to give his blothrud warriors some final advice.

"You could stay," O'vette told Tilli as she straightened up the Num's cloak.

"I know, but my mission isn't over. The Charm Stone was thrown into the Govi Glade, so it could still cause this same issue elsewhere. It needs to be found and removed from history."

"You could always come back once you finish."

"I might just take you up on that. I would enjoy living out my life here, but there would have to be some concessions."

"Concessions?"

"Yes, I've seen innovation that you can use without compromising your legacy."

O'vette grimaced at the idea.

"You already have done this with Pruva's suggestions, and you've adapted the techniques to help you with several trades. Can you be open to new techniques without losing what your identity of master craftworkers?"

Her stern expression slowly softened to a slight grin. "Perhaps it's time to grow."

"I'm glad to hear that, and I'd love to return to help."

O'vette nodded. "Until then, you all will be missed."

Tilli took a moment to look at everyone that had gathered to send Goothr, Pruva, and her off. O'vette and several of her craft masters were dressed in ceremonial gowns for the occasion. This included Bishhall, who stood proudly at O'vette's side with his new lantern.

Off in the distance, was the giant, Dwall, with an eye patch and cloth wrapping around his many wounds. After they had removed the crystal from the back of his head, the mognin returned to his normal gentle giant demeanor.

Dirk and Chaos stood near Dwall as they said their goodbyes to Goothr. The two blothrud warriors were confused as to who to follow after Goothr leaves.

"Dwall is taller than you, so he will be leader now," Goothr said to them, while pointing at the mognin. "I need to leave with Tilli so I can protect her."

"There was no saving Tilli. You should protect Ayva," Dirk replied.

Goothr opened his mouth to correct him, but decided against it and just nodded in agreement.

Tilli watched the four of them and smiled. "Looks like you have new help to move heavy materials," she said to O'vette.

"We do; as long as they are willing to help, they can stay," Bishhall stated, as though he could make that decision himself.

As the locals moved around the busy streets performing their daily duties, a cloaked figure approached Tilli and O'vette without being noticed until it was too late. The comfort of being safe within their own village had worked against them.

The mysterious person rushed in and pushed Tilli to the ground before grabbing O'vette by the neck and leaning her up against the half wall of the well. It was Greyson. He had escaped from the city through the portal to the Govi Glade and fought his way past the treerats to the village. Injuries from the trek and from the previous battle in his quarters left him limping and hunched over in pain.

"If I can't have you in life, then I shall have you in death!" Greyson pulled out a decorative blade. It was the very one that Eldor'Craft had custom made for him and his Alchemists had enchanted. "Once your soul is trapped in here, I will take my own life to join you."

O'vette screamed as she tried to fight him off, but he was too strong and driven with too much desire to be stopped. He pulled the weapon back and prepared to stab her.

Time seemed to move slowly as Goothr and his blothrud friends ran towards her to help. The same was true for everyone who watched the unexpected event come to fruition. There simply wasn't enough time to respond.

The horrifying sound of a metal blade slicing through flesh filled the air. It was a clean slice that extended all the way through the body. Blood dripped from its point onto O'vette's clothes, staining her fine white coat with bright red specks. There was no going back. The deed was done.

Greyson shook uncontrollably as he peered down to see the end of a blade poking out of his chest. It had penetrated his torso and gave him but moments to rationalize what had happened. The very blade he had given Tilli in the market had been used by her against him.

Tilli pulled the blade back out of Greyson and waited to see if another strike was needed to stop him.

O'vette moved away and gasped for breath now they she was free from his clutches.

Still shocked, Greyson fell forward, landing on the short wall and dropping his enchanted dagger into the well before he rolled onto the ground staring at her. "I loved you," he muttered.

"No. You loved controlling me," she replied. "But I lied to you as well. Ayva was indeed your daughter," she finished as she watched his eyes roll back. Greyson was dead.

Everything had happened so quickly, and Tilli was still piecing it all together. She had reacted without thinking and her actions began sinking in.

O'vette and Tilli stood a few yards apart, staring at each other in some disbelief.

Instinctively, Tilli said, "I'm sorry I got blood on your outfit... again."

The village leader glanced down at her coat. "I think I can forgive you this time."

The two began laughing as Goothr and the rest started arriving. It was finally over, and the relief of the freedom was truly overwhelming.

As O'vette and Tilli enjoyed their personal bonding with laughter, a green dragon arrived on the scene. "I see. I'm busy making sure all of our gear is ready while you stand around and make jokes." Landing on Goothr's shoulder, he spotted Greyson's dead body near the well. "Did I miss something?"

"O'vette will tell you all about it. We need to be on our way."

"Oh, no you don't. You're not leaving without me." Standing firm on Goothr, Pheosco wasn't planning on staying behind.

Tilli gave O'vette a final goodbye hug and turned to head toward Pruva at the far end of the road. "Why would you come with us?" she asked Pheosco. "You and I barely get along."

"True, but your grandparents sent me here to ensure you're not going to muck up the future. And I'm betting you're heading back to the Govi Glade to do just that."

Tilli sighed as she walked with Goothr down the street. "You're going to be a pain in my backside for a long time, aren't you?" she asked the green dragon.

"More than you know."

Epilogue
Mel'tayn

The battle had left a mess in Greyson's quarters. No one stayed around to clean the room up or attend to the broken door. The Alchemists had returned to their posts to announce the fate of Greyson and the end of the war. They knew the collapse of the city would follow and a migration of spell casters began to the south toward EverSpring.

The great experiment of a civilization using enchanted items for everyday chores was over, now that there was no one in command to continue driving the vision.

Leaderless, it didn't take long for the pillaging to begin, and thugs to start fighting for their turf within the city. Internal feuds broke out, eventually leading to a city-wide fire that burnt down most of the wooden walls and crates of goods, leaving the bear stone walls that had existed since the time of the ancient Notarians.

Mel'tayn had witnessed the destruction and stayed clear of being a casualty. With his shredded wing, his flying days were over. He now fought with the stray dogs and cats for food found in out of the way closets that the humans had overlooked.

It was in one of these dark closets where the black dragon heard the footfalls of boots entering his private stash. Mel'tayn swiveled around and hissed at the intruder.

The silhouette of the man didn't react. Instead, he stood defiantly. "Ah. There you are," came a familiar voice.

Clutching the rotten potato he had been chewing on, the dragon hissed again. "This is my space. I claim all that is in it."

"I see. Irluk would have wanted better for you." He then reached over and pulled an oil lantern from a shelf. "Have you given up on saving her?"

Growling, Mel'tayn couldn't quite place the voice. "What would you know of my master's wishes?"

"I know she trusted her life with you. She expects you to bring her Runestones to her," the man said as he opened the lantern side to light the wick.

Spreading his damaged wings, he snapped back, "My days of salvaging her items are over with these wings."

Unexpectedly, the man nodded toward the dragon and the creature's wings regrew to normal within moments. "No excuses."

He spit out a bad bite of potato at the man's boots. "You're an E'rudite! And you're hunting down my master. I won't help you. I can't help you. Irluk and the Runestones are in two different times in history. Even if I wanted to assist you, I have no way to reach either of them without blindly jumping into a Govi Glade sphere."

"Well then, it's fortunate for you that I know a few things about time travel." Lighting the lantern, the man's face was exposed. Deformed from two large gashes, one over each eye, his eyes were gone and the skin on his eye sockets had sunk deep into his skull.

Mel'tayn gasped at the sight. "Schullis?" he asked with a hint of fear in his voice.

"Yes, it is I. And it's about time you and I start changing time to our favor, which includes returning Irluk to her rightful place of power over the Alchemists."

***
KEEP READING!
Your next Adventure awaits with the Thorik Dain series
***

www.AlteredCreatures.com

Altered Creatures Epic Adventures continues with the following books:

Nums of Shoreview Series (Pre-Teen, Ages 9 to 12)
Stolen Orb (Book 1)
Unfair Trade (Book 2)
Slave Trade (Book 3)
Baka's Curse (Book 4)
Haunted Secrets (Book 5)
Rodent Buttes (Book 6)

Thorik Dain Series (Young Adult and Adult)
Treasure of Sorat (Prequel)
Fate of Thorik (Book 1)
Sacrifice of Ericc (Book 2)
Essence of Gluic (Book 3)
Rise of Rummon (Book 4)
Prey of Ambrosius (Book 5)
Plea of Avanda (Book 6)

Tilli of Kingsfoot Series (Young Adult and Adult)
Hidden Magic (Book 1)
Final Days (Book 2)

Santorray's Privations Series (Adult)
Betrayed
Hunted
Outraged

Look for other upcoming stories of
Ambrosius
Darkmere
Myth'Unday
Dragon & Del'Unday Wars
and more…

CHARACTERS Pronunciation Guide

Alchemist: al-kuh-mist
Ambrosius: am-broh-zee-uhs
Asentar: as-en-tahr
Avanda: ah-van-duh
Bakalor: bahk-uh-lohr
Bredgin: bred-jin
Brimmelle: brim-uhl
Bryus: brahy-uhs
Darkmere: dahrk-meer
Deleth: del-eth
Dovenar: doh-ven-ahr
Draq: drak
Ergrauth: ur-grawth
E'rudite: ee-roo-dahyt
Feshlan: fesh-luhn
Gluic: gloo-ik
Goothr: goo-thur
Grewen: groo-ehn
Gway: gwey
Hugh: hyoo
Humeth: hum-uhth
Irluk: ur-luhk
Kee: kee
Ovlan: ov-luhn
Pruva: proo-vuh
Schullis: skuhl-is
Thorik: thawr-ik
Trewek: troo-ehk
Vesik: ves-ik
Wyrlyn: wur-lin
ZiXi: zix-ee

LOCATIONS Pronunciation Guide

Carrion Mire: kar-ee-uhn mahyuhr
Corrock: kawr-rok
Cuev'Laru: koo-ev lah-roo
Cucurrian River: kew-kur-ee-uhn
De'Ceit: dih-seet
Della Estovia: del ehs-toh-vee-ah
Dor'Avell: dawr-uh-vehl
Doven: doh-ven
Dra'boric: druh-bawr-ik
Eldoric: el-dor-ik
Farbank: far-bangk
Govi Glade: Gah-Vee
Kiri: kee-ree
Krual'Dor: kroo-uhl dawr
Lagona: luh-goo-nah
Luthralum: loo-thrawl-uhm
Lu'Tythis: loo-tith-is
Maegoth: mey-goth
Mai'Buss: meyuh-buhs
Mar'tayn: mahr-teyn
Ossuary: osh-oo-er-ee
Olva'Mathyus: ov-luh muh-thahy-uhs
Pelonthal: pel-awn-thawl
Pwellus Demanta': pwehl-us dee-mehn-tey
Pyrth: purth
Trewek: troo-ehk
Wierfortus: weer-fohrt-uhs
Woodlen: wood-len

SPECIES Pronunciation Guide

Blothrud (AKA Rud): bloth-ruhd
7' to 9' tall; Bony hairless dragon-like head; Red muscular human torso and arms; Sharp spikes extend out across shoulder blades, back of arms, and back of hands; Red hair covered waist and over two thick strong wolf legs. Blothruds are typically the highest class of the Del'Undays.

Brandercat: brand-er-kat
Large lion-sized cats that have scales instead of hair. They can change the color of their scales to turn nearly invisible.

Del'Unday: del-oon-dey
The Del'Unday are a collection of Altered Creatures who live in structured communities with rules and strong leadership. These include Blothruds, Wolvians, Brandercats.

E'rudite: EE-roo-dIt
The E'rudite aren't actually a species. They are typically humans that have been trained in the basic arts of the Notarian mind control powers which makes them much more powerful than others, but not nearly that of a Notarian.

Fesh'Unday: fesh-oon-dey
The Fesh'Unday are all of the Altered Creatures that roam freely without societies. Wolves, boars, raccoons, and most forest creatures are in this clan.

Gathler: gath-ler
6' to 8' tall; Giant sloth-like species; Gathlers are the leaders of the Ov'Undays. They are very curious creatures who take their time to investigate the true nature of things.

Human: hyoo-muhn
5' to 6' tall; Pale to dark complexion; Weight varies from anorexic to obese. Most live within the Dovenar Kingdom.

Krupe: kroop
6' to 8' tall; Covered from head to toe in black armor, these thick and heavy bipedal creatures move slow but are difficult to defeat. Few have seen what they look like under their armor. Krupes are the soldiers of the Del'Unday.

Mognin (AKA Mog): mawg-nin
10' to 12' tall; Mognins are the tallest of the Ov'Unday.

Myth'Unday: mith-oon-dey
The Myth'Unday are a collection of Creatures brought to life by altering nature's plants and insects.

Notarian: noh-tawr-ee-in
These thin human-like creatures have semi-translucent skin and no natural hair anywhere on their bodies. Their motions are smooth and graceful and they have incredible mental powers that appear to be god-like to the other species.

Ov'Unday: ov-oon-dey
The Ov'Unday are a collection of Altered Creatures who believe in living as equals in peaceful communities. Typically pacifists. Species such as Mognins and Gathlers are part of this clan.

Polenum (AKA Num): pol-uh-nuhm
4' to 5' tall; Human-like features; Very pale skin; Soul-markings cover their bodies in thin or thick lines as they mature. Exceptional eyesight.

www.AlteredCreatures.com

Historical Event		Published Novel
2nd Age Begins: Notarians Arrive		
Creation of Unday		
Training of E'rudites		
Creation of Notarian Structures		
Completion of Lu'Tythis Tower	2nd Age	TD5 Prey of Ambrosius
Fall of Notarians		TD6 Plea of Avanda
E'rudite & Alchemist War		SP5 Outraged
Mtn King Temple Established		TK1 Hidden Magic
Nomadic Living & Fighting		
Migration of the Ov'Unday		
Creation of Magical Items		TK2 Final Days
Creation of the Myth'Unday		
3rd Age Begins: Del'Unday Rule		
Del'Unday Expansion		
War of Del'Unday and Myth'Unday	3rd Age	
War of Del'Unday & Dragons		
Del'Unday Civil War		
Rise of the Alchemists		
Victor Dovenar's Revolution		
4th Age Begins: Dovenar 1st Wall		
7 Provinces Created in Kingdom		SP1 Exiled
Dovenar Kingdom Civil War		SP2 Captured
Assassination of Dovenar Knights		
Creation of the Grand Council	4th Age	SP3 Betrayed
Matriarch's Cleansing		SP4 Hunted
Destruction of the Grand Council		TD1 Fate of Thorik
Dovenar Provinces Secede		TD2 Sacrifice of Ericc
Reuniting against Del'Undays		TD3 Essence of Gluic
The Final Great Battle		TD4 Rise of Rummon
5th Age Begins: Frozen Lands		SP6 Defeated

Epic Fantasy